S0-BYZ-181

Lizzie flung herself down in the long, coarse grass, gasping that she couldn't run another step. At the same time the shelling stopped. Tom slid down beside her. The grass made a striped shadow over them.

Then there was only Tom's face above her, the dusty hair, the sharply boned cheeks, the violent eyes. There was no doubting the furor within him.

His lips tasted of dust, mingling with the dust on her own.

It was still blazingly hot and her body was on fire. But she didn't care. The sober part of her mind had vanished and she was someone else—a woman alive with feelings she had never known existed . . .

Fawcett Crest Books
by Dorothy Eden

AN AFTERNOON WALK	24020	$1.95
DARKWATER	23544	$2.25
LADY OF MALLOW	23167	$1.95
THE MARRIAGE CHEST	23032	$1.50
THE MILLIONAIRE'S DAUGHTER	23186	$2.25
RAVENSCROFT	23760	$1.95
THE SALAMANCA DRUM	23548	$1.95
THE SHADOW WIFE	23699	$1.95
SPEAK TO ME OF LOVE	23981	$1.95
THE STORRINGTON PAPERS	24239	$2.50
THE TIME OF THE DRAGON	23059	$2.25
THE VINES OF YARABEE	23184	$1.95
WAITING FOR WILLA	23187	$1.95
WINTERWOOD	23185	$1.95

Buy them at your local bookstore or use this handy coupon for ordering.

COLUMBIA BOOK SERVICE (a CBS Publications Co.)
32275 Mally Road, P.O. Box FB, Madison Heights, MI 48071

Please send me the books I have checked above. Orders for less than 5
books must include 75¢ for the first book and 25¢ for each additional
book to cover postage and handling. Orders for 5 books or more postage
is FREE. Send check or money order only.

Cost $_____	Name _____
Sales tax*_____	Address _____
Postage_____	City _____
Total $_____	State _____ Zip _____

* The government requires us to collect sales tax in all states except AK,
DE, MT, NH and OR.

This offer expires 1 October 81   8999

Dorothy Eden

SIEGE IN THE SUN

FAWCETT CREST • NEW YORK

SIEGE IN THE SUN

THIS BOOK CONTAINS THE COMPLETE TEXT
OF THE ORIGINAL HARDCOVER EDITION.

Published by Fawcett Crest Books, a unit of CBS Publications,
the Consumer Publishing Division of CBS Inc.,
reprinted by arrangement with Coward-McCann, Inc.

Copyright © 1967 by Dorothy Eden

All rights reserved, including the right to reproduce
this book or portions thereof in any form.

ISBN: 0-449-23884-9

Printed in the United States of America

23   22   21   20   19   18   17   16   15

SIEGE
IN THE
SUN

I

Lizzie Willoughby and Alice Partridge had had a conference at breakfast.

When the ship in which they had traveled from England had docked at Capetown, they had both received letters, Lizzie from her brother Evelyn, who said that because of the imminence of war with the Boers he had enlisted in the Protectorate Regiment and was shutting up his house in Johannesburg, and Alice from her husband in Mafeking, telling her most emphatically not to join him as the town was occupied by the army, and preparations were being made for an anticipated siege.

The two young women had not yet become used to the brilliance of the South African mornings. The sun streamed into Alice's sitting room. Outside the window there was a jacaranda tree in blue flower, unfamiliar and exciting. Acacia, pepper, the feathery tamarisk and palm trees grew in the hotel garden. Beyond the garden were the roofs of the city, and towering over them, like a theatrical backdrop, was Table Mountain.

After the long sea journey both Lizzie's and Alice's spirits had risen. Their surroundings were so stimulatingly new and strange, even though Capetown was full of rumors of war. Alice's three little girls, Henrietta, Fanny and Daisy, had been wildly excited. They had seen their first natives and wondered about their black faces. Henrietta had begged Mamma and Miss Lizzie not to be afraid. "I am sure they are perfectly harmless, Mamma." Henrietta was a busy and bossy six, Fanny five and Daisy, the quiet one, three and a half. They were all longing to see their Papa again, although Daisy didn't remember him and could only pretend that she did. She remembered his black whiskers, she said, but that was from the photograph in a silver frame that her mother kept on the table beside her bed. It showed

7

a handsome face which Lizzie, who had never met Bertie Partridge, privately thought self-indulgent. But no doubt he was the sort of jolly father his children adored.

Alice, who had told the nursemaid, Gertrude, to take the children for a walk so that she and Lizzie could be alone, discussed the letter she had just been reading.

"All that talk about a siege! I believe my husband is making excuses to keep me away. He always loves me so much more dearly when we are separated. Twice he put off our coming to South Africa. He hadn't enough money for our passages, he hadn't a house ready. As if I would have minded what we lived in so long as we were all together."

Lizzie, thinking of the trunks that had accompanied the Partridge family, and of the finery Alice had displayed on the sea voyage, held her tongue. She had never been able to imagine Alice in a small corrugated-iron house in a pioneer town.

Alice's large blue eyes were swimming in tears.

"I know you don't believe me, but I am perfectly certain Bertie is exaggerating the dangers of the situation. He has lived too long unhampered by a family."

Lizzie indicated her own letter.

"But my brother says exactly the same thing. I am not to go to Johannesburg because he has enlisted in the army."

"Oh, poor Lizzie!" Alice Partridge was a warmly sympathetic person. That was one of the things that had endeared her to Lizzie on the long voyage. "So what are you to do?"

"I haven't yet decided. I had been going to keep house for my brother. I expect I can find some similar position in Capetown until the war is over. I should hate to sit idly, doing nothing. The war may last a long time."

"With your looks," Alice said vigorously, "I can't think why you're not married. Oh, dear Lizzie, have I hurt you? Such a look of pain came into your face. Have you had an unhappy romance?"

Lizzie's fingers felt the other letter tucked into her skirt pocket, the one addressed to Lady Elizabeth Stafford.

She said calmly, "Let us talk about more important matters. What we are to do?"

Alice stood up, shaking out her lavender skirts briskly. "There's nothing to talk about as far as I'm concerned.

8

I intend joining my husband in Mafeking. You have made up my mind for me in the last five minutes."

"I?"

"By showing me how alone a woman is without a man. I sympathize with you, but I don't intend it to happen to me. I want to be at my husband's side. We shall take a train the moment the piano and the rest of our things are unloaded off the ship. Gertrude must begin packing when she comes back with the children. And I really am sure the danger is far more imaginary than real. How could a handful of Dutchmen dare to oppose the British? And why?"

"Perhaps they remember Majuba Hill," Lizzie suggested.

"What's that?"

"A battle they fought a few years ago against the British, and won."

Alice was put out, both by her own ignorance and Lizzie's tone.

"You sound as if you sympathize with the Boers."

"No, I don't, of course, but there are always two sides to a question. My brother has often written about the great wealth of the Witwatersrand. He said there was certain to be a struggle over it one day."

"I don't care about the rights and wrongs of this silly squabble," Alice said impatiently. "I just want to be with my husband."

"You will make several more mouths to feed in a town under siege and with food rationed."

"The little bit I and the children will eat!"

"Won't your husband be angry if you disobey him?"

Alice dismissed that with a shrug. "A wife's place is at her husband's side, especially in war. Look at those wives who were in the Indian Mutiny and the retreat from Kabul."

"Well, I think it must be very harassing for a soldier to have one eye on the enemy and one on the safety of his wife and children."

"But Bertie isn't a soldier. He injured his hip playing polo, and his leg has been stiff ever since. It has been a great handicap to him in his career. He came to South Africa to see if the opportunities were better here. He tried mining on the Rand, then moved to Mafeking and began building houses. He has great enterprise. He said

Mafeking is a thriving town now that the railway runs through it. Mind you, I never thought I would have to live in a frontier town."

"I keep thinking about the children," Lizzie said. "The climate will be hard on them, and the food, and if there is a siege, there will be horrid diseases like typhoid and cholera."

"They will have to be tough, like the children of pioneers."

Alice's flower-blue eyes had such a look of innocence that Lizzie was always startled when she caught glimpses of a firm and stubborn personality behind the dreamy innocence.

"I don't think you're seeing the situation as it is at all," she said. "I think you're in a dream of meeting your husband."

"After a whole year," Alice murmured. "And he wants a son. So do I. I do believe you might be the smallest bit envious of me, Lizzie, and that's why you're wearing such a disapproving face."

"Because I haven't a husband to go to? Perhaps I am. But the children are another thing. Would you leave them with me? You know I love them."

"Bless you, dear Lizzie! I know we only met on board ship, but I feel as if we have been friends all our lives, and there is no one I would trust more with the children. However, I couldn't bear to be separated from them. Nor they from me. Think how Daisy would fret."

Lizzie nodded, thinking of the shy Daisy's almost perpetual tears. The smallest hurt sent them rolling silently down her fat cheeks. What would a town under siege do to a child like that?

"Oh, Alice!" she burst out. "How can you subject them to it?"

Alice set her mouth stubbornly.

"I've told you the whole thing is exaggerated. So you had better stop worrying about us and begin planning your own future."

Her own future . . . What could that be for a woman tied by marriage to a man who no longer wanted her? Wanted was too weak a word. Rather, Humphrey couldn't endure the sight of her. The love he had once professed

10

to have for the young girl he had married had turned to a cold, vicious hatred.

He was not sane, of course. Only she and his doctors knew that. The night on which, after a disastrous quarrel, he had locked her out of his room and forbidden the servants to admit her was the night he had suffered his apoplectic stroke. After that he had been tied to a wheel-chair. A big handsome man of only forty-five, he sat quenched and helpless. But the stroke had succeeded in burning out his rage. In a quiet, doomed way he had made his wishes known. She was to leave him and the wreck of their marriage. Her brother in South Africa would welcome her. She was to use her maiden name and to put out of her mind forever the nine tormenting years of being Lady Elizabeth Stafford.

In the privacy of her room, with the warm tropical air flowing through the open window, Lizzie took the letter addressed to Lady Elizabeth Stafford out of her pocket and began to read it.

The awkward writing, written with Humphrey's crippled hand, said that he apologized for the communication since he had not meant to trouble her again, but he was alarmed by the rumors of war, and she might be wiser not to join her brother in the troubled area. He was well, he said. He was able to hold a gun again and had been taking some potshots at rooks. It passed the time . . .

Lizzie crumpled the letter and dropped it in the waste-paper basket. She found she had no feelings at all, no anger, not even pity, for that prematurely aged figure sitting in the wheelchair on the lawn taking shots at the squawking rooks.

Colonel Sir Humphrey Stafford, D.S.O., who would dearly have liked to be in the thick of an African war . . .

Instead, it was his wife who was intending to be. The letter, with its reminder of all the anguished frustrations of the past, had made up her mind for her. She was tired of playing an inert part in life. Staying in safety in Cape-town would only continue that part. Lady Elizabeth Stafford was dead, but Lizzie Willoughby was alive and was about to prove it.

"Alice!" she called peremptorily outside Alice's door. "Can I come in?"

Alice opened the door. She had been trying to repack

11

the opened trunks but was failing badly, the clothes billowing out.

Lizzie went to her assistance.

"You haven't folded these things properly. Have you told Gertrude you intend going to Mafeking?"

Alice shook her head. "Not yet. I'm afraid she'll be upset. She came back in a great state, saying that everyone is talking war and that the Boers have long beards and eat children, and goodness knows what nonsense."

"Then leave her here," said Lizzie. "I'll come with you instead."

Alice stared. "Whatever are you talking about? You have been severely disapproving for the last hour about my going. Lizzie, you don't really mean that you will come with us?"

"Yes, I do, yes, I do!" Lizzie laughed, hugging the disbelieving Alice. "I've grown so fond of the children. I would worry about them every minute of the time they were away. So the only alternative is to come with you. Actually, it might be a useful thing for me to do. I've had some nursing experience, and, if there's a war, nurses will be needed. I don't think I'm afraid of danger. I don't see why I should be when I have so little to lose. Only my life, and I don't suppose any of us will lose our lives. At least, one can't imagine it."

Alice, as if reality had touched her for the first time, stood arrested, her eyes widened, her face pale.

"If it is as bad as that, we can leave again," she said uncertainly. "My husband would arrange that." Then she brightened and sparkled, as optimism and illusion took hold of her again. "Oh, Lizzie, what a perfectly wonderful idea that you should come with us. I never did know how we were to say goodbye to each other."

II

The three little girls sat in a row on the hard seat. Although they had broken their long journey to have a night's rest at Kimberley, they were still tired, their cotton bonnets wilting about their hot faces, their petticoats crushed and grubby with the soot from the engine and the continual red dust that found its way into every crevice. They thought they had been traveling forever across the hard sunburned land, with the blazing blue sky so dazzling that their eyes watered when they looked at it.

Henrietta said her bootlaces were too tight and hurt, and Fanny, her faithful shadow, thrust out her dusty little boots, too, for inspection. Daisy rubbed her eyes, leaving streaks of dirt on her damp cheeks. She was, as usual, not far from tears.

Alice leaned forward to examine the offending bootlaces.

"Nonsense!" she said. "There's nothing the matter with them. Look at your picture books. Or look out of the window. You might see some more strange animals."

Yesterday the little girls had been kept happy and interested by the train journey and the newness of their surroundings, enlivened occasionally by the sight of a herd of wildebeest or zebra. But today the novelty had vanished. They were simply hot and tired and irritable, as was their mother as well. Lizzie had worn a blouse and skirt, with a light coat to put on in the evening when the heat began to decline. But Alice had dressed in a muslin gown trimmed with lace that had rapidly wilted. She had had to shed her gloves, though the elegant little straw hat still perched on her upswept hair. She hadn't realized it would be so hot and dusty and the train so uncomfortable. It was her unrealistic attitude again. She had even dressed the little girls in starched white cotton threaded with blue ribbon.

13

Their frocks were now a travesty, but no matter, they would soon be at their destination.

The train was crowded. It was rumored that it carried military supplies for Colonel Baden-Powell in Mafeking. There had been a great fuss when Alice had insisted on the small upright piano she had brought from England being loaded. There wouldn't be any time for piano playing, she had been told. Although she had disliked the railway men's bad manners, she had behaved with the charming courtesy she could display when necessary, and said she was sure the guns, or whatever it was they were loading, were necessary, but how could one small piano affect a war that hadn't even begun? She really couldn't allow her daughters to grow up completely uncivilized. And, apart from the piano, she couldn't do without a single one of her trunks.

She had had her way. Triumphantly, the journey had begun. But it was no longer so triumphant. Several times, at stops at small wayside stations, rough faces had been thrust against the windows and there had been jeers and threats. At Kimberley, the little party had been less than welcome. The hotels were full of soldiers, and the town no place for women.

Now there was only one other stopping place, Vryburg, before they reached Mafeking. It was rumored that Vryburg was almost wholly Dutch and very hostile. Lizzie was afraid, too, but more concerned for the children than herself. They had made a valiant journey, but they were now tried beyond endurance.

Henrietta's face was scarlet with heat, Fanny kept fidgeting and complaining and Daisy was in tears.

It was because she wanted to be excused, Henrietta said, and she hated the dirty toilet. This was not surprising, for long ago the tap over the cracked basin had run dry, and there was worse than the seeping red dust on the filthy floor.

However, there was nothing for it but to face the horrid place, and Lizzie, to Alice's faintly murmured thanks, took Daisy's hand and led her off.

They were the only women traveling in the long carriage. The rest of the passengers were men, mostly young, some dirty and unshaven and obviously straight from the Kimberley diamond mines, some neatly dressed as if their

14

departure point had been from behind a desk in Capetown or even London. There were two or three soldiers in uniform. Lizzie recognized their regimental markings, two from the Blues and one from Humphrey's old regiment, the Grenadier Guards.

It was not one of these young men, but an older man in a khaki bush jacket, who sprang up and actually held open the door of the toilet for Lizzie to lead Daisy in.

He was still there on guard, leaning against the rocking side of the carriage, when she came out.

"This is no place for children," he said.

"In there?" Lizzie shuddered. But he had meant the train generally. "Are you going to Vryburg?"

"No, Mafeking."

"Why? May I ask?"

"My friend's husband is there. The little girls' father."

"And you?"

"I'm only accompanying Mrs. Partridge. I had been going to Johannesburg to stay with my brother, but he wrote me not to come."

"And didn't Mr. Partridge write his wife not to come?" Lizzie looked at the stranger in surprise.

"You know Mr. Partridge?"

"No, but you just told me his name."

He was smiling. He had a nice smile, although he looked haggard and tired round the eyes.

Daisy wriggled in Lizzie's arms, wanting to be put down. Lizzie set her on the swaying floor and watched her stagger back to her sisters.

"Yes, Mr. Partridge did tell us not to come." She lingered, talking, because every extra mile the train carried them from Capetown increased her anxiety. The warnings they had had were no exaggeration. There were signs of unease everywhere. At Kimberley a young Boer had spat on the pavement after them. Alice hadn't noticed, but Henrietta had gazed entranced, and exclaimed loudly about his lack of manners. And no one could have failed to notice the number of Boers who were wearing bandoliers and carrying rifles. She was sure now that they had been utterly wrong to come. Perhaps this polite stranger could do something to reassure her.

"Do you know anything about the situation? Have you been in Mafeking?" she asked.

15

"Yes. And it's rapidly becoming a fortress."

Lizzie licked dry lips.

"Then—there is—"

"Yes, there is going to be a war, and very soon. Tomorrow, the next day. If I may express an opinion, I think you and your friend have been out of your minds to travel here, especially with young children."

Lizzie attempted a rueful smile. "Well, there we are, so we must make the best of it."

"Lizzie!"

Alice, still preserving her dignity in the fetching little straw hat, although it was not set at quite such a perfect angle as hitherto, was curious about Lizzie's acquaintance.

Lizzie said impulsively, "I don't know your name, but will you come and talk to my friend? Perhaps you can advise us."

The man joined them at once, saying pleasantly, "My name's Tom Wheeler. I'm a journalist, with a commission to make contributions to London newspapers. How do you do, Mrs. Partridge."

Alice held out her hand graciously. "Has Lizzie told you my name?"

"Yes, but not her own."

"It's Miss Willoughby. Lizzie, may I present Mr. Tom Wheeler."

The little interchange had restored Alice's spirits. She approved of Mr. Wheeler. He was only a journalist, to be sure, but he looked respectable, and was a great improvement on most of their traveling companions.

She began to talk about the long journey and the heat, giving Lizzie an opportunity to observe the young man more closely.

Young? No, he would be in his middle thirties, if not more. There were gray hairs in the dark locks that lay plastered damply over his high forehead. He had a square, dogged-looking face, with deep grooves about a rather bitter mouth. His eyes had a bitter look, too, except when he smiled, and then his whole face became gentle. She liked his smile. Otherwise, he had the sort of looks she might never have noticed had he not spoken to her.

"You shouldn't be going to Mafeking, Mrs. Partridge," he was saying. "General Piet Cronje is reported to be moving troops across the border, ready to surround the town."

"Cronje?" said Lizzie. "Didn't he fight at Majuba Hill?"

"Yes, and wanted to shoot all the British prisoners of war out of hand."

Alice shuddered, looking suddenly cold in spite of the heat.

"He must be a barbarian."

"No. Just a loyal Dutchman. A Boer, wanting to preserve the Transvaal and the Orange Free State for his country and perhaps add Bechuanaland also."

"That's where we are now? That's where Mafeking is?"

"On the border. It has great strategic importance. If there's any fighting—"

Alice quickly laid a hand on his arm.

"Please! Not in front of the children."

"Of course. There's no use in talking anyway, since you're nearly there. Your husband will have to tell you the situation. The little girls have had a long journey. How do they remain so good?"

Henrietta, always pert, took her opportunity.

"Daisy hasn't been good, Mr. Wheeler. And Fanny and I have been getting rather pernickety."

"Pernickety, darling?" said Alice, raising her eyebrows.

"That's what Gertrude says."

"Gertrude?" said Mr. Wheeler.

"We left her in Capetown. We have Miss Lizzie with us now."

Lizzie experienced a curious tremor, almost a shiver, as Mr. Wheeler's eyes rested on her. He might have thought her a nursemaid or a governess, but she knew he wouldn't, because he would observe the creamy shantung silk of her blouse, the small enameled watch she wore on a chain around her neck, her expensive shoes.

"And Miss Lizzie is preferable to the abandoned Gertrude?"

Henrietta and Fanny giggled, saying, "Oh, yes, much preferable." Daisy slid a hot sticky hand into Lizzie's. They were all small replicas of their mother, with their huge pale-blue eyes and fine skin. They had looked well enough on the ship and in a civilized hotel in Capetown, but here, against the background of the vast red land, they

17

looked terribly delicate, flowers to be withered in the scorching sun.

"Papa said there would be ponies for us to ride, and we have brought our piano." Fanny knew as well as Henrietta that politeness demanded no conversational lapses, even if one was very weary.

Mr. Wheeler had put his hand inside his coat pocket and brought out a small sketching pad.

"I can't imagine piano lessons in Mafeking at this time, but if you say so, I believe you. Sit still, please, all of you."

He sketched quickly and very cleverly. In no time at all, in spite of the jolting of the train, he had produced a likeness of the children in their crumpled bonnets. They were enchanted and demanded more pictures. "One of Mamma, Mr. Wheeler. One of Miss Lizzie."

He had long nervous fingers and he worked with absorption. Once he murmured, "I didn't expect my first sketches to be of such charming subjects."

"What were they to be of?" Alice asked, the weariness and uncertainty creeping into her voice.

He might have spared the children, but he did not intend to spare their mother. Lizzie had the feeling that he had judged Alice already, deciding she was emptyheaded and vain and quite criminally reckless in exposing her children to the coming danger. His judgment was in his brief laconic words.

"Of war, Mrs. Partridge. What did you think?"

III

At Vryburg, the last stop before Mafeking, a railway guard stuck his head in the carriage window and advised no one to alight who hadn't business there. When the journey began once more, Daisy fell asleep, her head resting on her mother's lap. The two older ones struggled against weariness, but presently they lolled drunkenly, supported on one side by Lizzie and on the other, obligingly, by Tom Wheeler.

So, now that their infant ears were closed to alarm, it was time to be told the truth about Mafeking. Even Alice must come out of her dream of a happy reunion with her husband and listen.

Lizzie looked at Mr. Wheeler over the tangled heads of Fanny and Henrietta, and begged that he give them all the information he could.

"A geography lesson, please, Mr. Wheeler. How big a town is it? How many people live there? What does it look like?"

"As to that, Miss Willoughby, you'll soon see for yourself. But I can tell you a little of its history, past and present, if you're interested."

His narration passed the time, and the information was deeply interesting. Above the rattle of the train Lizzie and Alice listened to the history of the place where, perhaps, they were to die.

A frontier town of no more than three hundred dwellings and a population of about twelve hundred people, it had taken its name from the Barolong language, Mafeking meaning Place of Stones.

In the immensity of the veld, said Mr. Wheeler, there was no need to be parsimonious with space. The little town straggled for a mile or more, with wide streets, each bungalow set on its own piece of land, and in the center a

19

spacious market square. There were shops, hotels, schools, a town office, a recreation ground, a hospital and a convent. The railway station was the vital center of the town. It was the link between Capetown, nine hundred miles away to the south, and Buiawayo, five hundred miles to the north, in Rhodesia. Mafeking, on the borders of Bechuanaland and the Transvaal, was a stopping place for miners on the way to the Rand goldfields, Boer and British settlers coming in to trade farm produce, railway workers to develop the already large railway depot, and officials to administer this important outpost of the British Empire.

Although Mafeking was predominantly English, Bechuanaland was occupied mostly by Dutch settlers, who, on a word, would desert the British Queen for their own Oom Paul Kruger, President of the Transvaal. If Mafeking should fall, the British Protectorate of Bechuanaland would fall too, and the whole of the vast rich stretch of land with its goldfields and diamond mines would be Dutch from the borders of the Cape Colony to the Rhodesian border.

So the little town, with its acacia and pepper trees, and imported shrubs that struggled to take root in the stony soil, with its iron-roofed bungalows that glittered in the sun, and the winding snake of the Molopo River that divided the English settlement from the native kraal occupied by six thousand members of the Barolong tribe, was suddenly invested with an importance it had never expected. And a danger it was ill-equipped to face.

Mafeking already had its claim to notoriety, for it was the place from which Doctor Jameson, the pioneer administrator and friend of the Prime Minister of the Cape, Cecil Rhodes, had made his ill-judged raid into the Transvaal with the object of overthrowing the Dutch government. The raid, which had taken place four years previously, had met with disaster, and although the British Government had disassociated itself from the harebrained scheme, the Boers had never forgotten their bitterness about it. In the event of war, Mafeking would be one place on which they would wreak their vengeance. Not one stone would be left on top of another, they vowed.

And now it was the eve of war, and the little town had become a hive of activity. In the heat of the day and on into the evening, when the wind that came from

20

the distant Kalahari desert had acquired its nighttime chill, the trench diggers labored, constructing a series of trenches to encircle the town. Roadblocks were formed of mule carts, and the big clumsy Boer trekking wagons were upended and placed sideways across the entrances to the town. They were also made into barricades in the Market Square where, if necessary, a last stand would be made.

However, the commander, Colonel Baden-Powell, had much more ambitious plans than homemade barricades for defense, and had set up a chain of outposts along a perimeter of five miles, which enclosed the native kraal with its highly important grazing ground and water wells in its circle. The crumbling old fort on Canon Kopje, used by General Warren in the Matabele War, was made into an effective outpost. Another fort was made at Game Tree, and at several other places on the open veld earthworks were raised, rifle pits dug and mines laid. Finally, as a sophisticated touch, telephone wires were laid to all these outposts and field telephones installed. These were instruments the Boer forces were not likely to possess. They gave Baden-Powell a superiority that was psychological as well as practical. From his headquarters next to Dixon's Hotel he could be immediately in touch with developments, and from his lookout on the roof powerful field glasses could bring almost all of the defense area under his personal observation.

He was supported in his command by a staff that was not only able, but of high social standing. He had Major Alexander Godley of the Royal Dublin Fusiliers as his second in command; his aide de camp was Captain Gordon Wilson, who was married to Sarah, daughter of the Duke of Marlborough and sister of Lord Randolph Churchill. No less a person than Major Lord Edward Cecil of the Grenadier Guards, son of the English Prime Minister, Lord Salisbury, was there; and Lord Sudeley's son, Captain Algernon Hanbury-Tracy, of the Royal Horse Guards, the Blues. Person for person, the English aristocracy could seldom have been so well represented, for there was also Captain Lord Charles Cavendish-Bentinck, the Duke of Portland's half brother, of the 9th Lancers, and Captain Charles Fitzclarence, who could boast of royal blood, of the Royal Fusiliers. The Earl of Romney's son, Captain Douglas Marsham, had joined the Police regiment.

Captain Ronald Vernon of the 60th Rifles stood well over six feet, and so did several of the others. They were splendid figures and added a great deal to the morale of the female population, who admired them sufficiently in their khaki, and would certainly have swooned had they seen them in the full glory of dress uniform.

However, if Baden-Powell's men were of the highest class, his weapons were not. Of the 745 officers and men in the garrison only 576 would be armed with Lee-Metford magazine rifles, the remainder having obsolete Martini-Henry single-loaders, which would not be very effective against their hard-riding, fast-shooting enemy. It was said that the Boers rode into battle with the new deadly Mauser rifle in one hand and a Bible in the other. They were rough, bearded, humorless men who had vowed to drive the British out of Africa.

They not only had the new Mauser rifles but siege guns, against which Mafeking's incredibly ancient muzzle-loading seven-pounders left over from the Matabele War would be ludicrously ineffective. Though, Baden-Powell had managed to obtain seven Maxim machine guns and a small variety of smaller guns, all of which needed considerable repair, and not one of which had a range of two thousand yards.

Enormous ingenuity, courage and initiative were going to be needed. But those were qualities in which the British excelled under pressure. The small handful attempting to triumph against fearful odds was their specialty. Let the ten thousand Boers said to be massing round Mafeking and boasting that they would be in the town in time for lunch attempt to keep their threat. They had a lesson or two to learn. General Cronje, so clever and wily, and reputed to be a man of truculent and stubborn energy, would find things very different from what they had been at the time of the Boer victory at Majuba Hill.

Colonel Baden-Powell had impressed the little town with his qualities of cheerfulness, energy, ingenuity and total refusal to panic. He was cool, calculating, shrewd and resourceful. The Barolongs had already given him their own title, *Impeesa*, the wolf that never sleeps. The English residents simply called him affectionately B. P., and were constantly reassured by the sight of the slight, straight, ginger-haired ginger-moustached figure with the keenly observant blue eyes hurrying here and there, supervising, giving orders, making jokes, behaving as if the coming attack were going to be a rather pleasant adventure in which everybody could participate.

The Irish nursing sisters at the Convent of Mercy had organized a casualty ward and equipped an operating theater. At the newly completed Victoria Hospital a capable and calm matron, Miss Hill, was in charge of her small band of nurses, both trained and volunteer. Doctor Hayes, the resident doctor, was being assisted by Major Anderson and Lieutenant Holmden of the R.A.M.C. Other preparations such as digging new wells in case the town's water supply ran out were being made. Most important of all, many bombproof shelters had been dug, for it was probable that the Boers would bring up one of their siege guns and shell the town.

A ration sheet, which would be changed from time to time as circumstances warranted, had been drawn up. The first rationing list, not yet put into effect, would be generous enough, owing to the foresight of a provision firm, Messrs. Julius Wiel and Company. There would be sufficient meat, bread, vegetables, coffee, salt, sugar and tea at the present time. If the siege was over by Christmas, no one would have suffered hardship by starvation.

Women would have to be ingenious with their clothes if they were to continue being interested in their appearance, and toilet preparations would be scarce. Children would have to go without sweets and be kept quiet underground if shelling persisted for long at a time.

This was all a challenge, and accepted as such by the majority. The town's morale was high, Mr. Wheeler said, and then, noticing Alice's white face, exclaimed, "Have I alarmed you too much, Mrs. Partridge? I became carried away. I find the situation enormously interesting. I have never been on the brink of a war before. But it's a very different matter for women and children."

Lizzie's arm tightened around Fanny. She said calmly, "At least you've prepared us for the worst, Mr. Wheeler. But I wish we had met you in Capetown instead of three parts of the way to our destination. It's too late to turn back now."

Alice suddenly said in a low, intense voice, "But I *must* see my husband. It's been over a year. He needs me."

She almost sounded as if she were trying to convince

23

herself. Had she thought her husband's letter an elaborate ruse to keep her from him because he didn't want her? The startling thought was too improbable. Yet it could explain Alice's refusal to believe in the danger. Now the long journey had almost reduced her to crumpled despair. But not quite. As Tom Wheeler, looking out of the window, announced that he could see the bridge over the Molopo River, and that shortly they would be in Mafeking, Alice pulled herself together and began to improve her appearance. She smoothed her hair, set her hat straight and drew on her gloves. If her parasol had not been packed, Lizzie thought with amused affection, she would have had it ready to unfurl.

Alice's own repairs made, she began briskly to shake the children awake.

"Come along, darlings. Henrietta, tie your bootlaces. Fanny, your hair ribbon has come undone. Ask dear Lizzie to be kind enough to fix it. Come, now, be bright and smiling. No tears, Daisy, my pet. In a few minutes we will see Papa."

All this caused a faint sardonic smile to curl Tom Wheeler's lips. He really did seem to have taken a dislike to Alice, with her innocent affectations. When the train slowly came to a halt, puffing clouds of filthy smoke so that for a moment the railway station was obscured, he touched Lizzie's arm.

"Have you anyone meeting you, Miss Willoughby?"

"No one at all. I am only here as Mrs. Partridge's friend, as I told you."

"Then perhaps I could help you with the baggage while that affectionate reunion takes place."

"Thank you, Mr. Wheeler." Lizzie was grateful. She hadn't wanted to intrude on Alice's meeting with her husband. "I'm afraid there's a good deal. Even a piano somewhere in the goods van."

"A *piano!*"

"Yes. Mrs. Partridge doesn't want her children to be entirely without social graces even if they have to live in this faroff place."

"Good God! Will that vain, empty-headed woman never understand that there's a war on? Every inch of space on this train was needed for military supplies. For guns. And what do we get? A piano!"

24

The word caught Alice's ears as she was alighting, followed by the crumpled and weary children.

"Do please, if you can, see that they handle the piano carefully, Lizzie," she called. "I'm sure it will be quite impossible to find a piano tuner in this town—Oh, Bertie! Bertie! You got my telegram. I'm so happy—"

The man who embraced Alice on the station platform and then swung the little girls one after the other in the air was a tall, heavily built man with a sunburned face and a carefully oiled and twirled moustache. He had warm brown eyes that, even in the act of kissing his wife and children, looked over their heads to Lizzie, alighting from the train. He stopped what he was saying, and Lizzie heard his surprised question. "Surely that's not the nurse-maid?"

"That's Miss Willoughby. Of course she's not a nurse-maid, but she offered to come instead of Gertrude. We met on the ship and became the best of friends. Lizzie darling, come and meet my husband."

Lizzie thought she knew immediately the kind of man Bertie Partridge was. Happy-go-lucky, roistering, good-natured, not too moral, but likable.

He immediately began to apologize for his clothes, saying that he had come straight from the trenches, and had to go back as soon as he had got his family settled.

"It's grand to see you, Alice, but you'll have to go straight back, you know. You shouldn't have disobeyed me."

Alice gasped, her hand to her mouth.

"Not straight back! We couldn't! That terrible journey."

"Well, you shouldn't have come on it. Couldn't you have stopped her, Miss Willoughby? No, I suppose you couldn't. I know how stubborn my wife can be."

"Bertie, you can't mean it," Alice persisted. "The children couldn't stand another journey so soon."

"They'll have to. B. P.'s orders."

"What do you mean, B.P.'s orders?"

"He's posted a notice in the square. If you don't believe it, come and I'll show it to you. Let's get on our way. I've got a mule cart waiting. We'd better come back for the luggage later. If I know you, there'll be plenty of it. Eh, my extravagant girl?"

He placed his arm affectionately round Alice's waist, and

25

a little of the dazed alarm went out of her face. Then he saw Mr. Wheeler and called, "Hullo, there, Tom. Didn't know you'd been to Capetown."

"I haven't. Only as far as Kimberley. They're preparing for a siege there, too."

"Are they, poor devils? Have you been helping my family? That's decent of you."

"I've been trying to tell them exactly what you've just said. That they can't stay here."

"No, by Jove, they can't. They'll have to be on that train tomorrow. Never mind, my love," he said to his wife. "We'll have one night in the house I got ready for you. Haven't had time to fix it up properly. I've been too busy digging trenches, and anyway, I didn't expect you." With a clumsy and not-too-clean finger he tried to dry Alice's tears. "Ever ridden in a mule cart before? Well, it'll be a new experience, at least. Etty! Fanny! And where's my baby, Daisy?"

He was doing his best in a difficult situation. He seemed glad of Lizzie's presence and said, "Stay with us, Miss Willoughby. I can see you'll be invaluable."

The mule cart, driven by a grinning Kaffir boy, was indeed a new experience. Cramped and uncomfortable, only the children enjoyed jolting down the dusty road to the town center. Alice shivered in the already chilly evening breeze, and Lizzie thought how red the pepper berries were. The small bungalows at intervals along the road looked mean and flimsy, both walls and roof made of corrugated iron. Had Bertie boasted of a house such as one of those?

Lizzie could read Alice's fears, and was even more conscious of them and her own shiver of apprehension when Mr. Partridge told the native boy to stop the mules outside Dixon's Hotel, a one-story building with a wide verandah, in the Market Square. There were small groups of people, mostly women and old men, standing about awaiting developments and glad of the diversion the new arrivals made. Two officers hurried out of the army headquarters next to the hotel, mounted horses, which had been held by Kaffir boys, and rode off in a flurry of dust. A platoon of men in civilian clothes was drilling in the square in response to barked orders from an army sergeant. The Union Jack flapped lazily over the army headquarters.

26

Even as Lizzie watched, a neat, compact-looking man with a ginger moustache came out and made his way toward the drilling squad. That must be Colonel Baden-Powell himself, she realized, watching the quick figure give a genial nod here and there as he went.

With absolute conviction she knew that if she stayed there she would trust him.

But Mr. Partridge was drawing her attention to the brief, uncompromising notice posted outside the hotel.

October 10, 1899

Forces of Boers are massed on the Natal and Bechuanaland borders. It is possible that they may attempt to shell the town, and although every effort will be made to provide shelter for the women and children, yet arrangements could be made with the railway people to move any of them to a place of safety if they desire to go. The men would, of course, remain to defend Mafeking, which, with its present garrison and defenses, will be easy to hold.

Those desirous of leaving should inform the stationmaster of their numbers (women and children) and the class of accommodation required.

A burst of singing came from the hotel saloon. It was the new song they had been singing in London, "Goodbye, Dolly, I must leave you, though it breaks my heart to go . . ." The cool wind whipped the women's skirts, making them shiver. As an anticlimax, Mr. Partridge said, "The piano, since you've made such a point of bringing it, can stay. It will be here when you and the girls come back."

"When will that be?" Alice managed to ask.

"Oh, in a few weeks. By Christmas, most likely. Those beggars on the veld can't hang out long. They haven't even got uniforms."

Alice suddenly clung to her husband, her head pressed against his breast, her hat fallen off into the dust.

"Now, my dear, bear up. I expect you're worn out. We'll make all haste for home. Back into the carriage. Boy! Whip up the horses!"

The mule cart, which was no more than a box on wheels, and the single skinny mule bore little comparison to a carriage and horses, but Mr. Partridge's gallant optimism brought a smile of acknowledgment from Lizzie, even if his wife remained helplessly in tears.

Alice's tears were so unstoppable that it was doubtful whether she saw anything of the raw, ugly house at which they presently drew up. The house seemed to Lizzie to have one advantage only—that it was at the end of a road and therefore a little isolated from its neighbors. There had been attempts to make a lawn, and some drooping shrubs struggled to live. There were shutters at the windows, and inside, furniture of a sort. Mr. Partridge had obviously done his best, but much more, Lizzie thought, than a piano was necessary if a person like Alice, with her fans and furbelows, were to settle happily here.

Mr. Partridge was flinging open doors, making a great stir to cover the house's shortcomings.

"We have a bathroom with running water. Very grand. Three bedrooms. You must see the fireplace in the sitting room. It's made of stones from the veld. Nice colonial touch, don't you think? Alice, my love, for the deuce's sake, stop crying."

Alice was valiantly attempting to do so, drying her eyes with a damp wisp of handkerchief.

"Mind you, it isn't a manor house or anything, but for Mafeking—"

"Yes, my love," Alice said tremulously, "I think it's beautiful."

Her husband regarded her a moment, pulling at his moustache. Then he said, "Anyway, the Boers will blow it to bits, most likely, so you won't have to live in it."

"But, darling, I want to. I think it's a dear little house. We can build a nursery—when we're settled."

"Oh, for heaven's sake!" Mr. Partridge burst out, his sunburned face taking on a choleric color. "Drop the make-believe. You think it's an awful dump, and so it is. But you'll have to make do with it for one night. Tomorrow I'll send a personal request to General Cronje asking him to direct a shell onto it."

"Bertie!" Alice raised huge damp eyes. "I only mentioned there wasn't a nursery. Otherwise it's all perfect. I feel like a pioneer already. If only we could stay."

"You can't, and that's final. Talking of nurseries when there are ten thousand hostile Boers crossing the border." He sighed heavily and impatiently. "You haven't changed

28

a bit. You're still living in the clouds. But I must say you're looking well. Or will be when you've washed your face."

"Is it dirty?"

"Very."

Alice gasped in horror. "Lizzie, why didn't you tell me?"

Mr. Partridge shrugged, meeting Lizzie's eyes over his wife's head.

"Miss Willoughby, shall we postpone the war while my wife attends to her toilette? Well, I'd better get back to the railway station and collect your trunks, and that ridiculous piano. Now don't cry again, I implore you. I shall enjoy strumming a tune when I'm not digging trenches."

"I wasn't going to say anything about the piano. I was going to say that if we must go back tomorrow there's no need to get the trunks. They'll have to return with us."

"You have a fine hope of that. The train will be packed with women and children. I believe there are nearly two hundred to go. There'll be no room for anything except a bit of hand luggage. If you've brought a lot of finery, let's hope it doesn't eventually deck a few Boer *vrouws*."

That, to Alice, was the last straw. When her husband had gone, limping noticeably (after a hard day in the trenches his bad hip must have been paining him), she sank to a chair, put her face in her hands and began to sob.

The forlorn head, with its tangled fair hair, stirred momentary sympathy in Lizzie. But she was tired, too, and the children were speechless and, unlike their mother, tearless with exhaustion. So Lizzie spoke with asperity.

"You're only upsetting the children. Crying won't improve matters."

"But it's such a horrid house!" Alice wept. "And I had to pretend to like it." She raised her wet face. "Do you think my husband believed me?"

"Not in the very least," Lizzie said cruelly. All that silly talk of nurseries. She had no patience. Didn't Alice believe anything of the existing danger? Had she successfully shut her lovely eyes to it all?

But she could say nothing more, for Alice was whispering desolately into her hands, "He never does believe me, Lizzie. Even when I try to make him see how much I love him."

29

IV

In the morning, the farewells were heartbreaking. Lizzie couldn't bear to look at Alice Partridge's white face because, now that real courage was required, she had proved unexpectedly equal to the occasion. She hadn't shed a single tear, but her eyes swallowed up her face. She held Daisy by one hand and Fanny by the other. Henrietta, forgetting she was a big girl of six, clung to her mother's skirts.

Alice had made her husband leave her the moment they had boarded the train. It was possible it might not leave for another hour so chaotic was the scene, but Bertie, she said firmly, must get back to his work. Every able-bodied man was needed. Mr. Partridge, after his farewells to his family, had seized Lizzie's hand and begged her to take good care of them.

"I will be forever in your debt, Miss Willoughby."

"Nonsense," said Lizzie, privately wishing that she herself were not boarding this hot, crowded train. She found she had a great desire to stay in the besieged town and give what help she could. But her first obligation was to Alice and the children, so she must reluctantly go.

She was not the only one reluctant to leave. She saw a young woman clinging to her parents, her face contorted with tears and fear.

"Go along now, Amy," her mother urged, and her father, a tall, sober-faced gentleman wearing a clerical collar, said, "God will take care of you, my child. Always trust in Him."

The girl tumbled in a damp heap beside Lizzie and sobbed piteously.

"Show a bit of spirit, Amy Brown," said a stout, elderly woman, looking remarkably like Queen Victoria, who sat opposite. "It isn't the end of the world."

30

"Then what is it?" Amy stammered. "T-tell me that, Mrs. B-Buchanan."

"It's a tiresome squabble between people who should know better," said the old lady tartly. "And I wouldn't be on this train if my grandson didn't want me out of the way. He can't put his mind to being a soldier while I'm about, he says. But I could have defended myself. I've got my husband's old elephant gun. You two ladies are strangers?"

She was the Queen of Mafeking counting her subjects, Lizzie thought. But she had a dour, tough look that was attractive on an occasion like this. There were enough already who were drowned in tears.

"Yes, we arrived yesterday."

"I thought you must be the two they were talking about. Foolhardy coming here, to say the least."

"Oh, no," said Alice coolly, her chin in the air. "I saw my husband, after a whole year's separation. That was worth making the journey for."

"And risking your children's lives? Sheer self-indulgence!"

Alice flushed with anger. Lizzie put a restraining hand on her arm. It would be foolish to start quarreling before they had even begun the journey.

The old lady's black bonnet nodded. Her petulant mouth quirked slightly.

"But I might have done the same at your age. Went lion hunting with my husband, and my son was born on safari. Shot the lion that mauled my husband to death, and twenty years later watched my son die of wounds after Majuba Hill. So now I do what my grandson tells me. And you, Amy Brown, who've never felt any emotion except timidity, think you've got something to cry about."

"It's l-leaving dear M-Mama and Papa perhaps to d-die."

"Face your troubles when they happen, girl. Good gracious, Miss Rose, are you bringing the whole school?"

The new arrivals, who squeezed into the already uncomfortably hot carriage, were seven or eight children, driven in like a small herd of alarmed goats, by a tall, poker-backed, severe-looking woman who was obviously the schoolmistress. She gave brief, sharp orders to the children. "Sit down quietly. Sit on your bags on the floor if there's no room. Mary, as the eldest, I put you in charge of the

31

little ones." Then she turned to acknowledge old Mrs. Buchanan's greeting.

"I have been asked by Mr. and Mrs. Fortescue and Mr. and Mrs. Parker to escort their children safely to England, where they'll stay with relatives until the war is over."

"Good gracious!" said Mrs. Buchanan again. "When was this decided?"

"Last night, at a meeting. We talked of ways and means. Neither Mrs. Fortescue nor Mrs. Parker would consent to leave her husband, so this plan was suggested as the only alternative. It's a responsibility I wasn't eager to accept, but one must do one's duty."

"They'll miss you, Miss Rose," Mrs. Buchanan said, and for some reason, either for pleasure or pain, a flush touched the schoolmistress' thin cheeks. She wore a shabby bottle-green costume and a black bonnet, beneath which her face was tightlipped and waspish. The children were plainly so intimidated that they didn't even cry. She looked as if she were much more accustomed to holding a ruler than the bottle of eau de cologne which someone must have pressed into her hand at the last minute and a bulging carpetbag.

Room was made for her bony haunches on the seat, and then her arrival was forgotten by the breathless entry of a conspicuously pregnant woman. A little girl clung to her skirts, and an untidy, highly aggressive little boy of perhaps eight years followed at his own deliberately slow pace.

"Billy!" said his mother fretfully. She looked around at the other occupants of the carriage with a helpless, exhausted air. "That boy can't be made to obey. He went off to see his pony and I was out of my mind that we'd miss the train. Billy, come and sit beside your sister. Be a good boy, do."

The little boy had dirty marks on his cheeks that looked suspiciously like the runnels of cried tears. He would have hated that fact to be known, and stuck out his lower lip defiantly. His grief, whatever it was for, would be secret.

"You'd think he'd have cared more for saying goodbye to his father, but no, it was only the pony that mattered," his mother went on to her audience at large. "And here's my little Annie not a mite of trouble."

"Well, sit down and rest, Mrs. Ryan, for goodness' sake," said Mrs. Buchanan. "We don't want another occupant in this crowded place before we get to the end of our journey."

Mrs. Ryan gave a high, nervous laugh and dabbed at her damp face.

"It's all right, it isn't due for two months yet. I mean"—she looked at the staring children in embarrassment—"the doctor says the event is better to happen anywhere but in Mafeking, with shells flying about. So Jim made me come. I'm that frightened, really. I didn't sleep a wink last night."

Alice whispered desperately to Lizzie, "How are we going to endure this journey? I'd rather have those rude Boers yesterday."

But a few minutes later they were on their way. With a great puffing and a screeching blast from the guard's whistle, the train was beginning slowly to leave the station. The little crowd left on the platform was suddenly silent, scarcely a handkerchief waving. They stood there in the blazing sun, a shabby, motley-looking, no-longer-ordinary, but lonely, brave, intrepid people being left to face probable death.

The undistinguished buildings and the dusty trees of the little town melted into the heat haze as the train puffed, with increasing speed, toward the open veld. The passengers sighed with resignation and dried their eyes and settled back for the long journey.

They had scarcely relaxed, however, before the journey was over. Mrs. Buchanan had just begun to open the hamper of food she had been thoughtful enough to bring when the train came to a jolting stop.

They were in the middle of the veld with nothing in sight except the parched, scrub-covered land, the railway lines running into the distance and the immense, blazing sky.

And one soldier on a horse.

Thank God, he was British. At first, panic had gone through the train as everyone thought this must be the first encounter with the enemy. But the lonely rider wore a British uniform. As soon as this fact was established the

33

passengers began tumbling out of the carriage, shielding their faces from the heat with newspapers, fans, handkerchiefs, even the lavender-colored parasol that Alice Partridge had unfurled and now held at an elegant angle, as if she were going to a garden party. What was happening? Why had the train stopped? They were only at the beginning of their journey; the first stop should be Vryburg, not this empty wilderness.

Amy Brown, the parson's timid daughter, clutched at Lizzie.

"What's happening? Why don't we go on?"

Mrs. Ryan held her little girl close. It was no use trying to do the same with her boy, for he had gone haring off to stand gazing up at the trooper on his horse.

Children began to whimper in the merciless heat. Miss Rose, the schoolmistress, gave a brief order to her charges to keep in the shade. Rumors began to drift from carriage to carriage—the railway lines were cut, there were ten thousand Boers in Vryburg, President Kruger had declared war . . .

There was a moment's silence from the wild conjecture, and everyone seemed to be listening for rifle shots. High in the burning sky two aasvogels circled lazily. A puff of wind blew hot dust into the already stifling carriages. Amy Brown gave several gasps and looked as if she might faint, Mrs. Buchanan shook her, urging her to pull herself together. If she was going to faint when there wasn't an enemy in sight, what would she do in real danger?

Lizzie saw a stir in the little group pressing round the driver of the train. They were arguing, and presently the cause of the unexpected stop, just twenty-four miles from Mafeking, became known. The trooper had ridden up to warn the train driver that to the south the Boers were across the line in considerable strength. If the train proceeded, it was likely to be stopped and the passengers taken prisoner.

"We must go back," Alice said, the barest hint of relief in her voice.

Mrs. Buchanan nodded emphatically. "We should never have left."

"P-prisoner of the Boers!" Amy gasped.

The clamor to return to Mafeking became louder. The army was there. Colonel Baden-Powell was there. Most

34

of the women had husbands there to protect them. And houses, of a sort. Here there was only the open veld, and if they were taken prisoner, who knew what dreadful things might befall them? No one yet knew how the Boers, with their beards and their rough manners and their reputation as sharpshooters, would treat women prisoners.

Lizzie picked up the silently weeping Daisy. The fair head leaning against her shoulder looked infinitely fragile. Back to Mafeking to face a long siege with this tender little creature? Henrietta and Fanny clutched their mother's skirts, trying to get shade from her parasol. They were excited at the thought of seeing their father again. He had been so jolly.

The train driver and the stoker stood uneasily.

"What's it to be? Risk going on? Or going back?"

"Go back! Go back!" The demand was almost unanimous. Only one shrill feminine voice said, "No, go on!"

"You be quiet, Katie Roos," someone said threateningly. "If you want to go to your husband, go. No one's stopping you."

"I can't. He's with Cronje. He's coming to take Mafeking, and you're all scared sick."

The young woman called Katie Roos, who had untidy red hair and a flaming face, had an English voice. Lizzie and Alice could scarcely believe it. How could she be so brazen, so traitorous?

"Married to a Boer farmer," said old Mrs. Buchanan in an undertone. "They had a farm at Setlagoli until he joined the army. She came to Mafeking to take refuge. She's a troublemaker, but she's not the only one. There are a lot of Dutch women in the town who don't keep their sympathies to themselves."

"Then why doesn't she go to Vryburg if it's pro-Boer?" Lizzie asked.

"That's what she's trying to do. She left it a bit late. Because we're going back. There's nothing else to do."

Already most of the women were clambering back into the carriages, gathering up their skirts as if the Boers were at their heels.

"You're cowards!" yelled Katie Roos. "You run away like mice!"

"Don't let her back on the train! She's a traitor!" shrieked an infuriated Englishwoman. "Let her stay there and be rescued by her famous countrymen. And I hope they rape her!"

She shouted the forbidden word aggressively, knowing she would never have dared to use it in peacetime. It was a weapon, of a sort, against apprehension, against the fear they were all trying to master.

"You'll all be blown to pieces by siege guns and shrapnel," Katie shouted back vociferously. "I know. I had a letter from my husband. He told me to get out before it happened."

"Then it's a pity, Katie Roos, that you didn't do so sooner." Mrs. Buchanan had established herself as the voice of authority, and spoke tartly. "Now you'll just have to come back and face the shrapnel with the rest of us. And if you, or your friends, try smuggling messages to the enemy, you'll find that we poor, scared, cowardly Englishwomen know how to deal with you. Now why are we delaying here? Get back in your engine, driver, and take us home."

The veld lay red-brown, stony and silent beneath the burning sun. When the trooper saluted and rode away into the heathazed distance and the train began its slow chugging return down the glittering rails, it was as if the group of chattering, voluble, excited people had never been there. They had passed like a running animal, a wind; the vast land showed nothing of their touch.

In a land of this size, Lizzie thought, one was less important than a speck of dust unless one were surrounded by dwellings, even the small tin bungalows of the town they had recently left. At least there was a hospital, churches, schools, a convent, even a courthouse and a jail, marks of civilization and a defense against anonymity in this wilderness.

She watched the lazily moving specks of the aasvogels in the high blue sky. Did they, too, sense the coming struggle, or were they looking for the simpler feast of a dead jackal or a meercat? And how was this trainload of women and children going to survive the dangerous days ahead?

Old Mrs. Buchanan, with her stubborn mouth and air of imperturbability, would do so very well. So would Miss Rose with her sharp lonely eyes, and the incorrigible little boy Billy Ryan, who was making faces to amuse Henrietta

36

and Fanny. Katie Roos, perhaps, for the very violence of her loyalty to her husband and her new nationality.

Lizzie thought about them, and wondered, too, how the rest would fare. The weak, hysterical Amy Brown, who seemed to be frightened of everything—illness, blood, the possibility of death, even of living. Dear Alice, with her harmless affectations and her fastidiousness—how was she going to come through the ordeal? And the little girls, and all the other children with their vulnerability to disease and privations?

And she herself, who had just begun to recover from that long-drawn-out agony in England. Perhaps her character had been strengthened by that and would be further strengthened in the weeks to come.

She wondered what was happening at this minute in England. There would be troops training at Aldershot (would Humphrey be fretting uselessly at his inaction?) and troopships lying at anchor in Southampton water. There wouldn't be any panic. This was only another small war which would be won quickly enough. The old Queen would inspect her brave soldiers, and there would be popular sentimental songs written, and wives would weep over departing husbands, and taxes would go up.

Here, far from the mists of fat, rich England, the sun would blaze down over the enormous alien landscape and those black specks circling in the very heart of the sky had an unexpected feast coming.

Lizzie shivered violently, although the carriage was stiflingly hot. She had had a sudden morbid vision of what was to come. Not character building, but dead and rotting flesh in the long heat of the day. That was what the coming war would be.

V

The return of the train into Mafeking station was, if not an anticlimax, at least an exceedingly unwelcome event for the authorities, who were now faced with the support and safety of one hundred and seventy more women and children than they had anticipated.

Certainly, some of those who had returned would be useful. Most, however, would be a further embarrassment in terms of health, morale and an adequate supply of food. The harassed adjutant, who had been hastily summoned to the railway station, could only give orders to all to proceed quietly to their homes. It seemed that a declaration of war was expected hourly, and at any moment the first shot might be fired.

Alice Partridge stepped off the train and, putting up her lavender-colored parasol, called gaily to her children, "Come along, darlings. Hold hands and don't dawdle. There's no Papa to meet us today. He's much too busy. We must just walk home." And, lifting her skirts fastidiously out of the red dust, she set off.

She must have expected Lizzie to follow, but Lizzie was occupied with supporting Amy Brown, who had half swooned and was clinging to her as to a last spar. Miss Rose was in trouble, too, for her little clutch of children were behaving as if they had been let out of prison and were shouting vociferously as they raced in the direction of their homes. She had lost control of them. Grasping at straws, she tried to seize Billy Ryan, ordering him to help his poor mother with his little sister. But Billy waited only until the flat, bony back was turned before he too sped off, not toward his home, but toward the kraal, where he had left his pony in the care of two Barolong boys. He could scarcely believe his good fortune that he was not after all to be separated from the one thing he loved in the whole world.

A nice-looking girl of about sixteen, in a neat print dress, had come to look for old Mrs. Buchanan.

"Linda, what are you doing here?"

"We saw the train coming. Mamma told me to come and see if you were all right. Were you shot at? Was anyone wounded?"

"No, nothing of the kind," Mrs. Buchanan said testily. "It's all been a fiasco. But I'm glad to get home. Give me your arm. Have you heard from Andy?"

"No, he hasn't had leave. But I promised him I would look after you if anything went wrong about the train."

"You're a pair of children," the old lady grumbled. "Involved in a war at your age. Well, come home with me and make a cup of tea."

"We're older than you realize, Mrs. Buchanan," the girl was saying earnestly as they went off. "I'm seventeen and Andy's nineteen."

"That doesn't mean you're grown-up. So don't count on wedding bells. I won't have a boy as young as Andy going off to fight while he's worrying about a child bride. That's final."

Miss Rose, so rapidly relieved of her charges, came to see if she could help Lizzie with Amy. She took one look at the collapsing girl and slapped her sharply once on either cheek.

Amy gasped and jerked up.

"Aren't you ashamed of yourself, Amy Brown? The only one to indulge in an attack of the vapors. You'd better let me walk home with you."

"T-thank you, Miss Rose."

"Not a bit. We both go the same way. There's nothing more to be done here."

This was true, for by now a large group of the town's citizens and railway workers had gathered. What with steam hissing, tired children crying, a cool wind whipping at the women's skirts and raising a swirl of red dust, and friends searching for each other, the scene was chaotic. The mayor, Mr. Whiteley, was raising his voice, trying to create some kind of order, and begging people to be calm.

This was useless enough, for he got nothing but a barrage of questions. Had the Boer force been sighted? Was the town surrounded? When would the shells start falling? Was it safe to go home, to put the children to bed, to undress, as no one fancied facing the enemy in her nightdress?

Lizzie, thinking she must hurry after Alice and the children, turned to go and found herself being greeted by the journalist from the train journey yesterday, Tom Wheeler.

"So you didn't get far, I hear, Miss Willoughby."

"No, not quite to Maretsani. We were stopped by a trooper who said there were Boers cutting the rails."

"Was there any panic? Describe to me what happened."

Lizzie frowned. She was very weary after all the tension and not in a mind to be interviewed.

"You should have been there, Mr. Wheeler, if you think you missed some news."

He was good-humored and paid no attention to her snub.

"Actually, I had my own adventure. I rode right into a party of Boers and they had the nerve to offer to buy my horse and saddle!"

"How awful! Were they hostile?"

"They laughed at me and called me a *rooinek*. Will you come over to Dixon's and I'll see if I can get you something cold to drink while we talk?"

"I ought to get back to Mrs. Partridge. She'll need help with the children."

"Does she own you?"

"Of course she doesn't, but—"

"Then spare me just ten minutes. You're the only one in all this rabble who is likely to talk intelligently. The people at home will want news. A lot of them with sons enlisting will be hanging on it." He took her arm. "If you're worrying about going into a hotel bar, this isn't Mayfair or Belgravia. It really doesn't matter what anyone does here."

She remembered how kind he had been with the children yesterday.

"Very well. Just ten minutes, and then I must go."

The bar seemed to be occupied mostly by war correspondents, judging by the greetings given to Mr. Wheeler.

"Well, Tom! What's the latest? Seen Cronje? Hear you were out looking for him. That's a dangerous game now."

But their eyes were on Lizzie, who had sat as demurely as possible at a table in the corner. She was finding her surroundings unexpectedly interesting.

"Have some whisky, Miss Willoughby?" Mr. Wheeler asked. "We'd better make the most of it while it lasts. Come now. Medicinally. You look as if you need it."

"Yes, it was an alarming experience. Very well, if you recommend it."

He went to the bar and brought back two whiskies only slightly diluted with water.

"Now," he said, sitting down, "what are you doing in this end-of-the-world place? Neither you nor your elegant friend belongs here, that's plain enough to see."

Lizzie frowned, her eyes wary.

"I thought it was an account of what happened today that you wanted."

"I do. But at this moment I'm more interested in you. Frankly, your face has haunted me ever since I met you yesterday. It's familiar, in some strange way. Have I seen it in London? What are you doing, Miss Lizzie? Running away from a husband?"

"That's impertinent," she said sharply, and added, "I have no husband."

He looked at her steadily for much too long. Then he said with perfect amiability, "Then tell me what happened today."

"It was very hot. The children found it extremely exhausting and frightening. We thought there might be Boers hiding behind outcrops of rock. There was a nasty young woman called Katie Roos who said horrible things. We all voted to come back to Mafeking, except her." She paused, sighing. "Is it always as hot as this here?"

"Yes, it's hot in the day and cold at night. In January and February it's very hot, enough to frizzle us all if we're still here. How would you say most people behaved today? Like gallant Britishers?"

"Oh, yes, of course."

"No 'of course' about it. We'll see various shades of behavior in the next few weeks."

"Yes, that's what I was thinking as we came back. About character building. There'd be some who got strong and some who got weaker."

41

"And some who pray for the war to end, and some who find it hypnotic and exciting and an escape."

"An escape from what?"

"Dullness, or personal complications that have no solution."

She realized that he was talking of himself as well as of her. He drank the whisky as if he needed it and got up to get another. She had scarcely touched hers. She sipped it as he stood at the bar, wincing at the raw, unfamiliar taste. How was it possible that in this little town at the end of the world someone had already recognized her? When he came back she said, "I don't know about personal complications, but of course you have known all the time who I am, though I can't imagine where you have seen me."

"Journalists are trained to have good memories. I went through a stint of reporting society functions. And yours is not a forgettable face, Lady Elizabeth."

Lizzie winced and said in a low voice, "My husband used to insist on showing me off. At least, in the early part of our marriage he did."

"But not recently?"

Mr. Wheeler's question was not inquisitive. He spoke in a quiet, sympathetic, concerned voice. Yesterday he had drawn pictures for the little girls, and today she found that he was the first person she could talk to without pain and humiliation about the nightmare of the last years with Humphrey.

"Our marriage was, unfortunately, not a happy one. A divorce was unthinkable, so I yielded to my husband's persuasions to begin a new life in another country."

"You have no children?"

"No."

"Then why is a divorce unthinkable? Why must you be tied all your life to someone you hate? How old are you?"

"Mr. Wheeler, aren't you a little forthright?"

"Twenty-five, I would say. Twenty-six?"

"Twenty-seven, if you must know. A great age."

"A woman's best age. And by bad luck or fate, or whatever it is, you are to spend it in an ugly little town in a state of siege. It's not exactly the place to make amends for past unhappiness or lost opportunities."

"That wasn't precisely why I came here," Lizzie said

dryly. "You misjudge me. I haven't only pleasure in mind."

"No, but pleasure is what everyone hopes for, isn't it? Otherwise, how would we face living at all? Well, we may have to do a lot of living quickly now that we find ourselves in the middle of a war. Drink up, Miss Willoughby. I promise you your secret is safe with me."

There was no time to say more, for the door leading to the street had been flung open and a man was shouting: "Kruger's declared war! B. P.'s going to speak. You'd better hurry if you want to hear him."

The unfamiliar alcohol had made Lizzie's head spin. She had to cling to Mr. Wheeler's arm, as to a bulwark, as they went out into the dusk to hear the solemn pronouncement from Colonel Baden-Powell standing on a hastily erected platform. A message had just come by telephone saying that Oom Paul Kruger, that brave, foolhardy, stubborn old man with his straggling beard, his broad-brimmed hat and shabby black frockcoat had declared war against the might of the British Empire. With tears streaming down his cheeks, the message said, he had made the fatal proclamation.

It was October 11, 1899.

Field glasses trained on the darkening veld showed no movement, but runners had come in with the news that the Boers were moving close, thousands of mounted men, stout bearded burghers with their sons riding at their sides, looking very unsoldierly in their sheepskin or leather jackets, but holding their rifles with practiced ease. In their wake was coming the slow line of trekking wagons loaded with supplies. They were under the command of General Piet Cronje, a seasoned campaigner, hard, able and resolute. With him were Generals Snyman, de la Rey and Hans Botha. So there was no doubting the importance placed on the capture of Mafeking, although some of the citizens still laughed about all the fuss being made for Paul Kruger's army. One would think a German Army Corps at least was expected.

The Town Guard had been hastily assembled in the Market Square. They were a mixed lot, with a dozen nationalities—English, Scots, Irish, Welsh, some loyal Dutch, Russians, Americans, Germans and Scandinavians. There were merchants, traders, pioneers. Some were ex-soldiers who had seen service at the Crimea, or against the Prussians in the siege of Paris. They were diverse in their looks, their clothes, their language, but they all had one thing in common—the defense of the town they regarded as their own.

Colonel Baden-Powell had walked up and down the lines inspecting this tough little company before he had mounted the platform and given his brief orders.

"All you have to do is to sit tight and when the time comes shoot straight, and you will soon send those fellows to the rightabout. Take my word for it, if you act as I fully expect you will act, the Boers will never enter Mafeking."

When he called for three cheers for the Queen the response was vigorous and followed immediately by three cheers for the Colonel himself. The people gathered in the cool dusk yelled themselves hoarse. It was a defense against the coming dark.

Nobody was anxious to go home. There was more comfort in being one of the crowd in the chilly, darkening square. But Mr. Brown, the Methodist missionary, took his shivering daughter's arm and said they must hurry home, where Mrs. Brown waited for them. She would be nervous, because early that day the Barolong girl, Mary, who helped in the kitchen, had fled to the kraal, preferring to take refuge with her own kind in this great terror.

They would kneel in the parlor, Mr. Brown said, and say a prayer for deliverance and perhaps sing a hymn.

Miss Rose was making her way to her lonely rooms attached to the school. She must write a letter to her only relative, her sister, in Exeter, in England. She would relate the day's events, how she had been persuaded, a reluctant and unlikely shepherdess, to escort several children to England, but the journey had been abortive. They had been turned back, so now she was here to help in every way she could, this clearly being God's will.

Miss Rose had come to South Africa several years ago with the noble plan of being a missionary. But something had gone wrong, no one knew what. She kept her own counsel. Whatever it was, she had not wanted to go back to England to confess failure. So she had settled, like a long-legged migrating bird, in the raw unfinished town of Mafeking and started a school. She wore the clothes she had brought with her ten years ago, out-of-date skirts and

44

blouses, washed thin and dingy with age. No one loved her, that was certain. The children obeyed her, for her sharp commands were intimidating. They thought of her as someone with a spelling book and a ruler, not as someone who ate and drank and slept and woke and loved and suffered as they did. She was a familiar and respected figure in the town, walking down the street with her thin nose in the air, sitting in church on Sunday, her flat figure clad in her Sunday costume of faded bottle-green, the one in which she had begun the journey today. But she successfully hid her emotions, and no one would have guessed now, from her composed face, that she was suffering, not fear, but a high exaltation. She was so sure that God had remembered her at last and given her important work to do.

Mrs. Ryan, exhausted from an endeavor that had been too much for a woman in her condition, had got her little girl Annie to bed, but Billy, her disobedient son, had disappeared.

She lay on the shabby sofa in the kitchen, complaining ceaselessly to her husband, until he sprang up impatiently.

"Stop it, Maggie, will you. I've had a hard day myself in them trenches. My back's fair broken."

"Where are you going, Jim?" Mrs. Ryan screamed.

"Out to get a beer while there's some left. It'll be rationed tomorrow, they say. Anyway, we might all be blown to bits by then."

"Jim!"

"Well, I tried to get you away, didn't I? It's not my fault you're stuck here. But since you are, you'll have to make the best of it. If we've got to die for our country, we've got to, though if I'd wanted to do that I'd have gone into the army at the start. Doesn't seem fair, having to die not of your own free will. But we'll have to make the best of it, Maggie. After tonight I'll most likely be sleeping in the trenches, so you'd better fix up with one of the neighbors to sleep here."

Then he was gone, and his wife fell back, her hands on her bulging stomach feeling the unborn baby stir and wondering where and how it would be born, certain its birth would be the death of her, if her husband's callousness or her worry over her children's safety didn't kill her first.

Billy, at that moment, was far from home. Star, his pony, had whickered with pleasure at his return, and he had leaped on her back for a gallop along the banks of the Molopo before it was dark. The wind blew his shaggy fair hair; his thin, freckled, plain little boy's face was alight with elation. His knees tucked into Star's fat sides. The roofs of the distant town glittered faintly. A few thin spirals of smoke rose from chimneys. The scattered scrub and thorn bushes were black against the stony earth. The troopers' horses, hundreds of them, were picketed just outside the town. Billy decided to beg some oats for Star from Corporal Smith. He knew there was enough fodder in the encampment to feed an army.

But of course this was an army. And that was queer because it was so quiet. The veld couldn't be full of thousands of Boers with a great gathering of horses and wagons. It was too quiet. A half moon was silvering the sky, and only a jackal howled.

Tom Wheeler had said a hasty goodbye to Lizzie Willoughby in the square. He had to hurry and get off his dispatch before the telephone wires were cut. He was living in a house vacated by a bank clerk when the threat of war became too real. A Kaffir boy Joey looked after him. The house had a flat roof from which Lizzie could watch the battle, if she cared to.

"Will there be one soon?" she asked, her excitement tempered by dread of the unknown.

"I don't know what else all this fuss is about. The Boers haven't brought up their long-range guns yet, so it will be safe enough on the roof. Are you sorry you came to this place?"

He was excited, too. She could see it in his taut face and gleaming eyes.

"No, I'm glad. I didn't in the least want to go today."

"It won't be the height of comfort."

"No, but it will be living, as you said."

"I said you might have to do a lot of living quickly, which is an entirely different thing."

"Yes. Yes, I know. I hope I'll be brave."

"You?" he said in surprise. "What else would you be?"

The friendly encounter with Tom Wheeler, the feeling

of being more sharply alive that the imminence of danger brought, gave Lizzie a lighthearted euphoric mood.

Alice was alone when she arrived home. She said at once, "What's that smell on your breath, Lizzie? Have you been drinking whisky?"

"How would you know?"

"I haven't been married to Bertie for seven years without recognizing that particular smell. What have you been doing, Lizzie? Isn't everything bad enough without your going inside hotels? You're not accustomed to doing that sort of thing, are you?"

"No, I'm not accustomed to it. I won't contaminate your children. But on the eve of war—Didn't you know war had been declared?" Lizzie looked at Alice's fine, drawn face, the shadows of weariness beneath her eyes, and made a decision. "A drink wouldn't be a bad thing for you, either. Where's Bertie?"

"Gone out. He said something about helping with an armored train—oh, I promised not to speak of it! It's supposed to be secret. The town is full of Boer spies, Bertie said."

"And the children?"

"Asleep. They asked for you. Daisy thought her dear Miss Lizzie had vanished."

"I'm sorry. I had meant to come at once. But Colonel Baden-Powell was speaking in the square, and Mr. Wheeler talked to me."

"Mr. Wheeler has taken a fancy to you. I noticed him looking at you. But be careful. He's probably married. Anyway, he'll be killed, most likely. Bertie, too. In a war, all the nicest, bravest men get killed."

"If I know your husband," Lizzie said, "he'll have some spirits in the house. Let's look."

"Why, Lizzie! I believe you're drunk already."

"No, but I intend to be. You, too. That's far better than sitting here shivering with fright."

Alice gasped when Lizzie, opening cupboards in the kitchen, came on the stock of bottles, obviously hoarded in anticipation of the siege. "Good gracious! I never knew my husband cared so much for alcohol." Her eyes gleamed. "I have never tasted spirits in my life, but I intend to now. Open a bottle at once, Lizzie."

47

They sat at the kitchen table drinking out of cups because Alice had not been able to find any glasses. She couldn't imagine a house without crystal and fine porcelain, but perhaps it didn't matter after all, since the Boers would probably take possession of it before long.

"Bertie said those fat *vrouws* would be wearing my clothes," Alice said resentfully. "But not before I wear them first. Why shouldn't one keep up appearances? Tomorrow I intend to buy material, if one can in this terrible place, and make curtains and cushions. I shall need two dozen yards of white muslin."

"How do you know the exact quantity?"

"Because I've been measuring."

"Not already!"

"But of course. The house is naked. It's indecent. The moment the children were in bed I got out my workbox and my tape measure. Bertie says he'll find a Kaffir girl to work in the kitchen so we'll have to make caps and aprons for her, too. Can you sew?"

Lizzie was beginning to laugh helplessly.

"Alice, there's a war on, and you're talking of dressing up an ignorant black girl like an English parlormaid."

Alice pouted. She was already flushed from the whisky she had swallowed.

"That's my way of fighting a war, behaving like a civilized person. I won't have my children brought up like savages. Have you any better suggestions to make?"

"Yes, indeed. I'm not wasting my time with a needle and thread. I intend to offer my services at the hospital tomorrow."

Alice's lip quivered.

"Will I be here—alone—with the children?"

"Not if there's fighting. You'll be in a shelter."

Alice put down her glass.

"Not with all those frightful people off the train! I won't do it. The girls and I will stay here. Lizzie, pour me just a teeny—I wonder why I suddenly feel dizzy."

"So do I," said Lizzie, giggling.

"You and that Mr. Wheeler! He *looks* married, and you must find out if he is or not."

"People can be married and still—friends."

Alice leaned forward, looking at Lizzie earnestly. "Dear

Lizzie, you look unhappy. Is that what was in your past? A married man?"

The room blurred. Lizzie wasn't certain whether she was laughing or crying.

"Who cares? There's a war on and one lives from day to day. From minute to minute."

"We're drinking spirits!" Alice exclaimed in horror, as if she had just realized the fact. "Imagine if that old lady who looked like Queen Victoria saw us."

"Or the schoolmistress."

"Or that milk-and-water parson's daughter."

"I think I came past their house. I could hear a hymn being sung. 'Shall we gather at the river.' "

Alice began to sing in a high sweet shaky voice.

> Shall we gather at the river
> Where bright angels' feet have tro-od . . .

Lizzie picked up the refrain.

> Shall we gather at the river.
> The beautiful, the beautiful river
> Gather with the saints at the river,
> That flows from the hills of God . . .

They both collapsed in laughter.

"Imagine if the parson heard us."

"Imagine if God heard us."

"Lizzie! I believe we're intoxicated."

"But not frightened."

"Let's clear this mess up before Bertie comes home, or he'll divorce me. He only wants an excuse."

"Alice!" Lizzie protested.

Alice gave her a sideways drunken miserable look.

"Sometimes I think so. Not always. If he got his son he'd be content. He thinks I'm only good enough to give birth to girls. So I've come all this way—to this horrible town—to p-prove—" Alice looked at Lizzie, the tears running down her cheeks. "That's the truth. That's why I came."

Lizzie said with careful solemnity, "Then you'll have to prove it. Won't you? War or no war. Just as I—"

"What do you have to prove, dear Lizzie?"

49

"I don't know. Just that I can live, I suppose."

"Bertie treats me as if I am—a sort of ornament—I and the girls. So I try to live up to it. That's partly why I brought that damn piano—" Alice pressed her fingers to her mouth, mirth struggling with her tears. "Goodness, now I'm using bad language. It must come out of the b-bottle—"

They both started giggling wildly again. Finally Alice said, with some semblance of sobriety, "We must go to bed, or we won't be awake for the Boers when they come. At least we've got through this dreadful evening. Better than singing hymns, or kneeling on hard floors praying."

"When the time comes for hymns," said Lizzie, "then we'll sing them."

"Would you believe it—two well-bred ladies. Oh, I'm so tired. Bertie won't get his son tonight. Poor Lizzie. You have to sleep alone."

"Not forever," said Lizzie.

VI

At one o'clock Bertie Partridge, so tired that he stumbled on his stiff leg, went home. The armored train was nearly ready for its first sortie, but all was still quiet. The moon rode high over a still landscape. From their vantage points, the lookouts stared across the veld until their eyes ached. No alarm was given. The night remained completely peaceful.

Just before dawn a wind rose and howled mournfully. This desolate sound provided a fitting accompaniment to the scene being enacted outside the house of Mr. Julius Weil. Mr. Weil had had a distinguished guest, none other than Lady Sarah Wilson, who had been accompanying her husband, Captain Gordon Wilson, on a shooting expedition in South Africa when war had been declared. She had come to Mafeking with him when he had joined Colonel Baden-Powell's Protectorate Regiment. Now that hostilities were about to commence the Colonel didn't care to have a daughter of the Duke of Marlborough in the town. Against Lady Sarah's wishes, he persuaded her to leave, to seek safety in the township of Setlagoli, thirty-five miles away, where there was a small hotel. Later it might be necessary for her to move again to a mission station in the Kalahari desert, but at present the urgent necessity was to get her out of the beleaguered town. A Cape cart and six mules had been acquired. This was driven by a Cape boy who had once been Doctor Jameson's servant, and who was completely trustworthy. Lady Sarah and her maid, a German girl, were to ride in the cart, and Lady Sarah's white pony was to be led by another Cape boy.

The farewells, in the chilly windy dawn, had to be brief. Utterly miserable, Lady Sarah set her face toward the veld. Already the sun was rising. Soon it would be scorchingly hot. They had thirty-five miles to travel with the wind blowing sand ceaselessly in their faces, and the sun beating down mercilessly. Lady Sarah would infinitely have preferred to stay in Mafeking and share the danger with her husband and friends. She had the cold feeling that she would never see any one of them again.

But orders had to be obeyed. The mules were whipped up, and the little conveyance creaked down the dusty road out of the town.

By midmorning Tom Wheeler's native boy Joey returned from a sortie of his own. He was an adept scout and had been out since midnight gathering information. There were big guns and wagons and many many men out there, he said. The men, with their long beards and strange assortment of clothing, sat and held *indabas*. Some of them played card games, and some sang hymns and said prayers. Joey knew all about the religious part, because the missionary, Mr. Brown, had taught his people to do exactly the same. He was indignant that the Boers, who were enemies, should be behaving in this way.

He had lain since early morning in the blazing sun, as still as a lizard on a rock, listening and observing.

Still, no shot had been fired.

As the morning went on, Colonel Baden-Powell crossed Market Square whistling. He was a compulsive whistler, it seemed. Or he may have been doing it to keep up people's morale.

The little knot of war correspondents gathered in Dixon's Hotel were waiting impatiently for something to send home in dispatches. Tom Wheeler wrote:

"Since there has been no movement by the enemy, life is going on much as usual. The ladies have gone out shopping. Most of them have lingered, with their shopping baskets, in Market Square to gossip and to cast occasional glances at the church bell, which is to be rung if an attack is threatened. All the small boys are hoping to be chosen for Major Lord Edward Cecil's Boys' Brigade which has been formed, at the suggestion of Colonel Baden-Powell, so that the boys may run errands or carry messages to the men at the outposts and in the trenches. On the principle that life must continue as normally as possible, some parents have sent their children to school. I hear that Mrs. Albert Partridge, newly arrived from England, is to give a children's party this afternoon to introduce her three little girls to other children. 'We must keep them happy,' she said. 'I regard this as more important at the present time than going to first aid classes and rolling bandages. After all, we may not have any sick or wounded, may we?' For a newcomer, Mrs. Partridge is setting a fine example of coolness but she is unduly optimistic. There will be sick and wounded, and dead and dying. This morning Father Ogle said a special Mass for the men in the trenches and guarding the outposts. More practical, if less optimistic, than Mrs. Partridge, Miss Hill at the hospital has prepared as many beds as possible. But it is still quiet, the sun gets hotter by the minute, and the color of the red pepper berries suggests only one comparison."

Six children went to the party at the Partridge house. Several of those invited were kept home by cautious mothers, and Billy Ryan had been detained for an hour in school for being rude and insolent.

Miss Rose sat at her desk marking school books while Billy's resentful pencil squeaked over his slate. "I must not be lazy and disobedient." He was waiting until Miss Rose turned her head and then he was going to fly. He sniffed loudly and regularly, determined not to let the furious tears come. Corporal Smith had said to him that morning that when things got worse there would be no fodder for his pony. "We have to look after the regiment's horses first, lad. You'd better be prepared. I hope it won't come to eating horse flesh, but if it does—" Billy had been too horrified to reply. He had simply stared aghast, and at last Corporal Smith had laughed and said that that old pony would be too tough, anyway.

So he missed the party at the Partridges', which was a pity because Henrietta and Fanny had liked him yesterday. He had amused them by pulling faces. Even solemn Daisy had laughed.

There were not as many delicacies as Alice would have liked, because she had heeded the instructions to be careful with food. But she had baked the little cakes herself, and iced them with pink icing, and made jugs of lemonade, and put on a freshly ironed gown. It had been an extremely busy morning with the trunks to unpack and the cooking to do. She had postponed shopping for material for curtains, after all. The important thing was to keep busy. She found then that she forgot to be frightened and was not so conscious of her headache, which had persisted all day as a result of her and Lizzie's quite unprecedented and extraordinary excesses of the previous evening.

Bertie had roared his head off when he had discovered what they had been up to. How could he help but find out, since the house stank of whisky?

"Just don't make a habit of it," he had said to his still-comatose wife. He had been too tired to think much of it, except that war did curious things to people. Imagine someone like his elegant Alice kicking over the traces like that.

The party today was much more her form. Keeping up appearances, a stiff upper lip, and all that. She'd show this hybrid town what an English lady was made of. He thoroughly approved. But they mustn't make so much noise that they didn't hear the alarm bell if it rang.

There was plenty of hilarity. Lizzie joined in, and Tom Wheeler and one or two others strolled along. The children played Find the Handkerchief and Ring a Rosy on the lawn, its carefully watered grass already wilting in the afternoon heat. Above the hilarity, Alice listened for the warning sound of the church bells, one part of her ready to vibrate to danger. But if a war had to be endured, this was the way to endure it, with her husband approving of her dash, even of her shocking libertine behavior last evening. And the children were happy. Daisy's solemn face sparkled at last.

So the first twenty-four hours of the war had passed, and still, in Bechuanaland, not a shot had been fired. But that evening a railway ganger came trudging down the line to report that the Boers were tearing up the rails to the south, and that therefore the second armored engine that had been expected from Kimberley could not arrive.

Colonel Baden-Powell decided the time had come to make his intended reconnaissance.

Bertie Partridge came home at midnight saying, "Well, the train's ready," and poured himself a stiff drink. Then he undressed and washed, and went to bed with his wife. If the thought had entered his head that a siege was scarcely the time to make a woman pregnant, he dismissed it. Dear devoted Alice had traveled a long way to be with him, and since one never knew whether or not this might

54

be their last night on earth, it would be foolish not to make the most of it.

Alice was not semicomatose with whisky tonight. She was very conscious indeed and went into his arms with a little cry that was half laugh, half sob.

Lizzie, unable to sleep in the next room, wished that the walls were not so thin. She turned on her pillow and tried to remember Humphrey's face, before it had got so choleric with bad temper, and saw Tom Wheeler's instead. She hadn't had an opportunity at the party that afternoon to ask him whether or not he was married. The question would keep.

Early the next morning everyone who was still asleep was aroused by the rumbling sound of the armored train steaming out. This strange contraption, like a monolithic insect, had been in preparation for some weeks. It comprised a number of open trucks covered with armor, drawn by an engine completely encased in steel. Its object was to crawl along the railway lines into Boer territory to see if any enemy patrols could be persuaded to show themselves.

It chugged slowly over the bridge of the Molopo and disappeared into the heat haze. Shortly afterward the first shots heard in Mafeking sounded raggedly in the distance. People rushed out of their houses. What was happening? Was there to be an attack? The shots died away and the rumors began. No one knew the truth and the waiting was exacerbating to the nerves.

Several Englishwomen turned on a little group of Dutch, whose spokeswoman was Katie Roos. There were accusations of "Spies!"—which was too much for Katie's hot temper. With eyes blazing, she declared shockingly that she hoped the town would soon be running with English blood.

There was a forward rush by the incensed Englishwomen, and a scratching and hair-pulling fight was prevented only by two members of the Town Guard, who begged the ladies to behave themselves. Wasn't it enough that the men were fighting?

Katie slunk sullenly back to her friends. Lizzie Willoughby, who had observed all this with disgust, nevertheless asked herself a cool question. If she had a Dutch husband with whom she was in love, and whose cause she believed to be just, wouldn't she be wholeheartedly on his side? Poor Katie, she must be hating herself for being a traitor to her own country, but was she already picturing her husband lying on the veld with the aasvogels circling, waiting to pick out his eyes?

After what seemed an interminable time, the train came rumbling back. The driver reported that a small company of Boer horsemen had been encountered. The train had opened fire, and the horsemen, leaving one of their number dead, had been put to flight.

After that, Colonel Baden-Powell had another card up his sleeve. Coupled to two good trucks, another engine steamed out of Mafeking. Twenty minutes later an explosion rocked the town. A column of smoke billowed into the air and the startled townspeople gazed in fear and dismay.

But the engine, detached from the two trucks, came puffing safely back into the railway station. The maneuver had been successful. Unaware that the two trucks were loaded with dynamite, Boer horsemen had opened fire on them and blown them sky-high.

The strategy had worked. The enemy now believed that the rumors of large supplies of dynamite held in Mafeking were true, and that therefore the report of minefields laid around the town must also be true. No reckless attack was likely to be made.

But another piece of information not so reassuring to the beleaguered people had come in. The railway both to the north and to the south was cut. So now they were really alone. There would be no more news from the outside world except that brought in by scouts or native runners.

Lizzie and Alice had a conference. Lizzie said she wanted to volunteer for work at the hospital, but she didn't like leaving Alice alone with the children. Alice, who had remained paper-white ever since the sound of the train blowing up, said she would be perfectly all right. Bertie had found a Barolong girl, a young creature who had a toddler at her heels, to help her. The girl's name was Maisie, of all unlikely names, and she spoke a little English. She had worked for English people and knew how to cook simple meals. Henrietta and Fanny and

Daisy were enchanted with the little potbellied black baby. Alice intended cutting down one of her own cotton dresses to clothe Maisie, since the poor thing had appeared in the most dreadful garment. It was quite likely that she would run off at the first sound of gunfire, but Alice, with a forlorn attempt at bravado, said she would probably be hiding under the bed herself, so she couldn't criticize other people. Anyway, Bertie had promised to come home to protect his family if an attack did begin.

"You're so much braver than I," Alice said admiringly to Lizzie. "I'd never stand the sight of blood."

"I don't know whether I can stand it myself," Lizzie said honestly. "I expect I'll soon find out."

There was an ex-army doctor at the hospital, a middle-aged Scotsman named Macpherson. He had given a lecture on first aid to the several young women who had come to offer their services, and at the end he had spoken to Lizzie.

"You've done something like this before, Miss Willoughby?"

"Yes, in London some years ago."

"A little polite charity work, I suppose?"

"Yes. I helped in an organization in the East End before I"—she had been going to say before she married, —"before I arranged to come to South Africa to stay with my brother."

"Then you have experience with sickness, typhoid perhaps?"

"Not with infectious diseases. Are you expecting typhoid?"

"We are. Also dysentery, enteric, perhaps cholera."

Lizzie had a sharp feeling of sickness.

"Among the children, you mean?"

"Not only the children. But they'll most likely be the worst sufferers, particularly the ones who have careless mothers. Ignorance, lack of hygiene, lack of water and good food, heat, flies, we have every kind of condition necessary to an epidemic. It's a pity you didn't get out of the town in time."

"Not me," said Lizzie. "But I wish my friend Mrs. Partridge had got away. She has three little girls who are quite unacclimatized."

"Bad luck," said Doctor Macpherson quietly. He had

57

sandy hair and sandy eyebrows and blue eyes that were steady and uncompromising. There was none of Tom Wheeler's haggard brilliance here. Lizzie decided that Doctor Macpherson would be completely reliable, if rather dull. All the same, she hoped that if she fainted at the first sight of blood, it would not be in his presence.

After the gigantic explosion that morning there had been silence again. But it was now a doubly deceptive silence, for scouts coming into Mafeking reported that the town was practically encircled. Major Godley, from his command of the outposts, reported rumors that a party of the enemy intended coming by Riet Vlei and up the river bed; another from Ramathlabama might attack Game Tree Hill.

Andy Buchanan paid a quick visit to his grandmother. He had a couple of hours off duty. He wanted a wash and a change of underclothing and a cup of tea. He burst out laughing at the sight of the elephant gun.

"Whatever do you think you can do with that old thing, Granny? Blow Cronje's head off?"

"I wouldn't miss if I got the chance."

"I bet you wouldn't. Granny—"

"What is it?"

"You wouldn't think of moving in with the neighbors?"

"I would not." The old lady shut her mouth decisively. Then she asked sharply, "What's the matter? Is something going to happen?"

There was a tension about him in spite of his grin and his casual air. Something on fire in his eyes. His father had looked just like that a week before Majuba Hill.

"An attack?" she asked calmly.

"Perhaps."

"Us, or the Boers?"

"How do I know? The C. O. doesn't confide in me. By the way, Granny, if you see Linda Hill, tell her not to go larking with any of those swanky officers or I'll have her hair out by the roots."

"Why don't you tell her yourself?"

"Haven't time."

Or courage? It must be terrible to face death if you were young and had never had a girl.

58

"I'll tell her tomorrow," Mrs. Buchanan said. "She'll be a day older then, more deserving of such a message."

"Aw, Granny. She's nearly seventeen. Old enough to be married."

"And you, too, I suppose."

"Sure," said Andy confidently, his eyes sparking.

Then he was gone, and Mrs. Buchanan knew that he would go through his baptismal fire that night or early in the morning, and that she herself wouldn't sleep a wink. So she had better get on with her knitting. It would be cold in the trenches at night. The men were going to be glad of hand-knit socks and mufflers.

Just before dawn, all the light sleepers in the town, or those who hadn't slept at all, heard the rifle shots. There was a fight going on out on the veld. No one knew what had happened except that the armored train had gone out to support the skirmishers. Rumors began to circulate that a patrol under Captain Lord Charles Bentinck had clashed with the enemy.

People began to gather in the square, listening, and watching the horizon to the east. There were heated arguments among Dutch women, strongly partisan, and the furious English. Mrs. Ryan, incompletely dressed, rushed out screaming, "The Boers are coming!" and promptly collapsed. She was carried back into her house and given first aid. No one wanted to cope with a premature birth at that moment.

As the firing grew heavier, Mrs. Ryan was not the only woman on the verge of hysteria. Alice Partridge got the girls dressed somehow (Bertie, on the first sound of firing, had rushed off on Town Guard duties, promising to be back as soon as he could); then she closed the shutters of the living room and locked the door. Henrietta said that it was too dark to see to button her boots, and why weren't they having breakfast?

"Because the Boers are coming to eat us up," Fanny said ghoulishly. Two enormous tears ran down Daisy's cheeks, and she held up her arms to her mother.

"What nonsense," said Alice. "Colonel Baden-Powell wouldn't let any such thing happen."

A particularly loud burst of gunfire rattled the window frames. Alice repressed her sick fear and gathered the little girls around her with a storybook. "I'll read to you until all that noise is over."

"But won't we go to school?" Henrietta wanted to know.

"Probably not today."

"Oh, goody! I'm glad there's a war."

"Not if the Boers come and eat you up," Fanny reminded her.

"It's too noisy," whispered Daisy, burying her head in her mother's lap.

At the hospital the matron gave sharp orders to the nurses and volunteer aids.

"Make up as many beds as there are. Put mattresses on the floor, if necessary. We must be prepared."

At the Convent of the Irish Sisters of Mercy the same thing was happening. And at his headquarters Colonel Baden-Powell put down his field telephone and made the decision to send Captain Fitzclarence with "D" squadron of the Protectorate Regiment to the support of Captain Bentinck. A troop of "A" squadron under Lieutenant Brady followed.

The dust raised by their horses' hooves settled. The khaki-clad figures melted into the landscape. Little distant puffs of smoke from the firing rose and dispersed. The Boer sniping, people said, was reputed to be deadly. The marksmen hid themselves in the branches of thorn trees or behind outcrops of rock. Unless they could be needled out, it would not go well with the British exposed on horses.

In her bedroom Amy Brown knelt with her hands pressed over her ears, trying to pray. "Dear God, please . . ." she kept saying, but that was as far as she could get with her request. Her father came in and patted her shoulder and told her to be brave, God would protect them. But supposing God had a whim to protect the Boers instead, Amy sobbed childishly.

Lizzie, working hard at the hospital, glad to be occupied, wondered momentarily where Tom Wheeler was. She made a guess that he would be as near to the battle as possible. Supposing, when the stretchers began to come in later, as they certainly must do, she were to recognize his face on one of them . . .

"Miss Willoughby, don't stand there daydreaming! We need more blankets from the storeroom. And tuck those sheets in properly. Do you want the patient to fall out of bed?"

Supposing there were no wounded to come in. Supposing all those young men who had ridden out eager for action lay dead on the veld . . .

VII

By midday the battle was over. Billy Ryan dashed into the Market Square saying that he could see troopers coming back, some walking. "The bloody Boers have shot their horses!" he shouted in the greatest indignation.

No one remonstrated with him about his language, for it was all too true. The armored train came puffing slowly back laden with wounded. Major Anderson, who had tended them under fire, waited for ambulances to take them to the hospital. There were sixteen casualties, two of them grave. And two dead left behind on the battlefield, as well as sixteen dead horses.

Andy Buchanan dismounted, saying excitedly that they had encountered hundreds of Boers. But the armored train had proved too formidable a weapon for the Boers. There had been terrible slaughter. The ground was thick with dead and wounded.

He himself had a scratch over one eyebrow. The blood had run down his cheek, making him look fierce and exhausted. Both Captain Bentinck and Lieutenant Brady were among the wounded.

In the midst of all the excitement and the relief that what had seemed such a terrible battle had resulted in such light casualties, an emissary with a Red Cross flag arrived at the outposts with a letter from General Snyman.

Battlefield near Mafeking

To COLONEL BADEN-POWELL:

I have been informed that you have several dead troopers on the battlefield. I will guarantee the safety of your ambulance wagons and party until 8 P.M. this evening should you wish to recover them. A party of my men shall meet your party and point out the bodies.

So the sad little party went out. They came back to report that the Boer dead amounted to at least sixty, and there must have been another hundred or more wounded. They also reported that their own dead had been robbed of rings, rifles and bandoliers, and that the Red Cross flag they had carried had been fired on and they had had to hastily retreat.

The scene of slaughter, the drained corpses and the blood drying on the ground, the smell of spent powder and death in the burning sun, the aasvogels floating in slow circles, had proved too much for the less hardened ambulance men. They came back looking yellow in the face, and silent.

The scene at the cemetery, too, later that evening when the sun had set, was too painful for many of the women and some of the men. The first blood had been spilled, the first graves dug in the hard red earth. How many more would follow before this foolish tragic war was over?

Already it seemed certain that soon the two gravely wounded men would lie beside their comrades. Father Ogle, the Roman Catholic priest, officiated and said that in the Convent the good Sisters were praying for the souls of the gallant men.

The moon was rising, and the yawning graves looked as black as the priest's cassock. No volley was fired. The rifle shots might have raised new alarm in the tired, nervous town. But the poignant notes of the "Last Post" sounded across the darkening landscape and were audible in the hospital, where Lizzie, shocked and exhausted by her first sight of blood and unmanageable pain, still lingered.

Sister Casey had told her to go home half an hour ago. Some of the men had light wounds; some had been operated on; but all were now settled for the night. Lamps were lit in the wards and put on the floor so as to make the minimum of light should General Cronje decide to bring up his big guns and shell the town. Some of the men slept; some, half unconscious with chloroform, groaned. The two who were likely to die before morning were behind screens. Lizzie had not been allowed to see them. But she could hear their peculiar, infinitely distressing, bubbling breath, and every now and then, from one of

63

them, a high-pitched scream that was slowly growing weaker. The matron, Miss Hill, stayed with them.

So they were not alone, Sister Casey said briskly to Lizzie. A good nurse never allowed her patient to die alone, if she could help it. Lizzie was to be back at eight sharp in the morning. There would be plenty to do then.

"I hate death. I hate it, I hate it, I hate it," Lizzie had kept saying under her breath. She hadn't fainted, and she hoped she hadn't flinched noticeably, although once she had had to rush away to vomit. But the chant under her breath had somehow kept her going, and somehow, she fancied, helped to keep death at bay. One of the boys was only sixteen, and he had lost a leg. He was going to have to hop about on a wooden one for the rest of his life, and how was he to get over worrying what a girl would think of him as a lover? Doctor Macpherson had made her hold a basin, and asked her to pass him swabs, which he used and threw, bloodied, into the basin. He seemed to have forgotten that she was new to this ugly side of life. Or else he knew that she was more likely to live up to the shocking challenge if her inexperience was not acknowledged.

Anyway, she had managed to survive, but now the long day was over she was trembling so much that she could hardly walk home. When she came within sight of the Brown house, she saw that there was a light in the parlor. Mr. Brown must be holding one of his prayer meetings. Indeed, it was inevitable that he would, for he would never let such a magnificent occasion for prayer pass unexploited.

What a thing to think, Lizzie told herself tiredly. Mr. Brown was good, sincere and probably terribly distressed by the day's happenings. But tonight she couldn't believe in comforting words, or reassurances of heaven for those young men whose breath escaped in bubbles of blood.

Neither did she think she had the energy to go home to see how Alice had fared. She would have to try to keep the shock out of her face so that the children wouldn't be upset. She didn't know how she could talk to them, or to Alice, who would want to cling to her for strength.

I'm not strong, Alice. I'm weak and shocked and sick, and I'm frightened to shut my eyes or I'll go on seeing the blood and the look in Peter Moody's eyes. Private

64

Peter Moody, a soldier at only sixteen, but with his career already over . . .

She turned to the only refuge she knew, and a strange one at that, the bar of Dixon's Hotel.

No one seemed surprised to see her come in alone. When she asked if Mr. Wheeler was there, the barkeeper said he hadn't been in that evening, and one of the other war correspondents asked her why she didn't go to Tom's house.

"He might be back. There's nothing left to see on the battlefield but corpses."

Lizzie realized that they all had hollow, exhausted faces. One of them was holding a blood-stained handkerchief to a wound on his temple.

"Do you know Tom's house? It's not a stone's throw from here. Opposite the church."

Joey came to the door.

"Baas away," he said.

"Where?"

Joey shook his woolly head. "Walking around, maybe. The big guns don't scare him."

Lizzie clung to the doorpost. She was suddenly so tired that she couldn't move.

"But the battle's over long ago."

Joey nodded amiably. He seemed to expect her to come inside, accepting her as his master's friend. So she did, stepping into a room whose only furniture was a table littered with papers and drawing materials, one chair and a leather-covered sofa. The bank clerk, although in a hurry to vacate Mafeking, had not been in such a hurry that there had not been time to pack his best possessions. Even the floor was bare.

Joey, obviously an exceptional servant, indicated that he would bring Lizzie some food. The baas would come in soon very hungry, he said.

Lizzie shook her head.

"Don't bring me anything. Wait till the baas comes. I'll just sit down for a minute."

She had to do that, because her legs were folding beneath her. She slid into the chair at the table, where Joey had politely set down a lighted lamp.

The light fell on an unfinished letter, the black writing

65

on the white paper springing into such prominence that her eyes could not help but read the words.

DEAR MILLY,
How have you both been? Has Edward begun the school you mentioned? Tell him that I expect to be proud of him . . .

So he was married, Lizzie thought flatly. Married and with a son. For who else could Milly and Edward be?

Well, what about it? She was married, too. To an angry, vindictive cripple who refused to see her, and who had never been able to give her a son.

Her hands lay on the sheet of paper, her fingers curling as she restrained a quite surprising impulse to tear it up. She managed not to, and was too tired to analyze her motives.

She opened her eyes a few minutes later to see Tom himself standing over her.

"Have you been here all night?"

"Certainly not." Lizzie stirred, feeling the aching weariness in her bones. "I must have just fallen asleep. Joey said you wouldn't be long." She pressed open her eyes, holding up the heavy lids with her fingers. "Why do you say all night?"

"Because it's almost daylight."

"It can't be!"

"It is."

"I don't believe it! I can't have slept all night sitting up in a chair!"

He looked down at her, smiling a little, his own face haggard with weariness.

"You must have been tired."

"I came here from the hospital."

He understood at once. "Bad?"

She nodded. Tom went to the door leading into the kitchen and clapped his hands.

"Joey! Wake up. Make some coffee. Plenty of it."

Then he came back and fell on to the couch, stretching his legs.

"I'm tired, too. I've been out all night."

"Why?"

"Doing some scouting. I'm improving my technique. I

got within yards of one of the Boer laagers. Heard them talking. They weren't very happy about yesterday's affair. About sixty dead. I saw the wounded being brought in. Dozens of ambulance carts. It was the armored train that defeated them. I gather they expected it to blow up, like the dynamite trucks the other day, and instead it fired back and picked them off their horses. However, their turn will come. There are thousands of them, and reinforcements coming in all the time. I heard something about a siege gun they're bringing in to blow us all sky-high."

"Is this true? Would they really shell women and children?"

"They're determined to take Mafeking."

Lizzie sat still, her eyes dilated with horror.

"If you don't like being woken up with unpalatable news, Miss Lizzie, you shouldn't be here."

"I was thinking of the Partridge children. Other children, too. That boy who lost his leg yesterday. And two others were dying."

"The Boers are counting their losses in tens, not in twos."

"Does that help ours who died? Or Peter Moody with his one leg?" She got up, her bones stiff. "I must go home to Alice. I'll have to make her believe about the siege gun. She's a great one for unreality."

"Wait for your coffee. Here it is now."

Joey had come in carrying a tray with steaming mugs of coffee. Tom handed one to Lizzie.

"And you're one for reality?"

"I've learned to be."

"Then you'd better tidy your hair before you go home."

She felt her tumbling locks and ineffectually tried to pin them.

"Shall I?" said Tom.

She stood submissively.

"Please. Who are Milly and Edward?"

"My wife and son." His fingers were expert. It seemed that he had experience either in doing or undoing women's hair. "You'd better tell your friend Alice you've been at the hospital all night. Or say what you like. It depends how much you worry about conventions."

Lizzie sipped the hot coffee, and felt warmth and a faint familiar stirring of rebellion.

"I don't worry about them at all, but I can't help thinking of poor Humphrey tied to a wheelchair while I'm doing the fighting-for-Empire stuff. He'd never believe it. He always despised me."

"Why?"

"Because he wanted to. Tom Wheeler, you're a prying journalist, but I'm glad for you all the same. I'm so glad for someone to talk to."

"I, too."

"You have"—she gestured to the unfinished letter—"Milly and Edward."

"You think that makes me immune from the need for other human communication?"

"You can have it in the bar at Dixon's Hotel. With your own kind."

"Can I be scared to death only in the company of the war correspondents for the *Times* and the *Pall Mall Gazette?*"

"Are you scared, Tom?"

"I was when I saw that particular sight on the veld."

She noticed how the skin was tight over his cheekbones, the hollows scooped beneath his eyes. Her own jaw ached with the effort to control her trembling.

"Come here whenever you like, Lizzie. But if I'm not here, don't worry. I'll be around."

"Around where?"

"Doing my job. Getting news."

"Will Joey know where you are?"

"Perhaps. Now that's enough. Get on your way."

She walked home slowly, wondering about her feeling of happiness in spite of the dreadful day yesterday and the certainty of dreadful things to come.

But she was ashamed of her happiness when she saw Alice's wan but valiantly cheerful face. She was giving Henrietta and Fanny their first piano lesson and sprang up when Lizzie came in.

"Oh, there you are at last! I've worried all night. Bertie said you must be at the hospital still."

Lizzie stooped to kiss the children, one after the other, noticing that they were immaculately dressed in starched pinafores with ribbons in their hair. Soon Alice was going to run out of starch, or water, or hot irons, and then would her morale collapse?

"No, I wasn't at the hospital all night. I have to go back there now. I just came to see how you were."

"Miss Lizzie, we heard the guns," Henrietta was saying in her hectoring voice. "Daisy cried. I didn't."

"Nor I didn't," said Fanny.

Daisy lifted her fat arms to Lizzie, and, when she was picked up, pressed her face, still haunted by yesterday's alarm, against Lizzie's bosom.

"She'll have to get used to it," Alice said. "It's nothing at all to be afraid of, as Papa and I keep telling her. That rather dreadful little boy, Billy Ryan, brought his pony to show the children and that cheered them up."

"She's called Star, and he says we may ride her," Henrietta said. "But Mamma says girls can't ride bareback. Is that true, Miss Lizzie?"

"If Mamma says so, then I expect it is."

"I won't have them growing up like outlaws," Alice said.

Alice, dear vain silly creature, the Boers are bringing up a siege gun. And Doctor Macpherson says there'll be typhoid and enteric. If the children want to ride a pony bareback, let them, while they can . . .

"Children! Run outside and play. Put on your sunbonnets, and don't go outside the front gate." Alice spoke distractedly, seeing something in Lizzie's face. As the children ran off she asked, "What is it? Why are you looking like that? Lizzie!" Her voice was a whisper. "There's blood on your skirt!"

"Oh! And I wore an apron, too. I'll wash it off."

"Was it awful? I could hear the 'Last Post' at the cemetery last night. Bertie had come home, thank heaven. We sat with the children until they went to sleep, and then Bertie told me about the battle. He said some of the wounded were desperately ill."

"Yes."

"Poor Lizzie, you look exhausted. Did you sit up all night?"

"Yes, but not at the hospital. I called to see Tom Wheeler and he wasn't home, and I fell asleep in a chair."

"In his house!"

"I didn't mean to. But I was so tired. When I woke

69

up it was morning, and he had just come in. Alice, you look more shocked than if you'd heard the Boers were through the outer trenches."

"Are you falling in love with this man?"

"Alice, what a romantic you are! How can I when he's already married? He has a wife called Milly."

It was really quite amusing to see Alice's shocked face.

"Lizzie, how can you be so *rash?* I'd never have believed it of you. I thought you were a lady. So did Bertie. He congratulated me on finding such a suitable traveling companion. But what with making me drink all that dreadful whisky the other night and now this—Lizzie, are you mad? Or have you always behaved in this way?"

"I only wanted to talk to Tom. And I'm only telling you this because you'll think about it all day instead of worrying about the Boers." Lizzie leaned forward and kissed Alice on the cheek. "There now. I have to go back to the hospital. I promise to come home tonight, if you don't think me too wicked to have in the house."

VIII

Later that morning there was a new excitement in the town. Katie Roos and her Dutch friends were put in jail. That would teach them to be so free in their remarks about wanting to see English blood run.

The mayor, Mr. Whiteley, said that he would like to see every Dutchman or woman under lock and key. This, however, was not possible. The jail was not big enough, and anyway not all the Dutch people in Mafeking had Boer sympathies. But the more hostile and belligerent of them had been rounded up before they could begin sending messages to the enemy.

Now the three other occupants of the jail—a Dutch horse thief called Viljoen, another habitual criminal, Lonie, and an Englishman called Carter, who was awaiting trial for diamond stealing and manslaughter—had plenty of company. Whether it was to their taste was another matter. One of the warders reported heated arguments between the newly arrived Dutch and the prisoner Carter, who seemed to have plenty of British loyalty, if not honesty.

The emissary who had brought the message that the dead and wounded might be taken from the battlefield had also brought a message from General Cronje suggesting that, since Sunday was a day for worship and peace, no Boer guns would be fired on that day or any Sunday in the future, providing the British forces respected the truce.

Colonel Baden-Powell, realizing the value of this arrangement, readily accepted. This one quiet day in the week would be an oasis, a morale lifter, and a time for much needed relaxation.

People could go peacefully to church or stroll in the sun without worrying about danger. Sports meetings and other festivities could be arranged. The children could play safely in the streets.

The Boers, of course, would spend their Sundays singing hymns or making brief visits to their families if they lived on farms within reach. Their wives would trek over with wagons laden with supplies, meat pasties and biltong, mealies and sweet potatoes, and warm clothing and boots.

The Boer soldier didn't have a uniform but wore his habitual clothing—a sheepskin or leather jacket, heavy boots, a flat-brimmed hat. Most of them were farmers who hoped to be home in time for the sowing of crops. They didn't expect their generals to linger too long over the capture of Mafeking.

On this first Sunday of the siege Mrs. Milsom, the bank manager's wife, with the help of Miss Rose and one or two other ladies who were good at organizing, gave a musical party. This ended with a spirited singing of "God save the Queen," everyone hoping the Boers, across the miles of quiet veld, would hear.

"The Queen, God bless her," someone said, and Alice Partridge remembered the afternoon ten years ago when, clad in white satin and ostrich feathers, she had made her nervous curtsey to the dumpy old woman sitting pouting and regal on her throne. She planned the same privilege for her children, though it was scarcely likely that they would curtsey to Queen Victoria, since the old lady wasn't immortal. It would have to be to the Princess of Wales, who would then be the new queen. Alice hoped she could plan it so that the girls all went together, since there was only a year between Henrietta and Fanny, and Daisy would never have the courage to go through that ordeal alone.

Coming out of the town hall into the brilliant sunlight, she lifted her lavender skirts out of the dust with one hand and held her parasol with the other. The little girls in their white Sunday dresses and floppy white hats walked behind her. They made a pretty picture. Major Godley and Colonel Hore, strolling by, off duty, bowed gallantly. A pretty, gracefully dressed woman in this place was something to see. Alice knew by their admiring glances that they thought her composed and brave. They didn't know that she could keep up this calm only by looking straight

72

ahead and never once letting her anxious glance stray to the sunlit, menacing veld.

Although Lizzie had kept the news from her, she had soon enough heard the rumors about the siege guns.

But the peace remained so complete that it was hard to believe there was a war on.

The next morning, however, provided a rude shock. At half past nine, when Andy Buchanan's girl, Linda Hill, was going to Weil's store to do some shopping, she stopped short as a sharp crack sounded and on the roadside earth spurted into the air. She screamed, and someone shouted to her to take cover. That was a shell that had just fallen. The terrible threat had really happened. The Boers had kept their promise to begin shelling the town.

Minutes later the alarm bells rang, and as the shelling began in earnest there wasn't a person to be seen. The Boers had moved forward two light guns and were aiming their fire at the railway station. They failed to hit it, but two shells struck the Convent, in spite of the Red Cross flag displayed.

Presently a new trouble occurred. The water taps ran dry. This could only mean that Boer patrols had taken possession of the water reservoir some two and a half miles out of the town. However, this move had been anticipated. Householders had been warned some days ago by Major Hepworth to fill every possible receptacle they had, and as a precaution several wells had been dug to provide drinking water. For additional supplies, the Molopo was conveniently handy. It would have to be the task of the women to see that their supplies of water were replenished at night or in the early morning before shelling began. Provided, of course, that the Boers kept this unholy activity to the daylight hours.

At the time they were given, the women had listened calmly enough to these instructions, but now they must actually be put in force, there was panic. What with the intermittent sounds of exploding shells, and the tap running dry, Mrs. Ryan began to scream that the Boers were poisoning the water and they would all die of thirst.

Alice Partridge, who at the sound of shelling had made the little girls hide under her bed, pretending it was a game they were playing, began to weep silently when she

73

found what had happened. She had to stand still for several minutes, willing herself to be calm, until Fanny's plaintive voice—"Mamma, *when* are you going to find us? We think this game is rather tedious"—made her quickly dry her eyes and go back to the bedroom. Bertie had told her that when the alarm bells rang she must take the children to the nearest bombproof shelter, but there hadn't been time. The shells had begun to fall before the church bells had rung, and Maisie, the Barolong girl, had snatched up her baby and fled for her life, probably not to reappear until the next day. Left alone with the children, Alice had been too afraid to make a dash through the blazing morning sunshine to the shelters.

Since the shelling had begun so early, there had not been too many children at school. Miss Rose had rounded up only seven in the playground and hustled them indoors to take refuge under the desks. Soon, as their first terror wore off and they grew bored even with the unusual sight of Miss Rose's angular body crouched on the floor, they began to wriggle and squabble. Miss Rose, after a glance out of the window showed her nothing but a cloud of dust a long way off, decided that probably the children would come to no more harm sitting up decently at their desks and ordered them to do so. She then got out the storybook kept for special occasions and began to read to them, her voice completely calm. It was quite a long time later that she noticed her audience numbered not seven but six. Billy Ryan had disappeared. He must have slipped out the one moment she had had her back turned. Probably he had gone to see if his pony was in danger.

Miss Rose sighed deeply, decided that she could hardly be blamed if the first victim of the shelling was such a foolhardy boy, and continued her reading.

Just after noon the spasmodic firing stopped, and a flag of truce was seen approaching the forward trenches. It was a wretched flag, only four dirty handkerchiefs tied to a cane, and the bearer of it, who came from General Snyman, had a message he was instructed to deliver in person to Colonel Baden-Powell.

He was blindfolded and led through the town to the Colonel's headquarters. There he was relieved of his blindfold, and Colonel Baden-Powell courteously invited him to stay to lunch.

The man, bearded and almost as dirty as his makeshift flag, looked surprised and said he preferred to deliver his message first. General Snyman wanted Colonel Baden-Powell to know that the Boers were outside Mafeking in force, with artillery, and he would like to give the Colonel an opportunity to surrender now and avoid further bloodshed.

"Bloodshed?" inquired the Colonel, his jaunty ginger eyebrows lifted. "Ask General Snyman when the bloodshed is going to begin. You can scarcely give us a chance to cease firing when we haven't begun."

He calmly gave orders that the envoy be given a substantial lunch, to show him that there was no lack of food. Then the puzzled man, who must have thought the English commander a queer, cool madman, was blindfolded and led out of the town.

When this had happened, the Colonel took stock of the morning's casualties. It was a ludicrous list, with only one fatality, a hen. A pariah dog had been wounded, and one hotel window smashed. The damage to the Convent was not serious.

However, although the relief was great, and the townspeople a little abashed about their moments of panic, it was doubtful if the damage would always be so slight. The little skirmish had been merely a curtain raiser.

This fear proved all too true, for three days later another messenger came in, bringing a letter from General Piet Cronje himself:

HONORED SIR,

Since it appears to me that there is no other chance of taking Mafeking than by means of a bombardment, I have to adopt that course with regret. I have to allow you forty-eight hours to prepare your people, black and white. You have to see that noncombatants leave Mafeking before the expiration of that time. If you do not comply with this, I will not be answerable for the result. The time allowed to you I reckon from Saturday 21st, at 6 A.M., till Monday morning, the 23rd, at the same hour.

There was no doubt why this letter had been sent. The armored train, setting out on forays, had been all too successful in picking off Boers, who had no weapons which were effective against its armor. The forts placed strategically around the town had been keeping any enemy patrols well-covered, and the defenses were constantly being improved. Moreover, the Boers had a healthy fear of the mines rumored to be laid. They had no experience of night fighting, which was the only time they might successfully have penetrated the defenses, and before they could decide to embark on such a perilous action, the ingenious British had devised another weapon, a system of searchlights, which were merely a couple of biscuit tins welded together with an acetylene burner inserted and made to swivel on a pole.

So General Cronje wrote his threatening letter, and Colonel Baden-Powell replied:

SIR,

I am sorry that you have to confess yourself unable to take Mafeking without bombarding it. But this course you are quite at liberty to take if you imagine it will help you. At the same time I would remind you that the present war is of one government against another—not of people against people. Now you purpose to inflict damage upon private property and a peaceful town, and possibly to injure women and children under the excuse of war.

I am much obliged to you for giving warning to the noncombatants to move away from Mafeking; but they do not propose to avail themselves of it. In return for your courtesy I wish to warn your people that I have had the ground at a distance around Mafeking prepared with dynamite defense mines. Some of these are self-acting; the others are fired from observation points. I am loath to make use of them except when special reasons of defense may demand it.

He added:

I would inform you that I have had to confine in jail several of your informants, women as well as men. I will have a yellow flag hoisted to show this position so that any responsibility for their injury will rest with you.

There was a sudden storm that night, with wind and lashing rain. But the morning dawned fair and hot, and the freshness of the air lifted people's spirits. Cronje was bluffing, just as Baden-Powell was bluffing about the number of minefields laid. He would never turn a big gun on a helpless town and massacre everybody in it.

Billy Ryan got up at the crack of dawn. Dressing as quietly as possible so as not to disturb his mother or Annie, he stole out of the house and gave a small whoop of joy as he sped on bare feet down to the field at the back of the Convent to get his pony. Star whickered and ran to meet him. Billy fed her the lump of sugar he had stolen from the tea table last night (sugar was to be rationed, and his mother had threatened him with a thrashing if he wasted any of it on his pony) and then sprang onto her shaggy back.

He would have despised a saddle even if he had had one. His thin muscular legs gripping the pony's fat sides, his fingers entwined in her mane, he was part of her.

Someone shouted to him as he galloped away. He didn't hear what they said and didn't look back. He supposed it was someone telling him not to cross the river and go on to the veld. Which was exactly his intention. He wanted to see those old Boers for himself. He also had a fearful and fascinated desire to see the scene of the other day's battlefield. He knew that there would be nothing left but spent cartridges and the bare bones of horses, picked clean by the aasvogels. But he still wanted to see.

His father had been in that action, one of Lieutenant Brady's troop who had come up in support.

He hadn't had a scratch, but was infuriatingly silent about the whole thing and simply said, when Billy pressed him for information, "Not in front of your mother, son," and had spent all his short time at home cleaning his rifle as if he were obsessed with it. There had been some splashes of blood on his puttees, which had made Billy's mother go very white, but his father had said it was only horse blood. Colin Jenkins' mount had gone down in front of him.

There would be no blood left on the battlefield because the rain last night would have washed it away.

The wind, which had fallen at dawn, was getting up again. It was whipping up dust storms, and Billy, after fording the river and getting up on to the veld, had to drag at Star's mane to stop her while he wiped the dust

77

out of his eyes. It was blinding him. He knew that he was riding in the direction of Fort Cronje and Fort Mackenzie on the railway line. He wasn't at all sure that he would be able to get past those defenses unseen. He intended to try. He wasn't afraid of being shot at. Everyone knew Star, and they could see he was only a boy without a gun. Though he wished he had one.

Then he stopped wishing anything, pulled up Star and simply stared. In the far distance there was an extraordinary sight. Billy's young eyes had no need of field glasses. He could see quite clearly the team of oxen, a score or more, slowly dragging an enormously long object like a giant black snake. What was it? There could never be a gun that size. Yet it must be a gun, for Billy, his heart pounding, could see its muzzle slightly lifted. A siege gun, such as people had been talking about. And he was the first person in Mafeking to see it.

Wildly excited, forgetting about his original intention of seeing the battlefield, Billy wheeled Star around, dug his heels into her sides and galloped down the slope, splashing through the muddy stream, and up the other side.

He rode madly toward the center of the town, a crazy small boy on a tiring pony, bringing the news of doom.

A tall officer stepping out of Dixon's Hotel stopped him.

"Where are you off to, son?"

Billy stuttered with excitement.

"Please, sir, to tell Colonel Baden-Powell about the gun."

"What gun?"

"The big one, sir." Billy pointed an excited finger. "Out there. I saw it."

The officer had taken Star's forelock and was holding her firmly.

"You're not telling me you've been out on the veld?"

"Yes, sir, I have. And I did see the gun. It's bigger than"—Billy was at a loss for a comparison—"than the church steeple."

"If you do that again, my boy, we'll have to take your pony away."

Billy's fingers entwined in Star's mane.

The officer was very angry. "Don't you know there are Boer sharpshooters out there? You could have been picked off your pony like a bird off a fence. One of our own men might have done it, by accident."

Billy's face went sullen.

"I thought you'd be pleased that I'd spied for you."

The officer was a little kinder. "We don't expect little boys to do that."

Billy stretched his wiry body, making it inches taller.

"I thought after that Major Cecil might have had me in his Boys' Brigade."

"I am Major Cecil, and I still think you're a little boy. And we know all about the gun. And I'm warning you, if you ride outside the town again, your pony will be confiscated." Then at last the officer smiled and let go Star's forelock, and patted Billy's arm. "Get off home to your mother, boy. And if ever you see that big gun lifting its muzzle, get into shelter as fast as you can."

The gun's presence was indeed no delusion. It was a Creusot siege gun, one of four which the Boers had recently purchased, and which the British troops, in an effort to reduce its terror, promptly nicknamed Creaky. There had been Boer activity at Jackal Tree Hill for several days, and this was now explained. They had been building a platform for the gun. It was actually in sight of the town.

Colonel Baden-Powell at once ordered trenches to be dug at all street corners and in Market Square so that people caught in the open during shelling could immediately take shelter. Hotels and stores deepened and widened their cellars, shoring up the walls and ceilings. A system of bells was organized as an alarm system at several points in the town.

But the biggest innovation was the women's laager.

There were approximately six hundred women and children in Mafeking. General Cronje had already expressed anxiety about them. He did not want to get a reputation for making war on children. Now that he had showed that his intention to bombard the town was no bluff, Colonel Baden-Powell decided that the women must be removed from immediate danger.

Rowland's farm, on the outskirts of the town, should be safe enough. There were trees and water. A Red Cross flag would mark the spot and the enemy be informed. A laager was organized and many tents pitched. It would not be comfortable living under canvas, but it might prove much safer than remaining in vulnerable houses. The women could not, of course, be forced to move out of town. The Colonel only asked that those who chose to remain should behave with the greatest caution, not strolling about recklessly, and not pretending to be too bold to take shelter.

As was to be expected, Mrs. Buchanan refused to move. She was too old to live under canvas, she said. Anyway, the Boer shells held no terror for her. The only concession she would make to them was to take shelter in the narrow trench, like a grave, that Andy had dug for her in her back garden.

Miss Rose, too, was reluctant to move. It wasn't from caution that she was eventually persuaded to do so, but because the children would no longer come to school. If she wanted to continue their education, she must do so in a tent set up for that purpose in the women's laager. All the school equipment, blackboards, desks, slates and pencils and reading books must be moved with her. Her own personal belongings could be carried in one small canvas bag.

The Milsoms, the Cathcarts, the Burtons, the O'Gradys (who had the largest family of all, nine children at home, and the eldest, a stripling of seventeen, fighting in Major Godley's company), the Smiths, the Nolans, Mrs. Ryan and her two, the sickly little Annie and Billy, who thought living in a tent like a real soldier would be a tremendous adventure, all trekked down the dusty road with their belongings.

Mr. and Mrs. Brown tried to persuade their daughter Amy to go, but Amy had had enough of seeking safety in strange places. She preferred to take refuge in her small familiar bedroom, creeping right into bed like a caterpillar into its cocoon and pulling the blankets over her ears when the firing began. Besides, Papa could not go and Mama would not leave him, and Amy, stiffening her small stock of courage, thought it her duty to stay with them. She could never make herself help in the hospital, as Lizzie Willoughby was doing, but Papa had said there were many other things she could do, such as visiting the jail, now overflowing with prisoners.

The picture of Amy Brown timidly offering solace to

those furious Dutchwomen would have been funny if it hadn't been so pathetic.

"Aren't you afraid they'll scratch your eyes out?" Lizzie asked her practically.

"Oh, I expect they'll be behind bars."

"Well, I wouldn't want to offer any kind of sympathy, religious or otherwise, to Katie Roos."

"Papa says we must look at the other side of the picture," Amy said. "He says we don't do any good by nurturing hate, and I must imagine how I would behave if I were imprisoned for loyalty to my country in a Boer jail."

Turning the other cheek, singing hymns and preaching love was not Lizzie's way of fighting a war. Doctor Macpherson had told her that morning that Peter Moody, who had lost his leg, was going to die. Gangrene had set in, and it took all her self-control to approach his bed. Even when she made herself overcome her revulsion to the terrible smell, she didn't know how to look into his haunted eyes.

There was a woman called Mrs. Davis who was a superb sharpshooter, and who had insisted on taking her place in the trenches. Wearing a blouse, long skirts and petticoats, she was there among the men, who had already stopped laughing at her and were full of admiration for her skill.

That, Lizzie had decided, after her last conversation with Peter Moody, was what she would like to do. At the beginning she had contemplated the other side of the picture. But not any longer. She wanted revenge for Peter's tortured face, for those young strong bones that would shortly have to be discarded into the earth.

She was also worried about Alice and the children. There had been a painful scene last evening when Bertie had made the decision that his wife and family must move to the women's laager. Alice had cried and said that already he was tired of having them with him, for what other reason could he have for sending them to live in squalor with all those common women, Dutch and German, as well as low-class English? Had he thought what the sanitary conditions would be like? And what were they to do all day, living in a tent?

It had taken Bertie an hour of patient persuasion before Alice could be induced to see reason at all, and even then only a compromise was reached. She would try living in the laager for a month. If she found it impossible, and if by that time their house was still standing, she could come back.

"A whole month," sighed Alice, thinking it an eternity.

"It'll go in a flash," said Bertie. He was satisfied enough with the promise he had wrested from his wife because a month would surely be long enough to show how the tide was running—for or against them. Privately, he didn't think they had much hope unless a relief force arrived pretty quickly. This was unlikely, since Colonel Baden-Powell's acknowledged task was to pin down as large a Boer force as he could, diverting them from other fields of the campaign. So the only thing to do was to keep a stiff upper lip and pretend that all was fine and dandy. He wished to God Alice had stayed in Capetown, as he had told her to.

Lizzie reluctantly agreed to move with them. The children no longer thought any of this a game. Neither Alice nor Lizzie had been able to keep their spirits up enough to deceive the wide apprehensive eyes and ears of the little girls.

"There's a big gun coming that swallows up children," Henrietta said.

"Now, for goodness' sake, who told you that?"

"Maisie. She's going to take her little black baby and run away."

"Maisie is an ignorant Kaffir," Alice said. "I certainly don't expect my children to be either ignorant or cowardly. There is a big gun. I won't deceive you. But we're moving to a place where it can't reach us."

"What about P-Papa?" Fanny sobbed. "Won't the gun swallow him up?"

"A big brave man like Papa! What nonsense you talk."

Alice was doing her best, although her hands shook so much that she could scarcely pack. Books, dolls, games, sewing boxes to keep little fingers occupied. They could all come home every Sunday, Bertie had said, and wash their clothes and have piano lessons and go to church.

It wouldn't be so bad. It wouldn't be for long. After all, Bertie said, if it hadn't been for all those minefields, most of them fake, laid around the town, the Boers would have ridden in days ago. But with their losses at Signal Hill, with the armored train constantly patrolling, and with one or two of the mines deliberately exploded as a warning, the enemy was cautious. They would knock down a few houses with the big siege gun and terrorize the stubborn inhabitants of the town into surrender.

"They don't know the British," Bertie said, pulling at his moustache. With hard physical labor he had got thinner and looked very handsome. But his leg was troubling him. His limp was much more pronounced. Pain, and frustration that he couldn't get into the front-line trenches, made him short-tempered.

Packing resolutely, and somehow keeping a trembling smile on her lips, Alice comforted herself with the thought that it might be as well if Bertie didn't have his family underfoot, all the time.

The women had to make their move largely without the help of their husbands or male members of their families, for they were all engaged in digging shelters. All the weekend, every one of them who could hold a spade dug for his life. The heat was sweltering, but this was no excuse to slacken work. The shelters dug were roofed with steel rails, girders and corrugated iron brought from the railway yards. Hotel owners and storekeepers enlarged and shored up cellars beneath their buildings. For people who might be caught in the open when the alarm sounded, shallow trenches were dug at street corners and in Market Square.

This fury of activity was supervised by Colonel Baden-Powell himself, who strolled about observing everything, giving an order now and then, whistling cheerfully or bestowing his reassuring smile on a nervous woman or child.

Billy Ryan was now not the only little boy who had seen the big gun. It had been erected on Jackal Tree Hill and stood there with its long snout in the air for everyone to see. Beyond it, when the air was perfectly clear, it was possible to see the Boer encampment, estimated to hold ten thousand men. There were no more than a thousand who could bear arms in the little town.

At the end of that long Sunday Alice and the little girls, followed by Lizzie and Bertie, carrying bags, moved to their new quarters.

Everyone expected to be woken at dawn by the roar of the first shell from the gun.

It was a very long night.

After Bertie's departure, Alice sat on the edge of her campbed, unable to bring herself to undress. Fortunately, the little girls had thought this a great adventure. Tucked up in their beds, heads and tails, Fanny and Henrietta at the top, Daisy at the bottom, they had whispered and giggled until they had fallen asleep. Lizzie wanted to sleep, too. She had to be at the hospital early, and she had learned already that she must discipline herself to rest if she were to be ready for the demands made on her in the wards.

Her life was taking on a rhythm. Hard work all day in the grueling heat, an hour or so each evening to give Alice support and to play with the children, then leaden, exhausted sleep. This was the way not to think about Tom Wheeler, whose face had remained too persistently in her mind. If she wanted a light flirtation or the stimulation of masculine conversation, there were plenty of good-looking officers who would be glad of a little feminine society. Life was extremely dull for them, for, although they were constantly on the alert, the enemy remained elusive. They were spoiling for a fight. And spoiling for good-looking young women, too, of whom the supply was extremely small.

But when accosted by any of them, although she smiled courteously (who knew when their strong bodies, too, would lie torn and bloodied on the veld?), her eyes went beyond them to look into the heat haze. She hadn't seen Tom Wheeler for several days. She hadn't wanted to look for him too pointedly, but it was surprising how elusive he had become. One could almost suspect he was not in the town at all.

"Alice, go to bed," she said wearily.

"It's so awful," said Alice.

"I know it isn't very comfortable, but let's hope it won't be for long."

"I was thinking of Bertie. I made him promise to sleep in a shelter, but I know he won't."

"The Boers don't attack at night."

"But who knows when they will?" Alice leaned forward,

her eyes wild in the lamplight. "I'd rather die with Bertie than live without him."

"Stop that kind of talk, please. Think of the children."

"I do. They're the only reason I agreed to come down here." Alice's fingers began to grope with the buttons of her blouse. She summoned up her shaky smile. "Well, I suppose we must make the best of it. Tomorrow I'll fetch a rug to put on the floor. And the trunks could be covered with a piece of chintz and a cushion or two."

"You'll have the place looking like a sheik's in the desert," Lizzie murmured sleepily.

Alice stood up to let her skirt slip to the floor. She pulled on a warm dressing gown, buttoning it snugly.

"But while we stay here I'm never going to undress any more than this. I simply won't be caught by the Boers in my chemise."

IX

Colonel Baden-Powell had no intention of waiting meekly for the big gun to fire on the town. He took the offensive.

At six o'clock on Monday morning, just as General Cronje's time limit expired, there was the rattle of musketry. In the night two of the precious seven-pounders had been moved out of the town on to the railway line to get within range of the Boer guns. Under Captain Williams and Lieutenant Murchison, they opened fire and almost immediately scored a hit on a Boer gun.

After that there was brisk firing from both sides, which did not cease until noon. The expected roar from the great siege gun did not come. People's tense nerves began to relax. Most of them had obeyed Colonel Baden-Powell, and had taken candles, food and books underground, but when the great gun remained silent they began to emerge warily, blinking in the blinding sun, after the stuffy darkness in the shelters. They saw a body of Boer horsemen massing in the distance, but when the armored train puffed busily across the bridge over the Molopo, the Boers galloped away, after firing only a few shots.

By evening, even the most timid ventured to come out into the open for fresh air and conversation that was almost gay. The terrible day that they had thought was going to be their last was over, and they were still alive.

Except Peter Moody.

Doctor Macpherson and Sister Casey had been with him as he died. He would be buried quickly, just before dark that evening, a brisk affair, because by tomorrow evening there might be more burials to cope with.

He had been a Methodist, and his mother, who didn't look much more than a girl herself, asked Mr. Brown to take the service. His father, in the uniform of the Protectorate Regiment, with five of his fellow servicemen, carried the coffin and then stood to attention at the graveside. There was one trumpeter to sound the "Last Post." It seemed almost absurd, for someone who had been scarcely more than a schoolboy.

Lizzie and Amy Brown were among the small knot of people at the graveside. Lizzie had gone because she was still so burningly angry at Peter's death. She couldn't forget his frightened eyes. He had faced the Boers with courage, but death was a mean enemy, too vast to contemplate. He had sobbed with pain and terror. He was going to disappear forever. He couldn't believe it. He couldn't even lose consciousness, but had screamed and sobbed until the end. And refused to pray.

But now the prayers were said into his unhearing ears, and the hymn sung.

> Shall we gather at the river
> Where bright angels' feet have trod . . .

It was a quiet evening, with a luminous sky. The trumpeter's notes, although played softly, must have carried a long way, almost into the Boer encampment.

Lizzie had bitten her lip until it was bleeding. She let Amy Brown walk beside her, their arms linked closely for warmth and comfort.

"He was so young," said Amy, for the twentieth time.

"There'll soon be plenty of others to keep him company."

"Oh, Lizzie, do you think so?"

"For goodness' sake, Amy, face reality. There aren't ten thousand Boers out there for fun. That gun isn't there for fun."

Reality. That was what Tom Wheeler had talked about. It was nearly a week now since she, or anyone she had asked, including Joey, who had said noncommittally, "Baas away," had seen him. She was so afraid, in his desire for news he had gone out on the veld and been shot by a Boer sniper.

In Market Square, to Lizzie and Amy's surprise, there was a scene of wild elation. A runner had come in with news. There had been a notable British success at Elandslaagte in Natal—the 9th Lancers had charged and put the

Boers to flight, with severe losses. So already the tide of the war was turning. Now it was certain to be over before Christmas. Mafeking would be relieved before any of the elaborate defenses had been put to the test. Those fool-hardy Boers, thinking they could defeat the British army. One could almost feel sorry for them.

People were gathered in groups, talking excitedly and jubilantly. Someone touched Lizzie on the shoulder. It was Mr. Parslow, the correspondent for the *Daily Chronicle*.

"The friend you were asking about is in Dixon's bar, Miss Willoughby. If you want to talk to him, you'd better do so while he's still conscious."

Caring little for anyone's seeing her relief and delight, Lizzie flew across the Square, pushed open the door into the bar of Dixon's Hotel, and was immediately engulfed in an atmosphere of smoke and noise.

In spite of the people surrounding him, Tom saw her at once. He was perched on a stool at the bar. His eyes met hers over the vociferous crowd, and for a moment they stared at one another; Lizzie saw his unshaven face, his weariness, his startling thinness, and she stood rooted to the spot, knowing the truth. A runner had come in with the news about Elandslaagte. Tom Wheeler was the runner!

Tom was waving his hands, motioning people back. "Make way for the lady. Well, Miss Lizzie. This is a pleasure."

He slipped off the stool and stood swaying slightly. She realized, with a shock, that he was drunk.

"Have a drink, Miss Lizzie. Sam, is there any whisky left? If there is, let's drink it. No use waiting until we're all dead."

Lizzie exclaimed, "But they said there was a victory."

"There's also a notice pinned to a tree in Vryburg, my dear Miss Lizzie. 'Mafeking speechless with terror. Kimberley trembles.' And, 'Africa for the Dutch, and the English in the sea.' Mind you, they're a little in advance with their news, because they say as well that the burghers started firing on Mafeking with the big cannon and that the town is on fire and full of smoke. But that's for tomorrow, I imagine."

The dark eyes, terribly tired, lightless with weariness, rested on her.

"Elandslaagte is a long long way away, Lizzie, my dear."

"You were the runner," Lizzie said.

Tom attempted to bow, and swayed perilously.

"Now we know all about each other. True?"

"No."

"Never mind. I got my dispatches through. One can't live in limbo, you know."

"Tom, you're not drunk, you're exhausted."

The lopsided smile was slow in coming.

"You see too much, Miss Lizzie. I've walked about forty miles. Very hot out there. I can't stand it the way the Kaffirs can. Had to report. Had to have a drink. Now I'll go home." He made his unsteady way out of the bar and along the darkening street. He hadn't asked her to accompany him. She wondered if he could guess how much she had wanted to.

That night she dreamed about circling aasvogels in a burning blue sky, and a lonely figure stumbling across a limitless expanse of beige-colored parched earth. London and her past life had never seemed so far away. It might almost not have existed.

Miss Rose had used quite a lot of ingenuity in fixing up an outdoor schoolroom. She had persuaded two taller members of the Boys' Brigade to hang a piece of canvas from one tree to another, and in the shade this supplied she had arranged packing cases for desks and set up a blackboard. The first morning she had a gratifying attendance, mostly because the mothers were glad of some occupation for their children.

Even the Partridge girls came, Daisy at the heels of her elder sisters, though she scarcely knew what to do with a slate pencil, let alone her alphabet. But Billy Ryan decided to sit beside her and give her the benefit of his advanced knowledge. He drew faces on her slate, making her giggle. Miss Rose, about to rap with her ruler on her desk, suddenly desisted. Perhaps she decided that Daisy was only a baby, and too solemn, and it was nice if something in this very unchildish situation pleased her.

School, on this morning, lasted no more than an hour.

Just after ten o'clock Miss Rose, having settled the little ones with picture books, had just got out her spelling book and told the older children, in her dry voice, to get slates and pencils ready, when the alarm bells began to ring.

Slates clattered to the ground. There wasn't one of the children who didn't know what the bells meant. The monstrous gun was going to shoot them dead.

"Now quietly!" Miss Rose ordered, her voice lost in the din of screaming children, running into the arms of anxious mothers, who had appeared from all directions of the laager.

"Go to the shelters with your mothers in an orderly manner," she called uselessly.

For the children had bobbed into the earth like jack rabbits, the little girls' white petticoats like vanishing scuts.

In the dark shelters, smelling of earth and candle grease, the women and children crowded together, waiting. They had thought there would be a terrible explosion of sound within minutes of the warning. But time went by. Was it a false alarm? Were the Boers playing on their nerves, trying to bring them to trembling submission without bloodshed?

Alice Partridge, with Henrietta and Fanny on either side of her and Daisy on her lap, thought that she would explode herself from her effort not to shake with fear. Every muscle was tense. Her jaw ached and her eyes felt as if they would start out of her head. Where was Bertie? she kept wondering. Had he taken shelter? Supposing she and the children emerged safely into the sunshine and he lay dead, blown to pieces by the terrible gun. Or supposing it was he who emerged, and she and these babies with their dandelion heads and soft skin remained here in this stuffy darkness—forever . . .

She felt sick. Yesterday, with a feeling of slightly frightened joy, she had thought she might be pregnant. It was much too soon to be sure, yet she was almost certain that she carried the seed of Bertie's son.

To be born in this dreadful town? Or not to be born at all?

"Can't they get it over with?" one of the women said edgily. "What are they waiting for? To see the whites of our eyes?"

It was Miss Rose who, surprisingly, had some knowledge of the gun's manipulation.

"The barrel would have to be raised and aimed, first. That would be when the lookout gave the alarm. I believe it takes a little while to load and fire." She gave a tight smile. "Which gives us quite an advantage, since we have time to take cover."

"Well, next time I'll bring my knitting," said Mrs. Ryan, trying wanly to joke. The airlessness of the shelter made her too feel sick. Annie had had dysentery this morning. She hoped the child wasn't sickening for something. Billy sat with his jaw stuck out and his fists clenched as if he were scared to death, but he was probably only thinking of the safety of his pony.

Then, abruptly, the boom came, to be followed by a terrible rushing overhead, and then, blessedly far off, a dull explosion.

The women looked at each other's white faces. Unconsciously everyone sighed. It had happened. The gun had been fired, and they were still alive. Of course, no one knew what had happened in the town, but suddenly they were optimistic. If they could survive, so could other people. It wasn't quite as terrifying as they had expected it to be.

But far off they could hear the alarm bells ringing again. They settled back, prepared for a long wait.

In the town much the same thing was happening. In the shelter in which Amy Brown and her parents had taken refuge there were eleven other people, which made quite a crowd, since this was only a converted beer cellar. The walls were still lined with beer barrels and bottles of wine. A direct hit would make a fearsome mess. But the shells, coming now at the rate of one every five minutes, roared overhead and landed somewhere in the distance.

Amy was deeply ashamed that she was the only one to be in a state of hysteria. One woman even had the aplomb to remark that the shell made a song as it went overhead, and another begged that everyone should be quiet so that she could hear the song. It was a song with a shattering finale when the crash and the sound of falling glass came. There was a crackling, too, and a smell of smoke. Something was on fire.

One of the men, having got the rhythm of the firing,

ventured to emerge into the open between shots and came back to report that he could see two houses hit and a lot of wreckage lying about. The fire came from some drums of oil that were blazing. Two or three men had been hit with splinters, but so far no one seemed to be seriously hurt.

After nearly an hour there was silence. The lookout on Cannon Kopje reported that the gun's barrel had been lowered. It was safe to come up for air; there would be time perhaps to make tea and have something to eat.

At the hospital, the matron and nurses who had remained on duty, trying not to wince when the walls shook and dust filtered down, took deep breaths and began to be optimistic again. They had fared much better than the Convent, which had been hit once more, though no one had been hurt. Since it was the only two-story building in the town, it was too conspicuous a target.

Lizzie helped to take tea around to the patients. She found to her satisfaction that her hands did not tremble at all, although she still felt frightened and extremely anxious. What had happened to Alice and the children, and to nervous Amy Brown, and to Tom Wheeler, who without doubt would be tempted to stay above ground to observe what was happening?

Doctor Macpherson thanked her when she took him a cup of tea.

"You all right, nurse?"

"Yes, thank you, doctor."

"Not frightened?"

"Very."

Did he think she wasn't human? Perhaps he wasn't himself, for he looked absolutely calm, his blue eyes regarding her with their usual cool intelligence.

"Well, it's over for a bit. You'd better have some tea yourself."

"Yes, I will."

"Nurse!"

Already he was treating her with formality, as if she were a permanent part of the hospital staff.

"Yes, doctor."

"I must say I think all you nurses behaved splendidly. Except Nurse Jennings, whom I found with her head buried in sheets in the linen cupboard. But she's very young."

He was kind in his quiet way. Observant and fair. Lizzie felt respect for him, though she was a little uneasy about the way he made excuses to detain her in brief conversations.

"Well, go and have your tea, nurse. We may be busy this afternoon. Some casualties are inevitable. They may be arriving at any moment."

But only one man arrived, to get a splinter taken out of his arm. He said that the damage in the town was slight; the wide streets and the houses set far apart had made difficult targets. Unfortunately, the respite was brief. Early in the afternoon the firing began again, not only from old Creaky, but from all the Boer guns. A long, tedious, airless afternoon had to be spent in the shelters and cellars, and it was not until the cool quiet of the evening that people could emerge to relish the fresh air and the silence.

Their ordeal had only begun, as they discovered to their dismay when they were awoken by the alarm bells at dawn the following morning. Some scrambled into clothes; some had the forethought to grab some food for breakfast; but most, in a pellmell rush to the shelters, were still in their nightwear. They supposed ruefully that they would eventually get the technique of taking shelter to a fine art. Like Alice Partridge, they would never undress completely. Alice had had only to throw a coat over her petticoats, and gather up the children and fly to safety.

Lizzie had not left for the hospital, so was able to help with the frightened children, Daisy inevitably in her silent tears. Lizzie thought anxiously that already their faces were too pale, their eyes too large. Alice had had trouble in persuading them to eat the food she cooked on a small oil stove. Later, Lizzie thought worriedly, they might be glad to eat anything at all, but now they wanted fresh fruit and milk puddings.

Other children were faring less well than the Partridges. Annie Ryan looked extremely sickly, and there were several others who were wan and listless. Some of them had mothers whose ideas of hygiene were elementary. Lizzie couldn't help remembering Doctor Macpherson's predictions. These women could represent a menace not only to their own children but to others who, like the little Partridges, were kept scrupulously clean.

Most of the morning had gone by before the firing slackened. In a temporary lull Lizzie, who was worrying about the hospital, and two or three of the more venturesome women emerged and looked anxiously toward town. One would have expected, after all that noise, that it would be a smoking ruin.

But again, miraculously, few direct hits had been scored. A thin wisp of smoke rose from the Convent, indicating that it had once more been unlucky, but the damage must have been slight.

In the blessed silence, the sun beat down and the pepper trees swayed in a slight breeze as if this were a normal peaceful day.

Lizzie decided to make a dash for the hospital. If the alarm bells rang, she could take shelter on the way. As she picked up her skirts and hurried along the dusty road she saw a small figure running for his life in the opposite direction. It was Billy Ryan, escaped from the supervision of all those women, flying toward the native kraal to see that his pony was unhurt.

The town was coming to cautious life. There were small knots of people staring intently across the veld. Lizzie heard her name called.

"Miss Willoughby! Miss Lizzie!"

She turned sharply, seeing Tom Wheeler's spare form. He was beckoning to her.

"I promised you a sight from my roof one day. You can come and see it now."

Her heart thudded. "A battle?"

"Boer horsemen sighted. Hurry up."

With both terror and a curious elation, she ran after him across the square to his house, and allowed him to assist her up a ladder onto the flat part of the roof.

On neighboring roofs there were other watchers, intent figures in whom curiosity was stronger than fear.

"There," said Tom, pointing.

The sun was blinding. It was a little while before Lizzie could pick out the cluster of horsemen, black ants on the dry dust-colored land. But more and more of them gathering. As they came closer they were a solid black mass, moving with alarming swiftness.

Lizzie clutched Tom's arm.

"How many?"

"I don't know. B. P. estimated five hundred. I think there are a lot more than that."

"Are they going to charge the town?"

"Looks like it." Tom's voice was dry, laconic. "Damn, I wish I had field glasses. I had to contribute mine to the army."

"Why don't our guns fire?" Lizzie begged. While that black mass was so far away, it would only be like killing ants. It wouldn't be bleeding, agonized bodies in the dust. Even if it were, it would be better than having Henrietta and Fanny and Daisy, poor Alice with her large frightened eyes, and all those other women clutching terrified children to their skirts, ridden over and slain.

"They'll have their orders. Wait until the enemy's within range."

The minutes were endless. Lizzie's head began to ache from the fierce sun.

"The Boers are probably working on the assumption that after that bombardment the town is in ruins and everyone left alive ready to beg for mercy."

"They must be stupid."

"Are you not going to beg for mercy, Miss Lizzie?"

"Not if they hurt Alice's children. I'd shoot them myself."

"They're deploying," Tom said, his eyes narrowed to slits as he stared across the veld. "They're going to attack in two directions."

Horses and men were now clearly visible. A little cloud of dust followed them. Lances of light were flung off their rifles. Lizzie was rigid, waiting for the first sharp cracks.

There was not much longer to wait. One arm of the Boer force, riding in to the native kraal, was struck by a heavy burst of rifle fire from British forces concealed along the edges of the kraal. Not only the British, but the Barolongs, who had been much angered by the Boers' habit of stealing their cattle, were defending the kraal. Some of them had been issued Snider rifles and were only too eager to use them.

Major Godley, too, from his headquarters in one of the advanced forts, was making good use of his seven-pounder. The Boers seemed to have miscalculated the amount of opposition they would receive, for under the barrage of fire they came to a halt. Many were seen to fall from their frightened, milling horses. Some of the horses fell, too, and presently there was a turnabout, and the whole company of them, except those left on the ground, were speeding off into the distance.

Some scattered firing was heard to the northeast, where the second attack had been begun, only to cease almost at once. In less than ten minutes the landscape had cleared and was still. Even the puffs of smoke had disintegrated into the luminous air.

Lizzie realized that she was wet from head to foot with perspiration. She could scarcely unclench her fingers. Her jaw was rigid.

"Well, that was a bit of a fiasco," Tom said disappointedly.

"Thank God it's over!" Lizzie turned on him. "How can you be disappointed?"

He grinned. "I'm one of a strange breed called newsmongers. Our hearts are made of pieces of shrapnel."

He took her hand. "Let's get off this oven. You're pale. But you stood up to it well for a woman."

"Supposing it hadn't been a fiasco. Supposing they had got through the defenses."

"They didn't, and that's all that matters in war. The hard facts." He squinted into the distance. "They have some casualties out there. They probably won't be picked up until evening, poor devils." When she shivered, he said, "You be thankful there won't be a stream of wounded coming into your hospital."

"I know. I'm growing my tough skin. I can't do it all at once."

"Don't do it completely. One of us is enough for that."

One of us . . . She looked into his hard eyes. But they were not always hard, she remembered. That day in the train they had been remarkably gentle.

"Tom, you're too thin," she said.

"I'm fit. And what's my thinness to you?"

"The same as my tough skin to you, I suppose."

"Lizzie." He seemed about to touch her, then didn't, holding his hands firmly to his sides. "No, we both have things to do. But I like to think of your face to come back to. It's soft and pretty and English. I think of it when I'm hot and thirsty."

After that so recent display, the veld now bristled with danger. "You're going out again?" Lizzie asked.

He nodded. "But hold your tongue. The town's full of spies. B. P. wants to scotch this rumor that Mafeking has fallen. I'm going to get across the border to a telegraph post."

She pressed her hands together. He gave a short laugh.

"You've got a look on your face as if you're watching that battle all over again."

"I was."

"Then don't. Grow your tough skin. Goodbye, Miss Lizzie."

The guns went on intermittently all the long afternoon. Then at last there was silence, and in the growing shadows of the evening it was possible to see the Boer ambulance wagons making their slow progress across the veld. The lookouts, watching through field glasses, estimated by the number of ambulances that there must have been nearly eighty bodies picked up, either dead or wounded. In the cemetery in Mafeking there was only one new grave to be dug.

X

It was Sunday again and in the outposts a certain amount of fraternization went on. The Boers called out greetings to the British and boasted that they were well supplied with comforts. Their wives trekked over from neighboring farms with wagons loaded with food, cakes, Boer rusks, meat pasties and biltong, as well as warm clothing for the chilly nights on the veld. On Sundays, too, those who had homes in the vicinity were allowed to go off and visit their families.

It was very different for the besieged inhabitants of Mafeking. If they didn't want to be killed by shells or exhaust their food supplies, they must surrender soon. Why didn't they do so now?

But if they were watching through field glasses the activities in the town, the Boers must have been a little baffled and surprised by the carefree attitude displayed. There were cricket matches and children's games being played on the recreation grounds. In Market Square a band played waltzes and polkas—such light music must have been shocking to the hymn-singing Boers on the Sabbath—and women dressed in their Sunday gowns strolled about enjoying the open air after the last claustrophobic days in dark and stuffy bomb shelters.

Mrs. Buchanan in her best black silk, with her black jet-trimmed bonnet, attended church and then sailed across the square, a regal figure, to cast a benevolent eye on the children's games.

She talked to Alice and Bertie Partridge. Alice, in spite of her immaculate lilac gown and parasol and air of gaiety, was too pale, and had had to resort to a dash of rouge on her cheeks. She clung to her husband's arm and laughed vivaciously when she saw her children scoring points in the game of rounders that Miss Rose had organized.

"You can count yourself fortunate, Mrs. Buchanan," she said, "that you don't have to live in the women's laager. One week has already been an eternity for me. My husband says it's wise to stay there, for the sake of the children's safety. But we all slept at home last night, and I was up at dawn washing and ironing our clothes. It's the only opportunity I have to keep decent."

Mrs. Buchanan's sardonic eye went over Alice's crisply starched appearance.

"You might eventually decide safety is worth a ruffle or two, Mrs. Partridge."

"Alice is a great one for keeping up appearances," Bertie Partridge said, a trifle smugly. "It adds to the pleasure of the scene, don't you think?"

"In this climate," said Mrs. Buchanan, "I'd hesitate to dress little girls in petticoats and boots and socks. They must be overcome with heat. This is Africa, Mrs. Partridge."

"Are you suggesting they should go native?" Alice asked in horror.

"Certainly not. Their delicate skins wouldn't allow it. But the thinnest covering is all that is necessary."

She spoke a practical truth, for Daisy, looking extremely wan, her bonnet drooping about her face, had come to take her mother's hand, whispering that she didn't like the rough games. Henrietta had fallen and got a great smudge of red dust across her white muslin skirt, and Fanny was scarlet-faced with her exertions.

"Wait until January and February," Mrs. Buchanan said grimly.

"Is the heat worse then?" Alice asked her husband.

"It is a bit ovenish. If the war's over, I'll move you off to a cooler part."

"Will it be over?" Alice clung more tightly to him. She was realizing that she had to live for Sundays. During the long squalor and boredom of the week she had to think of this day of freedom, of being able to wash and dress decently, and cling to Bertie's arm, and behave in a civilized fashion. She had caught more than one admiring glance from strolling officers. She hoped Bertie had noticed. It pleased him so much when she was admired. It

99

excited him, too. Perhaps, in the cool dark of the evening, before he insisted on taking them back to the women's laager, he would hold her in his arms.

Linda Hill, in her Sunday-best gown of pink striped cotton, lurked about, hoping Andy Buchanan would have some leave. It had been a whole week since she had seen him.

Amy Brown had just gone home after visiting the prison with tracts. Her cheeks were still burning with humiliation. She had never been so laughed and jeered at. Those Dutch women had no intention of being patronized by a psalm-reciting Britisher, especially one so timid and ineffectual as Methodist Parson Brown's daughter. It was terrible to see the women confined, like animals, in the small compound, but worse to hear their unrepentant jeers.

Even more upsetting had been her encounter with the diamond thief and murderer, Mr. Carter. He was certainly guilty of the theft of diamonds, because he had been arrested with them in his possession, but the alleged attempt at murder was as yet unproved. Yet, although rough and unshaven, he had had quite a nice polite manner. She hadn't known how she had got up enough courage to visit him in his cell, but when she did so, it had been quite easy after all. He told her not to mind those rude women. He had heard the shouting, and could tell her that they had the worst manners he had ever encountered in women.

He took one of her tracts and read it aloud, without seeming to be scornful, and when she had said she must go, he had begged her not to.

"You smell so nice, Miss Brown."

What a remark to make! Amy gathered up her skirts and murmured something about its being only Windsor soap, and heard herself adding, to her astonishment, "I'll bring you a piece, if you like. They say it's going to be rationed soon, so one has to make the most of it while it lasts."

When the door clanged shut after her, the poor man pressed his face against the bars and cried, "Why don't they let me out to fight? I could be tried afterward, couldn't I? Can't you speak to someone for me, Miss Brown?"

Amy muttered confusedly that she would say something to Papa. She went away, thinking that a man who could commit a murder—if Mr. Carter had done so—should be quite splendid at killing the Boers, and it was certainly foolish not to let him. Only yesterday that terrifying woman Mrs. Davis had boasted that she had toppled a Boer off his horse as he rode away. Wasn't that murder?

It was certainly very difficult to go to Papa's afternoon service and listen with a quiet heart to his words of faith and hope and charity. For the first time in her life they didn't make any sense at all.

They didn't make sense to Lizzie, either. She had gone to sit in the cool austere church because she couldn't bear walking about outside in the afternoon sunshine and knowing that she would not encounter Tom Wheeler.

It was out of all reason the way she was beginning to miss him. What had happened between them? A friendly encounter on the train, a drink in Dixon's bar and the relief of sharing the secret of her past, a brief conversation in the dawn after her first traumatic experience of pain and bloody death, a battle watched together. That was all. But it was a great deal.

She tried to analyze her emotions, deciding that since their encounters had always taken place in the vulnerable moments of extreme weariness or danger, she was exaggerating his importance to her.

She had been lonely for so long.

War was a great stripper of pretensions and illusions. She knew herself now as a person whose emotions had not yet been deeply touched, but who had plenty of them and a great longing to expend them. Supposing one were to die tomorrow, or the next day, as poor Peter Moody had died, not having loved . . . It would be a negation of all God had made one for.

God . . . Mr. Brown, in his unpretentious pulpit, was saying, "Let us now rise and sing hymn number 306, 'Art thou weary, art thou languid, art thou sore distressed.' "

The medley of voices, much more eager than musical, had a haunting quality that made the tears come to Lizzie's eyes. Amy Brown took her arm sympathetically. There were tears in Amy's eyes, too. But then, she was

101

such a quiet religious little thing, she was probably only thinking of God.

The next day it rained heavily. When the veil of rain eased and the thunderclouds cleared away there was a new alarming development to be seen. The Boers, like moles, had been pushing their front lines forward, and suddenly an outpost was observed not three-quarters of a mile from the Mafeking main defense line. Sufficiently large to give shelter to fifty or more men, it was obviously meant to be the headquarters of a new assault on the town.

Colonel Baden-Powell did the only possible thing. He took the offensive and ordered an attack on the outpost that night.

Fifty-three men of "D" squadron, under Captain Fitzclarence, paraded for orders. As soon as darkness fell they set out across the veld, bayonets fixed, two lamps set above the rooftops in Mafeking guiding them. When the lamps were seen in a direct line, the men would know they had reached their objective.

To divert the Boers' attention, two other parties were sent out to engage the enemy in spasmodic fire, at the Brickfields and at another point on the Molopo.

This diversion was so successful that the unsuspecting Boers in the trench about to be raided were going on with their work, talking and whistling, when suddenly the roof crashed in upon them, their lamp went out, and all they could see were the pale faces of the attackers and the gleam of the terrifying bayonets, a weapon unfamiliar and hateful to them.

Pandemonium reigned. There were wild shots and screams, horrors both in the dark stifling trench and the open air, for those who escaped into the night air and began to flee across the veld toward their laager were mistaken by their friends for attackers, and were shot down as they ran.

It would be morning before their dead could be counted.

Mrs. Buchanan was aroused late that night by a knocking on her door. She sat up in bed, trying to steady the violent beating of her heart. She was too old for these sudden frights. One night her heart would stop.

Especially if the visitor were the one she expected, a

102

messenger to inform her that her grandson lay dead on the veld.

She got clumsily out of bed, groping for her dressing gown, calling, "Who is it?"

"It's only me, Mrs. Buchanan. Linda."

"Linda! Have you lost your senses, girl?" Mrs. Buchanan grumbled. She struck a match and lit the lamp beside her tumbled bed. She hadn't been sleeping very soundly herself, after listening to the distant guns. "Come in, child. The door isn't locked."

Linda came stumbling in.

"I was so frightened. I couldn't sleep. I know Andy's out there."

"Perhaps he is. Perhaps he isn't." In her bones, Mrs. Buchanan was pretty sure he was; her men had always been in the thick of things. She had long ago trained herself to sit quietly and wait, as this girl would have to if she was determined to be serious about young Andy.

"How can we wait till morning to know?" Linda sobbed.

"We'll have to, and that's all there is to it." Both women lifted their heads, straining their ears to listen. The spasmodic firing had died down. The battle seemed to be over.

Mrs. Buchanan looked at Linda's tousled head and tear-stained face. Bless her, how loyal the child was. And growing older by the minute. She had been a pig-tailed schoolgirl not six weeks ago. But this disheveled, anguished creature was no schoolgirl. The pain in her face was a woman's.

Mrs. Buchanan said, "Tch tch," quietly, thinking that she might have to change her own views.

"When do you have your seventeenth birthday, Linda?"

"Just before Christmas. The twentieth of December. Mamma has always said I'm unlucky, I have to share my birthday with Christmas."

"And I suppose you'll consider yourself grown-up then."

"Oh, I think that already." Linda sniffed and tried to tidy her hair. "Even if I'm behaving like a baby now."

"That's a matter of opinion," said Mrs. Buchanan. "But I gather that my grandson thinks you're a grown woman, just the way he thinks he's a grown man. Well, perhaps you'll be having a triple celebration this year—your birthday, Christmas, and your wedding."

She didn't know what had compelled her to make such

103

an astonishing statement. Two o'clock in the morning was clearly a time in which she took leave of her senses. But it was outrageous and unforgivable that these two children should have been thrust into maturity in such an agonizing way.

"Mind you," she said tartly, determined not to get damp-eyed herself at the sight of the child's suddenly glowing face, "I don't believe Andy's yet asked you, and for all I know he might not have the slightest intention of doing so. But perhaps we'll get through the night a bit more happily if we go and get out my wedding dress and veil." She gave a self-derisive smile. "You wouldn't think I'd have been sentimental enough to keep them, would you? But I have, all these years, against ants and goodness knows what. And believe it or not, I was as slim as you are in those days."

"And how old were you, Mrs. Buchanan?" Linda ventured to ask timidly.

"If you must know—seventeen."

At first light there was what the residents of Mafeking feared was to become a familiar sight, the white flag held aloft on a stick and the line of ambulance wagons moving slowly across the veld. The truce, mutually agreed to between Colonel Baden-Powell and Commander Botha, was to allow both sides to pick up their wounded and dead.

People lined the streets of the little town as the British wagons returned. They learned, to their relief, that losses had again been slight, only six dead and nine wounded. But Mrs. Murphy, whose husband, a barkeeper from one of the hotels who had joined the Protectorate Regiment, was wailing with grief because Pat, the drunken ould sod, was missing and no one knew whether he was a Boer prisoner of war or whether his body lay undiscovered in some hollow on the vast veld. Jim Ryan was also missing, and his wife was in a state of collapse.

The enemy had estimated losses of at least fifty men.

And Colonel Baden-Powell had made the decision to recommend Captain Fitzclarence, who had fought with the greatest gallantry, for the Victoria Cross.

It was nice to give the whole painful and bloody business a touch of glory.

As it happened, Andy Buchanan had not taken part in

that particular action after all. He was able to parade in good health that evening at the graveside of his companions. He then had two hours' leave, and was at first mystified, then delighted with the transformation that seemed to have overtaken that formidable old woman, his grandmother. She was literally pushing him into Linda's arms.

"Do you think the Boers are going to get me, Granny?" he asked.

"I think nothing of the kind. I've merely withdrawn my objections. Linda's a good girl and older in her ways than I had thought. So if you're set on marrying her I'll give you my blessing."

"I'm set on marrying her at some time, Granny," Andy said soberly. "I'd thought I'd get the war over first, but if you think I'm not being unfair to her—I'd do anything rather than hurt her."

"That's a bit out of your hands, boy," the old lady said gruffly. "We must just take what precautions we can. Well, what are you sitting here for, wasting your time with me? Go off and see her. She's been waiting since two o'clock this morning."

It was good to see the strain go out of the boy's face. He was a real soldier now and learning to cope with the constant rapid transition from death to life. That plump smooth-skinned child in his arms would be life enough for him for the next hour or so.

It rained again that afternoon, and the heavy showers turned the women's laager into puddles of mud. Alice didn't know how much longer she could go on living like this, in alternating mud and dust. Since so far the shells from the big gun had been almost completely ineffective, with the exception of a little damage to property, she had asked Bertie last night if they couldn't move back to the house. She promised faithfully that she would run to the nearest shelter the minute the alarm bells sounded.

But Bertie wouldn't hear of it. He said the fight had only just begun.

"Come on, dear girl. You're managing very well. You're still being the lady of the manor, eh?"

Alice looked at her soiled draggled skirt. She had let the children go out to play in filthy pinafores, for what was the use of putting on clean ones? They would come back just as filthy. If it were not for the oasis of Sunday, when she could plunge into the washtub and make them all reasonably respectable again, she would have died of shame. Bertie was unkind and insensitive. He should have known how dirt and squalor shriveled something in her.

Or was he insisting on their staying down here because he enjoyed the freedom of being alone? Had he not genuinely wanted his family to join him in Africa? Had he hoped she would have stayed in England?

In the misery and boredom of the long days all her old uncertainties troubled her. But perhaps this extreme anxiety was due to her state of health. She had told no one, not even Lizzie, that she suspected she was pregnant. Soon enough, when her morning sickness, with which she was all too familiar, began, the secret would be out. How was she to live through the shattering heat of the summer in this condition and give birth to a healthy boy for Bertie?

To make matters worse, the first case of typhoid had been reported. It was Annie Ryan, Billy's sister. She had been taken to the Convent for nursing, and her mother, weighed down with the baby she was carrying, did nothing but cry.

Alice was carefully boiling all the water the children drank, but she shuddered at the crude toilets they must use, and when she found them that afternoon playing with Billy Ryan she scolded them so sharply that Fanny as well as Daisy burst into tears.

Only Henrietta, who was getting out of hand with this unnatural life they were living, stood her ground.

"But, Mamma, Billy's our best friend. Why may we not play with him?"

Billy, lurking a little way off, dirty, uncared-for, his bony knees and bare feet covered with mud, his hands in the pockets of his deplorable pants, his tousled hair growing down over his jacket collar, his face surly and suspicious, was the last companion Alice would have dreamed her well-bred children would have.

"Because he may have germs, darlings," Alice said cruelly. Her instinct to protect her own children made her smother any feeling of pity she might be tempted to have for the ragged urchin lurking within hearing. She made

106

herself forget that he had been the first to make timid Daisy laugh with his antics.

"His little sister has been taken to the hospital," she went on. "She's very sick, and it won't be safe to go near Billy in case he gets sick, too."

"Will she die?" Henrietta asked.

"Of course not."

"What a pity. Billy doesn't like her very much. He'd rather have us for his sisters."

"Henrietta! How can you speak so callously about poor little Annie."

Alice's outraged gaze went to the unspeakable boy who was already corrupting her children with his dreadful manners.

"She's only a mother's pet," Henrietta said contemptuously, and Fanny, peering through her tangled, fair hair, asked if not playing with Billy meant they wouldn't be able to ride on his pony, too.

"Star hasn't got germs, Mámma," she said earnestly.

"He doesn't let you ride that animal!" Alice exclaimed.

"He does," said Henrietta. "Even Daisy. But he holds her hand. He says she's little and might fall."

"He holds my hand," echoed Daisy in her shy whisper.

Alice, in a panic, poured water into the enamel washing basin and plunged Daisy's plump hands into it. She scrubbed them unmercifully with the carbolic soap she had managed to buy at the chemist's, then ordered Henrietta and Fanny to wash their own hands just as thoroughly. After that, she brushed their hair, one tangled head after the other, and made them put on clean pinafores. Only when they were their usual tidy selves did she relax, feeling that the germs were banished. But she would not let them go out to play again. The sun was too hot, she said. Daisy, she thought, looked a little pale. They must stay in the shade of the tent flap and look at their picture books and do a little of their sewing. They were hemming handkerchiefs to send Grandma for Christmas. By some means, Alice maintained stoutly, the mail would get through by then.

She didn't let herself think about England in the daytime, but at night, when she so often lay sleepless on the narrow campbed, she let her mind drift over every inch of the manor house in Dorset in which she had been born and

107

brought up, and to which she always fled, as a harbor, when Bertie was away or going through one of his financial crises. Her father was a retired judge, and her mother a frail, elegant creature who had spent a great deal of her married life on a couch. Whether this had been necessary or not, Alice had never known, for Mamma seemed to have plenty of strength when she gave a garden party or one of her musical soirees.

The Elizabethan manor house was beautiful. Alice let her drowsy mind take her up and down the stairs, through the west drawing room and the east drawing room, the library, the paneled hall with its cavernous fireplace, the kitchen and pantries and stillroom, the little sunny sitting room Mamma lay in in the afternoons, the bedrooms and the attics, the herb garden, the rose garden, the spinney. When sleep finally claimed her she dreamed of green lawns. And woke reluctantly to the miraculously beautiful clear African dawn that would grow into such a harsh blinding day.

XI

There had been another Boer attack, this time on the fort on Cannon Kopje. The Boers, led by General Cronje's son, had played a trick. They had left their horses some distance away, and in the early dawn had crept through shoulder-high grass toward the fort. Only an occasional ripple stirring the grass indicated their approach. Colonel Walford, commanding the precarious fort, had forty men surviving after the initial bombardment. He estimated the steadily creeping Boers at a thousand.

Yet the bearded Boers, determined with one effort to sweep the *rooineks* off their crest, had failed.

The fire from the British had been too withering. There had been no cover. The last two hundred yards before reaching the summit of Cannon Kopje represented a deadly open space that seemed suicidal. Already too many of their comrades lay dead on the rocky slope. The dark line wavered. Suddenly it turned and began to melt away, sliding helter-skelter down the slope into the shelter of the long grass.

Had they underestimated the number of British holding the fort? Had they expected every man to be wounded or dead from the bombardment to which the vulnerable fort had already been subjected? Had their leadership or their courage faltered? No one could answer those questions, but it was soon realized that had Cannon Kopje fallen, it was unlikely that the victorious Boer army could have been kept out of Mafeking.

The little fort had been held at a price. Colonel Baden-Powell, riding out to inspect the damage and to congratulate the tense and blood-stained victors, found eight officers and men dead and a large number of wounded.

He could not count the Boer losses. How many bodies lay lifeless or shuddering into lifelessness in the treach-

109

erous long grass? Only the circling aasvogels knew. But a close watch on the Boer ambulances making their slow way toward the scene of the battle suggested that more than a hundred victims were carried away.

As well as the stretchers of wounded being carried into the hospital and the Convent, there were other tragedies. Two more cases of typhoid and the first of the dreaded enteric fever were diagnosed. In addition, although the women's laager was distinctly marked with a Red Cross flag, shells had fallen and a seven-year-old boy had been hit in the spine. He had been taken away, screaming in agony.

Alice thought she would never forget his screams. Her own skirts, to her horror, had been splattered with his blood. She had been about to duck into the shelter into which she had just bundled the little girls. A moment sooner and she would have missed the dreadful scene. Now it was forever imprinted on her mind, and she kept substituting Henrietta's or Fanny's or Daisy's face for the agonized one of Willie Morton. She wouldn't let the children out of the shelter all day, although they fretted and fidgeted and grew bad-tempered with boredom.

They had grown tired of the game of pretending they were moles or fieldmice, or meercats, the latter an animal they had never seen, although the African-born children talked of them with familiarity. A useful animal, too, for Major Godley had observed their burrows in an exposed part of the veld where it had been thought too rocky to dig trenches. If an animal could make a hole, so could a man. He had constructed a small, very exposed fort, called Fort Ayr. The Boers said contemptuously that the *rooineks* were putting up resistance in a few meercat holes and sent their shells sailing over the new fort, with its ineffective seven-pounder gun, into the town.

They must have been smarting from their failure at Cannon Kopje, for they continued the shelling indiscriminately, ignoring the Red Cross flags on the Convent, the hospital and the women's laager.

The guns had been quiet for at least half an hour before Alice would allow the children to come out of the dark stuffy shelter. Then it was evening. The cool sweet air revived them a little, but they were now unnaturally quiet.

The women in the laager hadn't cared much for Alice. She put on too many airs for them. They thought her vain and silly. But hardship was drawing them together. Mrs. Bolton sent over a piece of the cake she had somehow managed to bake in a camp oven. It might tempt the children's appetites, she said, since she had noticed how pale they were growing. And Mrs. Murphy sent her eldest, Kathleen, to see if she could be of use.

Kathleen, with her tangle of red hair and tough little Irish face, proved to be a godsend. She was used to looking after her tribe of smaller brothers and sisters and had a way with the telling of a fairy story that soon had the children entranced.

When their faces were washed and their hair brushed, Alice was able to tidy herself and then leave the children with Kathleen while she walked a little way from the laager to meet Bertie. He usually came down in the evening for an hour or so, before going back to his task of helping to repair trenches damaged by the day's shelling or taking over lookout duties. Not that this visit did much to cheer her up, for he was in a permanent state of despondency himself. He found it so galling being kept out of the front-line fighting, as if he were aged and decrepit.

He was decrepit, damn it, with his bad leg, but not so much so that he couldn't shoot straight or use a bayonet. He thought himself much more hardly done by than his wife, who was safely out of harm's way in the women's laager.

But it seemed she wasn't out of harm's way, after all. When she had managed to tell him the story of that day's tragedy and had shown him the blood staining her skirt, she begged to come back to their house.

"I can't stay down here, Bertie. It's so dusty and dirty and there are flies everywhere and germs. I'm terrified the children will get ill. And now they're shelling us as well. It isn't any safer here than it is in town."

"Of course it's safer. B. P.'s protested about the shelling of the Red Cross flag. I happen to know that. A messenger went out this evening."

"And how much notice will those brutes take of a protest? If you'd heard that child screaming today you wouldn't dream of subjecting us to this any more."

111

Bertie stood in the dusty road pulling at his moustache. He was tired, his leg ached badly, and he didn't care for Alice when she was distraught like this. He almost felt repelled by her, with her untidy hair and blood-spattered gown. She had come to meet him like this deliberately, he thought angrily, to soften him. If only she knew that he found her white anguished face quite ugly. She was another person. The person he loved was the serene, sweet-smelling, well-groomed one. It was a wife's duty to present only a pleasant image to her husband. If she couldn't do that, she should keep out of his sight.

Realizing his unfairness in these extraordinary circumstances, Bertie made himself speak persuasively.

"Now come, my love, be sensible. If you insist on coming back to the house it's more than likely it will be Etty or Fanny or Daisy the next time. I know you've had the odd shell down here, but not a tenth of what we've had in the town. There aren't many casualties yet, it's true, but there's plenty of damage being done to property. I wouldn't have a moment's peace about you. So bear up, old girl. This can't last forever."

"You don't care," Alice said.

"Now be fair—"

"You wish I'd never come to Mafeking."

"I certainly do that. Right into the middle of a war! You were stark, staring mad and if anything happens to the girls through your stupidity I'll never forgive you." Bertie's temper, never very controllable, was flaring.

Alice's eyes were very blue, very stricken, in her white face.

"Nobody cares for me," she said. "Not even Lizzie, now she's met that Tom Wheeler."

"I don't know about Tom Wheeler, but Lizzie's working like a black. Don't you know how many wounded came into the hospital?" The slight widening of his wife's eyes, indicating an increase in her pain, made his temper fade a little.

"Just be a bit more realistic, my love," he begged. "This can't go on for much longer. Tomorrow's Saturday. On Sunday you can come home for the day. Perhaps by Monday it'll be all over. Plumer's force will have got through."

Alice's shoulders drooped as she turned away.

112

"You could try being a little more realistic yourself. Your son will be born before Plumer or any relief force gets here."

Bertie had her by the shoulders and had spun her around.

"Alice! Is this true?"

She was suddenly so weary she could scarcely nod.

"I don't know for sure. I think so. After all, it's why I came here, why I was so stark, staring mad, as you say."

"Do you think it will be a boy?" he asked humbly.

"If it's born at all."

"Of course it will be born!" Bertie kissed his wife tenderly and put his arm around her. "You've got to take care of yourself. This is all the more reason to stay in safety in the camp. Come and I'll take you back now. You know, I believe this is one of the strange ways nature has. Immediately men begin killing one another, she sets about seeing that more babies are born. Did you ever hear the fact that the percentage of male children born is always higher than female in a war? Bless you, my love, we'll have our son."

Alice cried a little and they had quite a loving farewell, and Bertie whistled as he set out for the walk back to town. But his spirits ebbed before he was halfway home. Apart from the unlikely possibility of Alice's being able to bear a healthy child under these exceedingly trying circumstances, supposing it was another girl?

Colonel Baden-Powell sent a protest to the Boer commander.

We have never used, as you imply, a Red Cross flag on any fort or train engaged in fighting. The Red Cross flag has been used only in three places on the outskirts of the town, namely the Convent, the hospital and the women's laager.

With regard to the mines around the town, defense mines are a recognized adjunct of civilized warfare both by land and sea, and are in no way forbidden by the Geneva Convention.

As regards the natives now taking part in the defense of

113

Mafeking, they have taken up arms only in defense of their homes and cattle, which you have already attempted to shell and to raid . . .

But the indiscriminate shelling continued, and although, owing to the efficient alarm system, few people were hurt, the strain on nerves due to the danger, the noise and the boredom of long hours in the shelters was considerable.

And Tom Wheeler had not come back. With the influx of wounded into the hospital Lizzie had been working all day and half the night. She had taken to sleeping at the hospital, since there was no time for the long walk down to the women's laager. She was sorry about deserting Alice and hoped the children were not fretting for her, but in the meantime they would have to manage with the companionship of the other women and children. Alice would have to stop considering herself too good for the butchers' and the bakers' wives. Just as Lizzie had had to realize that the life of little Joe Blair, a cockney from Shoreditch, who could neither read nor write, was just as important as that of the several wounded officers whose needs she attended to.

She was still kept only to the menial tasks of washing patients, carrying bedpans and bringing meals to the ones who could eat. Some were beyond eating, and Joe Blair, who was wounded through the jaw, had to be spoonfed with infinite patience. Removing pails of bloody dressings was another task that no longer turned her sick. She found that the more tired she got the less emotion she felt, and the less the distant crash of shells worried her. Even when the hospital had another direct hit, and beds had to be hurriedly moved, through the choking dust-filled air, she was an automaton, her body performing the orders she heard the matron, Sister Casey, and Doctor Macpherson giving.

Little Joe, with his jaw swathed in bandages and his black alert eyes missing nothing, lay in the bed in which Peter Moody had died. Joe wasn't going to die, but perhaps his successor would. The man in the next bed to him, a cheerful Irishman from County Cork, did, unexpectedly, late one night. His wound suddenly hemorrhaged and in no time at all blood dripped through the mattress onto the floor, and Doctor Macpherson, working grim-faced, made a despairing cry, "If only there were some way to give him fresh blood I could save him."

But how could one replace the red stream that ran from a man's body? In less than an hour the large strong young man with his virile growth of black beard and his springing black brows lay dead.

The body, and the debris of its death, were quickly carried out. Sister Casey told Lizzie in a sharp whisper to mop up the blood; did she want her patients to wake in the morning and see it? Lizzie was thankful to work by the light of the little oil lamps standing on the floor. In the dimness the blood didn't seem so horribly sticky and crimson.

Afterward she stood outside in the chilly windy night, breathing deeply, not knowing whether she would faint or be sick or simply, like a female, burst into floods of tears. The last time she had been in this state of unendurable tension and horror she had gone to Tom's house. It was no use doing that tonight. She would only sit in the darkness, seeing visions of him lying face downward somewhere on the veld, his own blood spreading in a dark stain over the cold rocks.

It was a vision she usually managed to shut out of her mind. Tonight it came with unbearable vividness, and when a footstep sounded behind her, she cried out in shock.

"Is it too much for you, nurse?" came Doctor Macpherson's voice.

"It's you, doctor. You gave me a fright."

"I asked if that was too much for you."

"It was, for a minute. I'll get over it."

He held out a lighted cigarette.

"Here. Have a puff of this. Nicotine has a calming effect."

She took the cigarette and drew the smoke unwarily into her lungs. It made her choke. The tears streamed down her cheeks. She gave the doctor back his cigarette and got out her handkerchief to mop her cheeks.

"Between the two of you, you'll corrupt me," she said unsteadily.

"The two of us?"

115

"Tom Wheeler gives me whisky, and now you encourage me in the evils of smoking."

There was a little silence.

"Wheeler's not back yet?"

"How did you know he was gone?"

"The town's small. We're all waiting for news. We know who might bring it back." His voice was flat and factual. "I expect you'd like letters from home yourself. Have you a family who will be anxious about you?"

Was he prying? No, only in the perfectly genuine way of wanting to know more about her. She had noticed him looking at her quite often.

"Just my brother, and he's with the army somewhere in Natal. I've worried terribly that he might have been at Elandslagate. I don't know how I'll ever hear if he's safe."

"Then you haven't anyone in England?"

"No," she said calmly. "My parents are dead. I came to South Africa to join my brother because I was alone."

"I, too," said Doctor Macpherson. "I'm alone in the world. I suppose I should have married. There's no particular reason I didn't except that I hadn't found the woman I'd give up my freedom for."

Didn't . . . Hadn't . . . He was talking in the past tense.

"I thought it was only the woman who gave up freedom," Lizzie said.

"Did you? That's an old-fashioned idea. Well, nurse. Back to our job?"

Only two more significant things happened that week. The big siege gun, old Creaky, drawn by a team of oxen, was laboriously moved from Jackal Tree to another point east of Cannon Kopje. From the new emplacement its long barrel was raised, and smoke and fire belched forth. But on Sunday, in Mafeking, there was a new kind of sparkle and bang. A fireworks display in memory of Guy Fawkes was held. The Boers, surely by now getting tired of sitting so frustratingly close to their prey, must have wondered at the fizzy, lighthearted sparkling going on in the late evening. Hadn't the town had enough, yet, of explosions, even this innocuous sort?

Billy Ryan capered madly round the fireworks display. He lost himself in the enthralling present. He could even forget his anxiety for his pony. Several of the troopers'

116

horses picketed near the Molopo had been struck by shells and killed. This made Billy extremely anxious for Star's safety. Every night he went down in the dark to pat her and let her nuzzle at him and to beg some hay for her from Trooper Bates.

His sister Annie, they told him, was still very sick and perhaps was going to die. He didn't care about silly cry-baby Annie, she could die if she wanted, so long as God took her instead of Star. And perhaps instead of Daisy Partridge who, in her white sunbonnet and dress, looked like an overgrown daisy herself.

Almost immediately after the Guy Fawkes display there was another much grimmer display. Major Godley, with a force of ninety men, two seven-pounders and the Hotch-kiss, made an impudent attack at dawn on a Boer laager which had been made dangerously near the Molopo valley. After a concentrated fire into the encampment, with startled Boers coming awake and grabbing their Mausers, he and his party made off, escaping with only four wounded. Again, it seemed that the Boer casualties might be heavy. At least the purpose of the raid was achieved, for the next night the laager withdrew a mile or so and the danger of an attack up the Molopo valley was removed.

After this, there was some deliberately vindictive shelling, mostly in the vicinity of the women's laager and the hospitals.

Lizzie was constantly anxious about Alice and the children, but Sister Casey allowed her no time to brood over them. The hospital was getting fuller all the time. One ward was now devoted entirely to fever cases. When the wounded were brought in after Major Godley's attack on the Boer laager, Lizzie was able to look at their blood-stained bandages with less of the sickening feeling of dread. She was becoming accustomed to wounds, if not to the detached attitude that Sister Casey said was essential to a good nurse.

She was almost becoming so professional that she looked at the patients' wounds before their faces. That was how she came to get such a shock when she saw that the bearded blood-drained face lying unconscious on the pillow was Tom Wheeler's.

His body was emaciated, his cheekbones stood out like

knuckles. The stubbly dark beard made him look a stranger. That was why she hadn't recognized him immediately. His injury, fortunately, was slight. A bullet had gone through his right hand, coming out cleanly, and there was no infection. But there had been a severe blood loss, and that, combined with exhaustion and near-starvation, had brought him to this state.

At least that was what Doctor Macpherson was saying in his impersonal, clinical voice.

"Give him plenty of beef broth, Sister. He only needs building up."

He moved off to the next bed. If he had noticed Lizzie's white face, he gave no sign. But Sister Casey came back to give her a tart order.

"Don't stand there stargazing, nurse. Get on with your work."

She obeyed quickly, knowing that Sister Casey, an astringent old maid, was likely to move her to another ward if she guessed her interest in one of the patients. But her hands shook as she dusted and tidied and straightened beds and removed the usual dreary baskets of dirty linen. Every now and then the walls shook to the crash of an exploding shell. Old Creaky had been persistently active lately; indeed, the shelling was becoming so familiar that one scarcely allowed it to interfere with what one was doing. But occasionally there was the crash of breaking glass, and often showers of earth spurted up in the near vicinity. .

This was her nightmare come true, that one day one of the still forms carried in on a stretcher would be Tom's.

Doctor Macpherson had seemed quite unworried about his condition—there were more serious cases to interest him—but Lizzie hovered as near his bed as possible, determined to be within call when he returned to consciousness.

She was not the only one interested in his return to consciousness, for a little while after his admission one of Colonel Baden-Powell's officers came to sit by his bed. He had the matron's permission to do so. Mr. Wheeler might have information for which they were impatiently waiting. So little news had come into the beleaguered town in the last weeks that someone who had got through the lines was of the greatest importance.

It was nearly an hour before Tom's eyelids quivered. A moment later they lifted, and the dark, quenched eyes looked straight into Lizzie's.

"Don't try to talk," she said. "I have some broth for you. Lieutenant Mabley," she went on severely to the officer who was leaning eagerly across the bed, "allow the patient to recover. Be kind enough to leave him until he's had some nourishment."

"Running the place—already—Miss Lizzie? Got me—captive?"

"At least, I'm better than the Boers," Lizzie said.

She had raised his head and was spooning the warm beef broth into his mouth. At first it seemed as if his throat hurt too much to swallow, but presently he began to take the liquid thirstily. When the cup was empty he lay back and immediately fell asleep.

There was a brief bitter argument outside the ward. Lieutenant Mabley was complaining to Matron Hill that he had not been allowed to interrogate a patient for information, for which the Colonel was waiting. Did she give all her junior nurses such authority?

"The patient in question," said Lizzie heatedly, "is asleep after taking the first nourishment he has probably had for days. I only refused to allow him to be wakened."

The matron's lips tightened.

"I happen to know who the patient in question is, nurse. And I appreciate the Lieutenant's urgency." She was reluctant to take the side of a junior nurse, and an untrained one at that, who seemed to have become far too uppish, but her own training asserted itself. The patient's good must come first.

"But I don't imagine the war will be lost by waiting another hour or so for whatever vital information Mr. Wheeler may have. You must simply inform Colonel Baden-Powell the patient hasn't yet regained consciousness. Nurse Willoughby!" Her frosty eyes flicked over Lizzie. "Will you be good enough to go and help in ward three. One of the nurses has gone off sick. I'm sure you'll find plenty to do."

So Lizzie could not be there when Tom woke again. Full of frustration, she was tart with the patients and impatient with the other nurses. It seemed as if the time when she could go off duty would never come. Even then she didn't intend to rest. She intended to go straight back to Tom's bedside. If he still slept, she would sit there the night through, and defy Matron and everyone else. Tom was her friend, apart from Alice Partridge her only friend. She was entitled to be with him. If there was trouble she would go to Doctor Macpherson.

But she hoped not to have to do that. She had the feeling that the doctor's quiet disciplined face might register an emotion she preferred not to see, perhaps disapproval, or perhaps pain.

There was no trouble. It was her own affair if she wanted to sit up all night, Sister Casey said.

Mr. Wheeler had woken and talked to the Lieutenant and fallen asleep again. He was stronger and had asked to be shaved first thing in the morning.

The news he had brought back was far from reassuring. Both Kimberley and Ladysmith were under siege. Twenty thousand men under Sir George White were immobilized in Ladysmith, and the Boers were reported to be massing on the Modder River, which would cut off any hope at present of its relief. Such news meant that the relief of Mafeking was even farther away. It would be only the most optimistic now who expected hostilities to be over by Christmas. Rather, preparations must be made for a long siege.

The threatened rationing would begin, Lizzie thought. Supposing the food ran out. Supposing one had to watch the children getting thin and weak from malnutrition. A grown man like Tom Wheeler could stand it, but little children, like Henrietta and Fanny and Daisy . . . Even Tom's face in the dim light looked skeleton thin.

She had half dozed herself when she was aware of his eyes watching her.

"Lizzie! Is that you?"

"Yes, it's me."

"Am I as bad as that?"

"Oh, no. The doctor said you were not bad at all."

"Then why are you sitting up with me?"

"Because I was so glad to see you safely back," Lizzie said, too happy for anything but honesty. "Safely," said Tom wryly. "I have a bullet wound, and I'm dehydrated, and I had to shoot my horse three days ago when he stumbled in a meercat hole and broke a fetlock, and I had a touch of sunstroke, but I suppose you could say I'm safe."

"Yes. You are now. Can I get you anything? The doctor said you had to drink a lot."

"Fine. I'd like a large whisky."

"Oh, now—"

"All right. I'm in a hospital so I suppose I have to behave myself. How am I looking?"

"Terrible. That beard."

His thin fingers felt it.

"I agree. I doubt if even my wife would recognize me."

Lizzie stood up, saying calmly, "I did, so I expect she would. Now I'm going so that you can rest."

His weak, hoarse voice followed her.

"Do be a good girl and try to get me a whisky, Lizzie. I've been dreaming about it for days."

Lizzie bit her lips, restraining her angry disappointment. She had been wasting her time with her vigil at his bedside. He woke up and talked of whisky and his wife.

The sound of voices had made other patients stir. Lizzie said, "S-sh!" sharply and tiptoed out of the ward. Ten minutes later she was back with a medicine glass half full of amber liquid.

"It's brandy, not whisky. I stole it out of the medicine cupboard. Don't blame me if it kills you."

"Lizzie!" His weak voice shook with laughter. "You're a worthy successor to Florence Nightingale." But he was too weak to sit up. She had to lift his head and hold the glass to his lips. Which virtually would make her a murderer if the brandy did kill him.

It didn't, of course. It merely made him fall instantly asleep. And Corporal Robbins in the next bed was leaning over whispering hoarsely, "Couldn't you give me a nip, too, nurse?"

"No, I could not. And if you dare to tell Sister—"

"Bless you, love, I wouldn't breathe a word. If you're sweet on the lad, good luck to you."

The next day Tom was considerably stronger. The barber had come and shaved him, so that now the hollows in his cheeks were alarmingly visible, but his eyes were

121

bright, and in a day or two, the doctor said, he would be up and about, although it would be longer before he could use his hand. He had had a lucky escape, but one didn't suppose that would deter him from going out again. No, said Tom, not when he had found another horse. He had been trying to steal one from the Boer camp when he had been shot. He had had to lie low beneath a clump of thorn bushes all day. The bushes hadn't provided enough shade, and that was how he had got a slight sunstroke which had confused him and delayed his return. A lookout at Fort Ayr had spotted him staggering down an incline, and it was lucky he had not been shot again, this time more seriously.

Joey, his Barolong servant, came to visit him, alternating with joy at finding his master alive and nervousness of the hospital.

"You back safe, baas?"

"Certainly I'm safe, Joey. What else did you expect?"

"You get out of here quick," Joey said, his eyes rolling like a nervous stallion's.

"Why, I believe you're more scared of a hospital than you are of the Boers."

"Sure, bass. I plenty scared here."

"Well, get off home, you scoundrel. Get in plenty of food and liquor. I'll be home at the end of the week."

"Not plenty food or drink, baas."

"Yes, Mr. Wheeler, you're behind the times," Sister Casey said crisply. "Owing to the news you brought back, rationing's started. There's plenty of meat and bread, but I hear we'll be getting low on salt and sugar and tea. However, I don't suppose a shortage of tea will trouble you too much."

"Tell me the worst, Sister. Don't spare me."

"I hear that you can buy *pâté de foie gras,* if you wish. But all alcohol has been taken into store. It's to be kept for emergencies."

"Don't look so triumphant about it, Sister. I can make do with tea if I must."

"I don't believe that woman likes me," he added to Lizzie, who had come to make his bed. "If I can go for a week without a drop touching my lips, I can go for a month. Don't you believe me?"

122

"Except for an occasional stimulant in the night, certainly, Mr. Wheeler."

"Did I have something in the night?"

"You begged me for whisky and I brought you half a glass of brandy, which you swallowed with every evidence of pleasure."

"I don't remember a thing about it. Did you do that for me, Lizzie?"

He really was shockingly thin. His eyes burned in his bony face.

"Yes, I did it. But don't ask me to again."

He lay back, silent for a while, then he murmured something about thinking he had dreamed it. He had a brooding, moody look. Lizzie wanted to ask him what was wrong but had guessed before the words were out of her mouth. He had dreamed it had been his wife, Millie, who had given him the drink.

"Is your hand paining you today?" she asked.

"No. Yes, it is, and don't talk to me like a nurse. Where are my clothes? I've got to get out of here. I'm not sick. Joey can look after me. You'll be needing this bed for more urgent cases."

"In a day or two," said Lizzie. "At present you're an urgent case. Now try to rest. Corporal Robbins, will you ring the bell if Mr. Wheeler attempts to get out of bed."

"Oh, God! Cronje will shell us all out of our beds, with any luck. All right, Lizzie. I apologize. It's just that I loathe being helpless. I'll have to try to write my dispatches with my left hand."

"Can I help? You can dictate them to me if you like. Perhaps you'd like to write to your wife, also."

(*Dear Milly and Edward . . .*)

"Would you?"

"Of course."

"Ministering angel," he murmured. "When did you begin upholding the institution of marriage?"

The weary eyes held hers for a moment. Then, abruptly, like a child's, they closed and he was asleep.

That night Annie Ryan died, and two more children were admitted to the hospital with suspicious symptoms. In addition, Alice Partridge went down with fever. Bertie came to look for Lizzie. He wanted her to nurse Alice.

123

The hospital would have to do without her. It didn't look as if there would be any fighting or any wounded for a few days, because Cronje was moving out.

Unexpected as that news was, it was true. A cloud of dust on the horizon marked his departure. Obviously called to another theater of the war, he took two commandos and several guns. But General Snyman remained, and so did Creaky to constantly harass the town. The enemy was still very much in view. Nevertheless, the depleted numbers gave heart to the defenders. It was too soon to begin tossing their hats in the air, but at least they could be more optimistic. It was a pity that the hot season was approaching, and the sickness increasing.

XII

Alice was ill for ten days. Lizzie wanted to have her moved either to the hospital or the Convent for nursing, but she begged not to go. She didn't want to be separated from the children. She was convinced that if she let them out of her sight they would wither away. Apart from this feverish fancy, which it was wise to humor, both hospital and Convent were filled to capacity with various cases of sickness, and the doctors urged people who could be cared for at home to stay where they were.

One could scarcely call the uncomfortable tent home, and nursing with such limited equipment was difficult. Somehow Lizzie managed, and found that her most reliable helpers were an unlikely pair, Miss Rose and Billy Ryan.

Miss Rose not only briskly took charge of the children but somehow concocted surprising delicacies to tempt Alice's appetite. Billy hung about the tent, a ragged, tough little figure, waiting for a glimpse of his favorite, Daisy. Lizzie had qualms about seeing Daisy's trusting hand put into that exceedingly grimy paw, but since Billy had become her hero it would have been cruel to separate them.

It was impossible to move Alice into the shelters when the shelling began. She had to lie in the hot tent, growing hotter as the sun moved toward the center of the sky, and quiver at each distant crash. But Miss Rose undertook to keep the children safely underground, and occupied as well. For this purpose she kept a permanent supply of slates and pencils and reading books in what had become known as the "school," a portion of the deep trench across which a blanket had been hung to get some kind of privacy. Slabs of corrugated iron lay across the top to form a ceiling and keep out the sun.

These rattled faintly every time a shell burst anywhere near. At midday, the sun beating on them made the heat suffocating. But Miss Rose soaked towels in pails of water and made the children lay them on their foreheads, or wipe their faces and hands with them every time the little faces grew too scarlet, or too pale.

It was surprising how much more attentive Billy Ryan had become to his lessons now that he had the Partridge children to show off to. People said he was a hardhearted little wretch—he didn't seem to have cared at all about his sister's death or his poor mother's state, or even that his father had not been heard of since he had been reported missing. He would come to a bad end. Miss Rose, regarding him with her sharp eyes, was coming to another conclusion. He was as soft and pliable as anyone else when he was given love, the uncritical love that gentle, shy Daisy Partridge and his shaggy, aged pony gave him. But he would be much easier to love, she reflected, if he were given a good bath.

Annie's death had almost killed her mother. The only thing that had given her a feeling of desperate pride and importance was that it had been reported in the Mafeking *Mail*, the newssheet that two enterprising journalists were getting out each day. It reported sports events and the prices of food and small personal news, including the fact that Annie Ryan, aged two years six months, had been the first child to die of typhoid.

Mrs. Ryan had insisted on going to the burial, which had been held at night by the light of a lantern, as were all burials, so as not to be interrupted by shelling. Then she was distressed that two soldiers who had died of wounds were buried at the same time, stealing Annie's limelight. It wasn't fair. Her baby should have had more respect. "Suffer little children to come unto Me," Father Ogle said, in his gentle grave voice, but Mrs. Ryan wept hysterically because the other graves had the "Last Post" sounded over them.

She was scarcely sane. The sooner the new baby was born the better, so that she would have something in her arms again.

As Alice began to recover, Lizzie was ashamed of herself for not having enough patience and sympathy with her moods of depression. She had been a grudging nurse all the time, for she had not wanted to leave Tom Wheeler's bedside. She was especially disturbed when she heard that he had got up and walked out of the hospital before he was half recovered. He said his black boy would look after him. But what did an ignorant native know about dressing a wound and keeping it clean? A badly infected hand, and Tom's career as an artist, if not as a writer, would be over. Lizzie remembered too vividly Peter Moody's death from gangrene and worried inordinately.

When Bertie Partridge came down that evening to see his wife, Lizzie begged him to stay while she went into the town.

"What for? You can't shop at this hour. There's very little to buy, anyway. Everyone's been raiding the draper's for the children's fancy dress party on Sunday. And as for food, it's going to get deuced dull and scarce before long, if I know anything about it. I'd give a lot for a good English roast beef dinner, wouldn't you? How about you, my love?" He kissed Alice, lying on her narrow bed, and she said listlessly, "Food interests me remarkably little. You and the children can have all my ration."

"Oh, come now, my love, you're eating for two, remember? Perk up. You're getting better, Lizzie says. Be thankful the girls didn't catch this fever."

They hadn't, although Lizzie found them playing a macabre game, under the instigation of Billy Ryan. He was burying Annie all over again, only this time Daisy was the corpse. Henrietta, crying noisily when she could control her giggles, was Annie's mother, and Fanny her sorrowing friend. Billy, with Daisy's white hair ribbon tied round his throat for a parson's collar, was reciting what he could remember of the burial service. Daisy lay very still in her crumpled white dress, her chubby hands clasped on her breast.

Lizzie had rushed over and snatched Daisy into her arms, scolding angrily, "You terrible little boy! What a game to play!"

"It wasn't Billy, it was me who thought of it," Henrietta said offendedly. "Billy isn't the only person who knows about funerals."

"You interrupted us, Miss Lizzie," Fanny reproved. "We

were just going to sing a hymn. This one." In her clear high voice—Fanny had a good singing voice, which was one reason for her mother bringing the piano from England—she sang, "Shall we gather at the river, where bright angels' feet have trod . . ."

"Billy said I was going to see the angels," Daisy whispered disappointedly.

"One day you will. When you're very old." Lizzie set Daisy down, and told Henrietta to take her hand. "Run along now. Papa's here. He wants to see you."

Unduly haunted by what had been only a children's game, Lizzie was in no mood for Tom Wheeler's bad temper.

When she knocked on his door, he opened it and greeted her aggressively.

"If you've come to tell me I'm crazy, you're wasting your time."

"You are crazy. But I wasn't going to waste words telling you so. I've come to dress your hand, since I wouldn't trust what Joey would put on it. Cow dung, most likely."

"My hand's all right."

"Oh, Tom. Don't be so awkward. I only want to help you."

"Why have you selected me for your special care?"

"Because other patients at the hospital are discharged at the proper time and go back to their units where they have some supervision. Where's Joey? I'll want some warm water."

"Then you'll have to get it yourself, Miss Nightingale. Joey's gone out."

Lizzie looked at him inquiringly.

"He's one of the best native scouts we have. Didn't I tell you? He's gone out to get me some information. Must have something to write home about," he added flippantly. "The Queen must have news of her Empire."

"And how will you get your dispatches through when they're written?"

"The same way as usual, of course."

"It was only by luck that you got back last time."

"Are you suggesting that a soldier should never fight another battle because he survived his last one?"

"Don't listen to me," Lizzie said exasperatedly. "I'm

only a woman with soft ideas. I'll go and boil some water."

When she came back after an interval he was sitting in the dark. She could just make out his form.

"I'm so damnably weak," he said. "Makes me short-tempered."

"We're all getting short-tempered. Where are the matches? I'll need some light."

He tossed her a box, and she lit the lamp, waiting until the soft glow grew strong enough to illuminate the room. The table was in its usual state of disorder, but she saw that he had been trying to write with his left hand. The awkward letters sprawled across a page.

She unrolled the bandage she had brought, saying, "You really should be a little more gracious. I'm only trying to help you. I saw Peter Moody die from gangrene. I hope never to see anything like that again."

"The little heroine," he said in his weary voice. "Sorry, Lizzie. I didn't mean that. I am an ungracious fellow. I don't need to be told it. I can stand pain but I hate weakness."

"You lost a lot of blood. It takes time to get strong again." She unwrapped the bandages and studied his wound in the lamplight, relieved to see that it was healing cleanly. "This should be all right in a few days. You'll always have a scar."

"Will you mind?"

The different tone of his voice, suddenly intimate, made her heart jump.

"No, I won't mind. But it's nothing to do with me."

"As a woman, you wouldn't mind a scarred hand on your naked skin?"

"Tom!"

"Tell me. Because one thing I know, and that is that my wife wouldn't like it. She'd squeal as if she'd been stabbed."

"She hasn't been through a war," Lizzie said.

"War or not, are you the sort of woman who would mind that?"

"I wouldn't mind anything about a man I loved," Lizzie said evenly. "Naturally."

"Naturally. What a marvelous word. Naturally. It expresses everything." He was silent a moment, and then

129

said, as if seeking a safer subject, "How are the little girls?".

"The Partridge children? Well, but I worry about them. I hope they're not as delicate as they look. I expect it's the heat that makes them so pale. They're not used to it."

"Are you fond of children, Lizzie?"

"Yes. Especially Henrietta and Fanny and Daisy."

"I know. They were like a bouquet of orange blossom, I thought. With their silly, exquisite mother. I made a sketch of them on the train the day we met. It's there somewhere. Would you like to see it?"

"Very much."

"I was going to send it to the *London Illustrated News*. Call it 'Innocent Victims,' or something like that." He was searching among the untidy pile of papers. "You see, I can be sentimental sometimes. I like children, too. I love my own son. I worry like the devil about him. Here it is."

But Lizzie's eyes had fallen in fascination on another sketch. It was of a circle of African vultures, the ugly aasvogels, with hunched wings and bent heads, standing over the body of a soldier. Its caption was "Grace Before Meat."

"That," said Tom, "is what the sensational press will prefer."

"Have you seen something like that?" Lizzie asked in horror.

"Yes."

"It's horrible."

"It's not particularly pleasant. Lizzie, I've been trying to write to my wife and I can't."

"Then let me. I offered to in the hospital."

"It's a mental not a physical inability I suffer from."

She met his eyes above the lamplight.

"Yes, it must be hard for someone safe in England to realize what it's like out here."

"It's not a geographical difficulty, or a military difficulty. It's simply that I have nothing to say to her."

"Oh. You—what about that letter you had begun? Was it never finished?"

"It was not. What about you? Have you written to your husband?"

130

"That's a different thing entirely."

"Not different at all."

The laconic voice disturbed her. What was he telling her? That he felt about his wife—the unknown Millie—as she did about Humphrey?

But this was an entirely different thing, in spite of his denial. Millie had had his child.

"My wife," he was saying, "wanted a husband who conformed to her pattern. That's the whole story. She has a little suburban soul. But we have a son I love dearly." He rubbed his hand across his forehead and said, "I always wanted a son. I couldn't bear to lose him. Do you see?"

"Yes," she said, after a long time.

"Then let's get that letter written. You can help me. You'll know what to say. A few everyday things. The price of bread. What fashionable ladies are wearing in the siege."

Lizzie pushed the pen and paper at him.

"If you love your son, write to him. And write to his mother. Don't mix me up in it. It's not my trouble."

She was standing up, breathing quickly, as she looked for her shawl.

"I came to bandage your hand. That's done so now I'll go."

"Lizzie, you're angry with me!"

He had stood up to block her way.

"Don't be angry. Don't go."

"I will go. You expect too much. You used that poor Millie to have your son, and now you're using me to—"

When she faltered, he said, "To be my nurse, my amanuensis, my confidante, to give me a shoulder to cry on. Yes, it must seem like that." His voice was suddenly very tired. "You're quite right to go. It would be a great pity if you became the sort of woman who always fell in love with the wrong men . . ." He took her hand in his good one. "I told you I won't give my son up. So don't let me use you, Miss Lizzie. Guard against it. Anyway, God knows whether that letter would ever get dispatched. We'd probably be wasting our time writing it."

She was a coward. She ran away. She had provoked this situation, subconsciously wanting it, consciously exultant that Tom didn't love his wife, and now she ran

131

away from it. They could fall in love, and there would never be a happy ending. She was tired of unhappiness. She had to be practical, as Tom said, and guard against it.

She kept thinking of pretty suburban Millie, wincing away from the scarred hand, and it was difficult to concentrate on Alice's too-wide-awake voice.

"It will be fun for them, and they must go. I might even feel strong enough to go myself. I really do feel much stronger tonight. If we could get some blue ribbon and find some sort of crooked stick—Lizzie, are you listening?"

"I'm sorry. I was half asleep."

"Poor Lizzie. You're worn out. But do just hear what plans I have for the children's fancy dress party on Sunday. I intend my three to outshine all the rest. Bertie will be so proud of them."

They were in the middle of a war. Who knew whether they would come out of it alive. They had all had brushes with death, Alice with this fever, Tom on the veld, herself when a fragment of shell had struck the hospital and showered down dust, Bertie who remained above ground to man an alarm bell or stand to attention at a gun post when a raid was in progress, the children with their close proximity to the dread typhoid. So why was she being so cautious about protecting a future that might never exist? Why wasn't she just concentrating on the fact that it would be terrible to die, as the young men were dying, without having loved?

"Lots of white frills," Alice's feverish voice was murmuring. "I still have some starch left at the house. The three of them can go as shepherdesses. They'll look adorable."

Alice was obviously recovering, since she was once more concentrating on the image of herself as a lovely young mother with three beautiful children. But that might be hard to maintain with the hot summer and her now certain pregnancy ahead.

If anyone had thought that Cronje's departure would ease the pressure on the besieged town, he was mistaken. The Boers under General Snyman seemed to have made up their minds that it was foolhardy to risk the lives of more men by direct attack. They would sit as comfortably as possible in their laagers and confine their activities to a concentrated shelling of the town, especially of the women's laager, since rumor had it that that was where the major part of the British forces were lying in wait.

An average of seventy shells a day fell. But the Boers' aim was still poor, and the shells were made of such uncertain material that frequently they did not explode. It was soon discovered, during November, that the times when Creaky was elevated for firing took on a regularity, a few rounds before breakfast, a few before noon and another session at teatime. In between these times people became bolder, housewives doing their shopping and men strolling about in the sunshine. Sometimes they were too bold to bother to take shelter at all, but a few casualties caused Colonel Baden-Powell to deplore this foolhardiness. The Barolongs, who found the idiosyncrasy white men had for digging holes in the ground and then hiding in them very strange, stayed above ground themselves and consequently there were too many casualties in the kraal.

Andy Buchanan, as a consequence of his excellence as a marksman, had become a sniper and lay out on the veld for hours, trying to catch in a careless moment the Dutch gunners who manned Creaky. When he came home for a few hours' leave he worked on improving the dugout he had made for his grandmother in her back garden. It was now so commodious that she used it for bridge parties, or sewing parties at which the women mended uniforms or rolled bandages or made Union Jacks to fly over the forts. Andy wanted her to sleep in the dugout for safety, but she demanded to know why her old bones should be so specially protected. She preferred to die from a shellburst, rather than live with rheumatism crippling her from long nights spent underground.

The gentle Sisters of Mercy at the Convent, who had been working night and day with the influx of wounded and fever patients, asked for donations of sheets and blankets. Petticoats were contributed to be cut up for bandages. The lull in the fighting, since Cronje had departed, meant fewer wounded soldiers, but this was sadly compensated for by people suffering injuries from the shelling and by the slow steady increase in typhoid, dysentery and the dreaded enteric cases. News had come through that Sir George White's troops, shut up in Ladysmith, were dying like flies from enteric. And Colonel Plumer was still as far away as Bulawayo. Relief seemed farther off than ever.

Every now and then a runner got through, carrying a message written on tissue paper and concealed in the lining of his cap or the sole of one of his boots.

So far the news had been consistently bad. British forces everywhere were suffering defeats and enormous difficulties. They lacked food, equipment, maps and, often, intelligent officers. They would win the war, of course. They always did win.

But victory would not be before this Christmas, perhaps not even before the next.

Another suspected spy was jailed. He had been observed holding up three lighted matches to light his pipe. He pretended drunkenness—although spirits had been commandeered there were still plenty of bottles of wine available—but he could not have been as incapable as he would have had his captors believe, for when he was marched off his step was quite steady.

Amy Brown had continued her prison visiting, steeling herself to the distasteful task. She found the Dutch women, bored and worried about their families, were growing less hostile, although Katie Roos maintained her shrill aggressiveness.

"Don't give me any of that God is love stuff, Amy Brown. I can see the hate for me in your eyes."

Amy colored unhappily, unable to deny the truth of that. She did feel a revulsion for Katie, regarding her as a traitor of the deepest dye, but that incorrigible prisoner, Mr. Carter, whose hard black eyes sent shivers down Amy's spine, said, "Don't let her upset you, Miss Brown. She's worried about her husband. She thinks he might be killed. There's no way for her to find out, poor little wretch."

"Why are you sorry for her?" Amy asked.

"Oh dear, Miss Brown, do I have to teach you your religion? What are you doing here, if not turning the other cheek? You have a pretty cheek, too."

Amy's cheeks became hotter than ever. She wished Mr. Carter would stay silent and ignore her the way the

134

horse thief, Mr. Viljoen, did. He looked at her so intensely, yet his voice sounded sincere and respectful. Could a man like that ever be sincere? She kept remembering that his hand, a very strong-looking hand with dark hairs springing from it, had clasped the knife that had killed a man. Yet she always put on a freshly starched blouse and tied her hat ribbons with a distinct coquettishness beneath her chin before she went to the prison.

She told her mother that she could only stand the dirt and smells by feeling perfectly clean herself. She had looked at herself critically in the mirror before she left the house and found herself repeating the performance even more closely when she returned. Mr. Carter had said she had pretty cheeks. It was true that they were still flushed, and that certainly did add to her looks. But she still hadn't real prettiness. Her eyes were too pale a blue and her chin too small. It must be only her youth and her fair coloring that attracted that awful man.

She was nearly twenty-one and, hiding beneath her prim bonnets and her neat high-necked dresses, she had not been really noticed by any man before. She was deeply humiliated that the first compliment ever paid her should come from a criminal.

General Snyman was less tolerant than General Cronje had been. It seemed that the Sunday activities that went on in Mafeking annoyed him. There had been the children's fancy dress party, a baby show, a horse show and an exhibition of paintings. Cricket was played on the recreation grounds, and there was often a polo match.

Watching through binoculars, General Snyman was probably more offended that a besieged town could be so lighthearted than that impious use was being made of the Sabbath. He sent a message saying that he disapproved, and that if this frivolous behavior continued he would reluctantly be obliged to cease observing the Sunday truce.

It would be terrible if there was never a day when people could emerge safely from the shelters or give vent to their week-long suppression of high spirits by indulging in light-hearted amusements. Colonel Baden-Powell unhesitatingly decided to ignore Snyman's warning and continue as hitherto. For good measure he suggested a band concert and folk-dancing to take place on the following Sunday. The band was to play all the liveliest airs. The women might oblige by wearing their gayest clothes. In the long hot afternoon, the sounds would float across the veld, and the pretty hats of the women would enliven the scene.

It was the beginning of December, and there was no whisper of a relief force.

The only news that came into the town that first week in December was a letter from Lady Sarah Wilson to her husband. She was, startlingly, a prisoner of General Snyman. Her letter read:

December 2, 1899

MY DEAR GORDON,

I am at the laager. General Snyman will not give me a pass unless Colonel Baden-Powell will exchange me for a Mr. Petrus Viljoen. I am sure this is impossible, so I do not ask him formally. I am in a great fix, as they have very little meal left at Setlagoli or the surrounding places. I am very kindly looked after here.

Lady Sarah had spent an unhappy and very anxious two months, first at Mosita, on the farm of a colonial farmer, Keeley. His wife, who had four small children, was in a state of the greatest anxiety because her husband had gone on business to Mafeking just before the siege and had stayed on to defend the town. She was glad of Lady Sarah's company and made her warmly welcome. During those first days they heard alarming rumors— that the armored train had been blown up and all its occupants killed, that all telegraph wires into Mafeking were cut, that Vryburg had been taken without a shot being fired and the *Vierkleur* hoisted with much psalm singing and praying. The Boers were boasting that Oom Paul was about to take the Cape Colony, and then England.

Fortunately, Mr. Keeley decided to return home. Anxiety for his wife and children had preyed on his mind, and since it appeared that Mafeking was going to hold out for a long time, he was given leave to depart, riding for his life to escape the Boers.

It was an enormous relief to hear that the casualties in Mafeking had been so few, although Mr. Keeley said

136

the people were living like moles in the ground, owing to the persistent shelling.

After that Lady Sarah endured the boredom of her enforced imprisonment a little longer. There were more false alarms. A warning came that the Boers were swarming round Setlagoli and a commando would be coming to the Keeleys' farm the next day. With the help of her German maid, Lady Sarah buried her jewel case in the garden, and then all of the household spent a wakeful night. Mrs. Keeley decided the best thing to do was to have a good supply of coffee made to offer the Boers. But the long hot day went by and nothing happened. The mingled tension and boredom was becoming unendurable. Lady Sarah decided to defy danger and return to Setlagoli and her friends, the Frasers.

Mrs. Fraser had a story to tell about the Boers coming to the store and ransacking it, fitting themselves out with clothes, watches and chains, silk pocket handkerchiefs and, more practically, saddles and harness.

They had eventually gone away, just before the arrival of a Reuters correspondent, who had contrived to get through the lines from Mafeking. He brought with him a crate of carrier pigeons and suggested that Lady Sarah should use them as a means of communicating with Mafeking. If this could be done successfully, Colonel Baden-Powell would send her messages which she could pass on to the outside world.

But the first attempt ended in pure farce. The pigeon flew to the Boer laager outside Mafeking and perched on General Snyman's headquarters. The next day, inevitably, a party of Boers arrived asking for the English lady.

Lady Sarah did the only thing that seemed practical. She wrote to General Snyman asking him for a pass into Mafeking to rejoin her husband. While one Boer remained to guard her, another took her letter. He returned the next day to escort her for a personal interview with the General. All the way he boasted alarmingly about the English defeats. Fifteen thousand, he said, had been slain at the Modder River battle. And two thousand *Engelman* lay dead in Mafeking.

The forty-five-mile drive along sandy roads in the burning sun was an ordeal made additionally poignant when,

137

coming over a rise, the tired woman could see the roofs of Mafeking shining in the sun not five miles away. In the intervening space there were broken-down wagons and aasvogels hovering over the almost stripped skeletons of horses and cattle. She could not see a living soul on the flat grassy plains, although her driver assured her that everywhere there were Boer sharpshooters hiding in the scrub.

An additional ordeal was watching the sudden puffs of smoke and hearing the distant roar of the big siege gun as it began its afternoon shelling of the town. Weary and heartsick, she was almost at the point of believing the boastful Dutchman and his story of two thousand dead.

But at last she was taken through the laager, filled with the grizzly bearded Boers, and into a farmhouse which General Snyman had made his headquarters.

In the low dark room, seated on a bench, there were two old men with long beards and shrewd narrowed eyes. They were General Snyman and Commandant Botha. They both looked what they were, Boer farmers, in untidy suits with heavy watchchains across their waistcoats and heavy boots, their broad, flatbrimmed hats lying on the table beside them.

General Snyman was in a surly mood. Her arrival was an embarrassment to him. He would not hear of her suggestion that if he would not give her a pass into Mafeking, he exchange her for one of the Dutch women prisoners. The woman was of little use to him. She could stay in the jail in Mafeking. But, after a lot of reflection, he decided he might agree to exchange her for the Dutchman Petrus Viljoen. Certainly Viljoen was a convicted thief, but he could hold a gun.

This information was communicated to Lady Sarah's husband, Captain Gordon Wilson. While waiting with what patience she could for his reply, Lady Sarah was kept a prisoner in the field hospital, a small house half a mile away. She was shut in a tiny room smelling strongly of disinfectant which was obviously a crude operating theater. There was a broken-down sofa and a dilapidated washstand. The walls were riddled with bullet holes. Two Dutch women sullenly undressed and searched her, then brought her some execrable coffee. She spent an endless uncomfortable night, and the next day, being

Sunday, she was tortured by the long prayers and the hymn singing, out of tune, that went on for hours outside her window.

At last the reply from her husband arrived.

Mafeking, Dec. 3, 1899

MY DEAR SARAH,

I am delighted to hear you are being well treated, but very sorry to have to tell you that Colonel Baden-Powell finds it impossible to hand over Petrus Viljoen in exchange for you, as he was convicted of horse-stealing before the war. I fail to see in what way it can benefit your captors to keep you a prisoner. Luckily for them, it is not the custom of the English to make prisoners of war of women.

GORDON WILSON

It was desperately disappointing. More agonizingly, she could see Mafeking from her window and watch the explosions of smoke and dust after the big gun had fired. Was she going to be kept captive here for weeks? All day the Boers talked beneath her window, and at night snored loudly.

But at last, four days later, her purgatory ended. A messenger arrived saying that it was agreed she should be exchanged for the horse thief. It seemed that Lord Edward Cecil, the Prime Minister's son, had agreed to take on himself any censure the English Government might feel it necessary to make.

The Boers suddenly became courteous and wished Lady Sarah goodbye and good luck. She climbed into the mule cart that stood waiting for her and, whipping up the pair of mules, set off at a spanking pace.

A little distance from Mafeking a small party, carrying a white flag, escorted Mr. Petrus Viljoen, who looked extremely dejected. It appeared that he hadn't much wanted to be repatriated. He didn't bear any love for his fellow countrymen and preferred the comparative safety of his English jail.

This was the final touch to the whole tragi-comedy. Rattling along past the barricades, Lady Sarah was both laughing and crying as the men in the trenches cheered her wildly. In Market Square, Colonel Baden-Powell himself was waiting to welcome her. Lord Edward Cecil was there, too, and her husband, Captain Gordon Wilson. But the greetings had scarcely been said before Creaky malevolently began firing and the welcome ended in an undignified hustle into the nearest shelter.

The only other episode of any significance that week was an exceptionally heavy storm. It began with flashes of lightning and great cracks of thunder that terrified the children. The sky was so black, it seemed as if it must fall and smother them. Then the rain began. It was a deluge that flooded the shallow trenches, making them virtually unusable. Worse still, the women's laager bore the brunt of the storm. Over it, the heavens opened, and the flimsy tents were useless against the wall of water that descended. Some collapsed. Some simply dripped a steady stream on their unlucky occupants. Soaked and miserable, women emerged carrying their frightened children. They were a lot of drowned rats, with peaked white faces and streaming hair, waiting for the rain to stop and the sun to come out and dry them.

When at last the sun did come out the earth steamed. There was a glorious crisp clean smell, but the children failed to revive as quickly as the renewed earth. Some of them continued to shiver, and it was clear that there would be more fever beds filled in the hospitals.

They had also another blow to face. Colonel Baden-Powell after consultation with Captain Ryan had decided that the rations were too generous. They must be cut by two-thirds. The siege, although it was nearing its sixtieth day, was far from being over.

XIII

The children's fancy dress party was held, and there was also a gymkhana and a concert. Tom Wheeler organized a picture gallery, offering prizes for the best entries. He himself hung his sketch of the Partridge children, and Henrietta importantly pointed it out to everyone. Alice was better, although still weak and inclined to shed tears on the least provocation. There had been some more cases of enteric, but chiefly among the army. So far, the children had escaped that unpleasant and dangerous disease.

A runner had got through with a slim package of letters from England. The lucky recipients read theirs greedily. Alice had one from her mother, and her tears flowed once more. And Lizzie knew that Tom Wheeler had had one from his wife because she had been in Dixon's Hotel when the letters had been distributed. She saw him put the letter in his pocket, either because he wanted to read it in privacy, or because he didn't want to read it at all. She was ashamed of herself for wanting so badly to know what was in the letter, and for her sharp feeling of jealousy. Perhaps he would tell her about it later. He was much stronger and his hand was improving. He didn't need her care any longer. And he seemed to be avoiding her. It was the wisest thing to do. They both knew that. There was no future for them if they fell in love.

But with General Snyman obstinately sitting in the middle distance watching the town, was there any future anyway?

On the tenth of December Colonel Baden-Powell wrote a letter addressed to "The burghers under arms around Mafeking."

It read:

141

The main body of the British is now daily arriving by thousands from England, Canada, India and Australia, and is about to advance through the country. In a short time the Republic will be in the hands of the English and no sacrifice of life upon your part can stop it. The question now that you have to put to yourselves before it is too late is: Is it worthwhile losing your lives in a vain attempt to stop the invasion or take a town beyond your borders which, if taken, will be of no use to you? The German Emperor is at present in England and fully sympathizes with us. The American Government has warned others of its intention to side with England should any Power intervene. France has large interests in the goldfields identical with those of England. Italy is entirely in accord with us. Russia has no cause to interfere. The duty assigned to my troops is to sit still here until the proper time arrives and then to fight and kill until you give in. My advice to you is to return to your homes without delay and remain peacefully until the war is over. Those who do this before the thirteenth will, as far as possible, be protected, as regards yourselves, your families and property, from confiscation, looting and other penalties to which those remaining under arms will be subjected when the invasion takes place. Each man must be prepared to hand over a rifle and 150 rounds of ammunition. The above terms do not apply to officers and members of the Staats artillery who may surrender as prisoners of war at any time, nor to rebels on British territory. I may tell you that Mafeking cannot be taken by sitting down and looking at it.

Hundreds of copies of this letter were printed, wrapped around stones and thrown from the advance trenches toward the Boer lines.

Reports seeped into Mafeking that General Snyman was furious. His fury, however, was confined to more persistent shelling. No direct attack was made. It seemed that the reports of mines laid about the town, deliberately exaggerated by correspondents who were getting their dispatches through to England, was the reason for his hesitancy. They believed that the mines could be exploded by electric wires communicating with Baden-Powell's office. The Boers were not cowards, but they didn't fancy having their arms or legs blown off before their objective

142

was reached. Mafeking remained a plum aggravatingly out of reach.

The renewed shelling hit Dixon's Hotel, the Dutch church and, again, the hospital. This time one of the wards was demolished, and it was obvious that a new building would have to be found to house the patients. Also, in the town, a man was blown to pieces, and later one of his legs, a macabre relic, was dislodged from the roof of his house. When a piece of shrapnel flew straight through the chemist's window, Mrs. Peterson, who was at the counter buying a bottle of eau de cologne, slid to the floor in what was at first thought to be a faint. But on examination it was found she would not want her eau de cologne after all. It was too late to revive her. She had died of fright.

How was it possible to enjoy the approaching Christmas season in this atmosphere? Orders came from headquarters that festivities must be observed. Every child in the town was to receive a Christmas gift. Amy Brown and Linda Hill organized a center for this purpose, and every day the offerings came in, second-hand or homemade toys, picture books, shabby dolls that had been furbished in new clothes, some hoarded boxes of candy. Mrs. Ryan tearfully parted with Annie's favorite doll, sensibly realizing it might make another child happy. Henrietta and Fanny Partridge sat patiently sewing dolls' clothes which their mother had cut out of one of her silk petticoats. She had carefully unpicked the handmade lace and instructed the little girls in how to embroider the tiny frocks.

Henrietta and Fanny fretted at the tiresome occupation and were even more distressed when they found that they were each expected to give one of their own dolls toward the Christmas fund.

"But, Mamma, then I shall only have Emilia left," Henrietta protested.

"Never mind, darling. One has to learn to make sacrifices. Let me see that hem. I'm afraid your stitches are not as neat as they should be."

"Who is to see them?" Henrietta muttered rebelliously.

"That isn't the point. The point is to always take a pride in your work."

That old nursery admonition. It was all very well for

143

an orderly nursery in England where one knew that time went on forever. But here, when any moment a shell might blow them to oblivion? Alice bit her lips, handed the sewing back to Henrietta, made herself smile calmly and refused to let herself worry about what she was to make her baby's clothes from. They would be far from here, and safe, before the baby came.

The contributions piled up in the room that Amy and Linda had turned into a receiving center. Linda giggled at the homemade golliwogs and strange-jointed wooden dolls that some of the old men had made. She was always lighthearted these days because Granny Buchanan was going to let Andy marry her after Christmas. She was making a nightgown out of some Swiss lawn her mother had had put away. She cared very little that she would not be a well-equipped bride with a dozen of everything. She only wanted Andy. And then about ten children.

"Do you want to have children, Amy?" she asked.

Amy flushed.

"I suppose so, someday. I hadn't thought about it."

"Goodness!" Linda exclaimed in frank astonishment. "Then what do you think about? Not God all the time?"

"No, of course not. But—"

"If you don't think about them, you'll never have them," Linda said sagely. "You have to want things before you get them. Are you too scared?"

"I don't know. It's not a thing to talk about."

"Well, I intend to make the most of my life while I'm still alive. If the war goes on, or if Andy gets killed, I intend to have something. I know someone else who thinks like this, and that's Miss Willoughby."

"That woman!" said Amy disapprovingly. "Papa says she's being very foolish. She sees far too much of Mr. Wheeler, and everyone knows he has a wife in England."

"You can't help who you fall in love with."

"You can! You can so!"

Linda looked at Amy in surprise.

"Why, I believe you're secretly in love yourself, Amy Brown."

"I am not! Who is there for me to be in love with?"

"Why, the place is bursting with men, if only you'd open your eyes and look at them. I'd hurry, if I were you. None of us might be alive for long."

"Linda Hill, you're only a schoolgirl. Talking like that."

But it seemed as if Linda might be right, for the very next day she narrowly escaped death. A shell struck the house while she was sewing the precious nightgown, and her sewing machine was blown through the window, taking with it the treasured length of Swiss lawn. Linda was dazed and shocked. Her hair was full of dust and for several minutes she couldn't speak. But she was alive and unhurt. It was a miracle, not a bad omen. That night Mrs. Buchanan got out her wedding dress again and made Linda try it on.

It was a little too tight at the waist. Linda was a healthy young creature brought up in the colonies. She had never been subjected to tightly laced corsets.

But the waist could be let out. Otherwise the dress fitted perfectly. It was old-fashioned, and the lace had yellowed and rotted slightly, but none of this mattered. It was a real wedding dress, and Linda, even though her wedding was to take place in a town under siege, and a shell might fall through the church roof in the middle of the ceremony, would at least look like a bride.

The wedding was fixed for the first Sunday in the new year, provided Andy was able to get leave. He had wanted it the day after Christmas, but Linda had had a superstitious feeling that to be married at the beginning of the new year would be lucky. It would be the first week of the new century, too. She would be able to tell her children about it in time to come.

Lizzie and Alice were both invited to the Christmas dinner party to be held in Dixon's Hotel.

Although Christmas Day fell on a Monday, it had been decided to hold it on Sunday in case the Boers did not observe a truce on Monday. Lady Sarah Wilson had organized the Christmas tree, and a tea party with food supplied by the merchant Ben Weil, for the children. The brave pile of gifts was distributed. The mothers had dressed in their best, and the children, although a little pale and peaky, were washed and brushed and bright-eyed with excitement. They had had thrilling rides into town in conveyances organized by officers of the Protectorate Regiment, and now there were cake and sweets to eat, and new toys to play with, and the Commander-

145

in-Chief obligingly turned himself successively into a bear or an elephant and romped with them.

Henrietta Partridge watched to see who got the doll with which she had been so loath to part. The recipient was a stolid Dutch child who spoke only Afrikaans. She stood hugging the china-faced Mabel to her fat breast while eyeing Henrietta with hostility. Henrietta had an intense struggle with herself. She badly wanted to snatch Mabel back, claiming prior ownership. Good manners prevailed, but grudgingly. Her own gift, a string of beads, hadn't pleased her very much. She didn't care for Christmas in Africa at all.

Her sisters had fared better. Fanny had got a silver thimble, and Daisy one of the homemade golliwogs whose hideous face enchanted her. She sat rocking it in her arms crooning to it, a miniature beauty and the beast.

Billy Ryan, looking unfamiliar with his scrubbed face and flattened hair, got a bag of marbles, which delighted him. But he hadn't stayed long at the party. As soon as he thought himself unobserved, he had slipped out and made for the horse paddocks. He had managed to steal a bunch of carrots from the vegetable gardens so carefully tended by members of the Town Guard. Star must have her Christmas gift, too.

He was worried about her because grazing had been bad after the depredations of a swarm of locusts, and there were troopers' horses to be fed. Star's ribs were showing. Billy didn't realize that they were less prominent than his own. His spare body was little more than skin and bone. Ever since Annie had died his mother had given very little attention to preparing food, and any of the more tasty tidbits that came his way he saved for Daisy Partridge. He couldn't resist her look of delight and the uncritical love she bestowed on him.

As the sun went down, the weary, overexcited children, whose stamina was not what it had been before the siege, were taken home, and the dinner in Dixon's Hotel took place.

Lizzie had put on her dark blue silk dress and had done her hair elaborately, although it had been a scramble to get away from the hospital in time. Only three nurses were left on duty.

At the last minute Doctor Macpherson had asked to accompany her. She could scarcely refuse and felt ashamed of her lack of warmth. She hoped Tom Wheeler would be at the dinner and intended, if possible, to sit next to him. But Doctor Macpherson, neatly dressed in a dark suit, stayed persistently at her side. He had stopped calling her nurse on this occasion, and even more formally addressed her as Miss Willoughby.

Tom was late.

"You keep looking at the door, Miss Willoughby. Are you expecting someone?"

Lizzie answered frankly.

"Yes. I wondered if our ex-patient, Mr. Wheeler, would be here."

Doctor Macpherson's eyes narrowed slightly. But his voice was composed. It would never be anything else, Lizzie thought impatiently. He was a man who was always in control of his emotions. But she could never cease to admire his calm and his selflessness in emergency, and thought that if ever there was a reliable shoulder to cry on, it was this one beside her.

At the last minute, just as the guests were about to take their places at the long table, Tom came in. Some uninspired wit had composed a couplet which was printed at the top of the menu:

> *May Xmas find you glad and well*
> *In spite of Kruger's shot and shell*

Due again to the generosity of the merchant, Mr. Weil, there was turkey and plum pudding and an unlimited supply of wine.

Grace was said and a Christmas carol sung:

God rest ye, merry gentlemen! let nothing you dismay,
Remember Christ, our Saviour, was born on Christmas day.

Lizzie thought of the white-faced sad Mrs. Ryan, whose time was getting very near. And of Alice, who was beginning to suffer tortures from morning sickness, although she had steeled herself to come to this dinner to please her husband. She sat opposite Lizzie now, looking ethereal in her lilac silk, a gauzy scarf over her shoulders, her great blue eyes sparkling with forced animation.

147

Sometimes Lizzie thought that silly vain Alice was the bravest woman she knew.

Tom Wheeler did not sit near her, after all. He was engaged in conversation with Lady Sarah Wilson, and obviously being very amusing, for Lady Sarah was laughing heartily. Lizzie made the discovery that so long as Tom was in the same room as herself she was happy. She noticed that his hand was now unbandaged, although even from this distance she could see the unsightly scar.

"He may have trouble with that hand in future," said Doctor Macpherson, accurately reading her thoughts. "There may be some contraction in the muscles."

"It's his right hand."

"True. But at least he didn't lose it. Where did you spend last Christmas, Miss Willoughby? In London?"

"No. In the country." (A little place called Middlehurst where my husband has an estate . . .)

"That isn't very explicit."

"It was in a country house in Surrey. Where did you spend yours, Doctor Macpherson?"

"In Edinburgh. And my friends call me Alex."

"I must call you doctor in the hospital."

"Of course. In the hospital."

Lizzie sipped her wine and stole another look at Tom. He was still acutely thin, but she found his ravaged face, animated as it now was, disturbingly exciting. He happened to turn from Lady Sarah Wilson at that minute and caught her glance. Immediately he lifted his glass to her. His eyes were merry, concerned only with the present jollity.

"The more important thing," she said, politely maintaining the conversation with Doctor Macpherson, "is where we will all be next Christmas."

"In a more comfortable place than this, I hope. Do you intend going back to England after the war?"

"Oh, no, I'll go to my brother in Natal as I had intended to. If he's alive, of course."

"Come. No unhappy thoughts today."

Then Alice leaned across to say something, and Lizzie's neighbor on her other side, a woman whose husband was recovering from a wound in the hospital, wanted to know if she could take the patient a bottle of wine later.

148

They were all getting pleasantly relaxed from the food and drink. The fact that several thousand warlike Boers were sitting in laagers scarcely three miles away, consuming their Christmas dinner, if they indulged in one, seemed almost farcical.

But it wasn't farcical. Chairs had just begun to be pushed back at the dinner's end when Tom was at Lizzie's side. He took her arm and drew her a little away.

"I'm off at dawn. Have a happy new year."

"Oh, Tom—"

"Keep it to yourself. Have you any letters you want sent?"

"Tom, you can't even hold a gun yet."

"I'm a postman, not a sniper."

She looked at his face searchingly. She was wondering if she would ever see it again.

"No, I haven't any letters. England seems—my life seems to be here, now."

"Don't get too intense about it. This isn't real. This is living in another dimension. The siege won't last forever."

"I wasn't wishing that!" she said in horror.

"I don't suppose you were, but it is a way of shutting the rest of the world out—if that's what you want to do."

"Yes, I do want to do that," she admitted.

"So do I. Well, anyway, we've had a good dinner. It'll be something to remember when we're reduced to locusts and horse flesh." He took her hand and lifted it to kiss it lightly. "Now go back to your sober doctor friend. He's in love with you."

He had gone before she could answer, if, indeed, she had known what to answer. She watched him move through the crowd.

"Is Wheeler going home to get an early night? Sensible fellow," said Doctor Macpherson.

Not an early night, but an early morning. A figure, infinitesimal against the enormous stretches of the veld, moving toward the morning heat and the blazing noon. Tom, will you come back?

There was little time to spend worrying about him. Although he was never out of the deeper part of her

149

mind, Lizzie soon found herself too occupied for private worries.

For on Boxing Day an attack was launched on Game Tree Hill, from which one of the Boer guns had been wreaking havoc. In working out the plan of attack it was believed that many of the Boers would have been allowed Christmas leave, and the fort might be undermanned. Major Godley was in command, and in support he had experienced men, Captain Vernon and Captain Fitzclarence, Major Panzera and Colonel Hore.

The attack began at dawn. It was only half past four, and everyone, even the deepest sleeper, was awakened by the rattle of musketry. It was a clear bright morning with a slight breeze, the air cool and refreshing before the heat to come. Larks were already rising. In between bursts of gunfire their song was quite clear.

Hastily huddled into an assortment of clothes, the people in the town watched the distant action, the puffs of smoke, the antlike figures of men moving forward, running, falling. Already rumors were spreading that something had gone wrong. The armored train had been intended to take part in the action, but it had had to stop out of range, for the rails had been taken up. This must have happened in the night. Spies must have been at work. The Boers obviously had been warned of the coming attack.

So now Captain Vernon was making an unplanned thousandyard dash up the slope to the fort. He came under heavy fire. From the rooftops in Mafeking it was distressingly easy to see men falling. There was no sign of the burghers. Well under cover, they continued to pour a devastating fire into the oncoming troops.

The long grass rustled. The sun caught fire on suddenly bared steel. As fast as men fell more filled their places, and the bayonet attack on the fort began. It seemed to go on forever. Surely there could be nobody left alive, neither attacker nor attacked.

A large party of Boer horsemen, despite intimidating riflefire from the British outposts, were closing in. If Major Godley did not give the order to withdraw, his entire force might be trapped.

The Boer horsemen continued to come, from both north and west. Just as the distance diminished to a precarious few hundred yards, Godley at last gave the reluctant signal to withdraw.

To the anxious watchers there seemed an astonishingly large number of survivors. The gunfire had been so intense that it had seemed no one would come out of the little hell.

But slowly the men straggled back, stopping to help the wounded, some of them assisting, or even carrying on their shoulders, a man unable to walk. Stretchers were improvised. The ambulance wagons began to move up. As all gunfire ceased, a mass of Boer horsemen crowded around the fort, waiting with apparent amiability for the ambulances. They were the victors. They could afford, for once, to be amiable. They had already rifled the pockets of the wounded and the dead. They also had held Game Tree Fort, which had proved to be a blockhouse prickling with Mausers. No amount of courage, and there had been plenty of that, would have taken it with the weapons the British possesssed.

It only remained for the losses to be counted. Young Captain Vernon, who only the previous day had been one of the most active in the Christmas celebrations, had been killed. Captain Fitzclarence had a severe thigh wound. There had been two other officers killed and twenty-one men. Another twenty-three were wounded with varying degrees of severity. There had been many acts of gallantry, and later there would be two Victoria Crosses awarded.

The losses were a devastating blow, but their very severity made the besieged people more determined than ever never to yield. How could they now lose faith with so many brave men who were going to leave their bones in Mafeking?

Worse still, bad news had come in about other British reverses at Magersfontein, Stormberg and Colenso. The future had never been more uncertain.

Imperturbably, Colonel Baden-Powell gave orders for extra rations to celebrate the new year. And to drive away forebodings. A horse show was organized; Billy Ryan rode his pony, tucking his bare feet into her now much less robust sides. It worried him that she had got so much slower. There was a concert. And Linda Hill planned her wedding.

151

Andy had his leave arranged, three whole days, unless there was an unexpected attack. Mrs. Buchanan was going to move down to the women's laager for a few days and let the young couple have her house. Mr. Weekes, the Church of England parson, had agreed to hold a short marriage service immediately after the usual morning service. Linda insisted on dressing as a bride and having attendants. These were to be the three little Partridges, and they were full of importance and excitement. Their mother had spent an entire Sunday washing, starching and ironing their white muslin dresses and their blue hair ribbons.

At the end of the day she was worn out, but it was worth the expense of energy to see the children's excitement. Their eyes hadn't sparkled like that for a long time. It was the very first time they had ever been bridesmaids, and it didn't matter in the least that it was to be at a wedding held in a little church scarred from shellfire, with the bride wearing makeshift wedding finery, and the guests worn and peaked and shabby from their weeks of poor food, the daily hours spent hiding in bomb shelters, sickness and fear. Henrietta talked importantly of how they were to walk and stand. She, being the eldest, would be nearest to the bride. She only hoped Daisy would remember what she had to do.

Daisy gave her limpid smile and promised faithfully that she wouldn't cry once all that day. Fanny wanted to know if there would be delicious food, as there had been on Christmas Day.

Lizzie, on Doctor Macpherson's orders, had the whole day off.

"You women love a wedding," he said. "I've spoken to Matron. So go and enjoy yourself."

Sister Casey was inclined to sniff. Lizzie wasn't the only one who had been worked half to death during that nightmare week. Not only many of the wounded from Game Tree Hill had come in, but the incidence of infectious diseases was increasing. The real summer heat had begun. There was a plague of flies, and mosquitoes became an insistent whining pest. At night, when the wards could not be kept entirely in darkness, they hummed monotonously around the paraffin lamps on the floor and added to the sufferings of the wounded, some of whom could not lift a hand to defend themselves.

Lizzie had had about forty hours of sleep in the last ten days. She was in a trance of weariness which was, in its own way, a blessing. It made her able to look at the worst wounds without flinching. She had had the fortitude to sit all night beside a dying boy, holding his hand and talking quietly to him whenever he appeared to be conscious. He was eighteen and he kept talking about a girl he hadn't written to in England. She would be fretting. If only he had a pen and ink now . . .

"Tell me her name and where she lives and I'll write to her."

"Molly," said the boy. And he never did manage to tell Lizzie the girl's address. It seemed she had black hair like Lizzie's. At the end, just before his eyes rolled up, Lizzie saw his blurred gaze resting on her with some sort of ecstasy, and she knew that in that moment he had imagined her to be the absent Molly.

She wanted to tell Tom this small personal tragedy. But Tom was one person her weary mind refused to think of. If she allowed her anxiety for him to come into this nightmare too, she would never remain sane.

All the same, Doctor Macpherson had been right about a wedding doing her good. In spite of her lack of sleep, she got up in the early morning, when the air was still cool, and went around to people's gardens, asking for flowers. She wanted to make a small bouquet for the bride, and posies for the little girls to carry.

There were roses and cornflowers and yellow poppies. They would quickly wilt in the heat, and in the hot clasp of little fingers, but they would make a touch of gaiety to begin with.

Laden with her spoils, she went to Mrs. Buchanan's house where the wedding preparations were in full swing. Everyone had gathered there—Alice and Bertie Partridge and the excited children, the bride and her mother and father, and Miss Rose, who was displaying another unexpected ability. She was quite clever at dressing hair and would do Linda's in an upswept crown that would make her look much more adult.

But there was an air of quiet over the little party. The bridegroom had not yet arrived.

It seemed that he should have been there two hours ago. He would have come off nightwatch at dawn. But no one had seen him. He must have delayed to get the good wishes of his comrades. They had probably had an early morning issue of rum to wish him luck.

Mrs. Buchanan, rustling about in her best black silk adorned with little trembling cascades of jet, said that Andy had never had any idea of time. He would be late for his own funeral.

She hadn't meant to make such an unfortunate remark but wasn't going to apologize, even when Linda gave a small cry of horror.

"What an awful thing to say, Granny Buchanan!"

"Don't be so squeamish, child. You'd better get to know the man you're in such a hurry to marry."

The church bells were ringing for the morning service. It was pleasant to hear their leisurely peal instead of the alarm notes they so often sounded during the week. In another hour or so they would ring for the bride who sat in her old-fashioned wedding dress clasping her hands tightly to stop their trembling.

"Now you go in the bedroom the minute you see Andy coming," Mrs. Buchanan said. "It's bad luck for him to see you before you stand by him in the church."

Linda's eyes went back to the window, and the dusty red road leading to the trenches. They had not been off it for more than a moment or two at a time since she had finished dressing.

The children were restless, and Henrietta had fallen down and got dust on her dress. Alice slapped her sharply.

"For goodness' sake, can't you sit quietly. Such a great tomboy you're getting. On the sofa, beside Fanny and Daisy."

The little girls sat crushed together, like paper roses, their eyes growing as anxious as Linda's.

"When is the wedding to be?" Daisy whispered.

Bertie Partridge began to look uneasy. He walked about, pulling at his moustache, filling the small room and making it seem hotter than ever. Suddenly he said, "I'll walk down to the barracks. See if I can dig out this reluctant bridegroom. Do you think he's got stage fright, Linda? Ha ha!"

The women were glad for him to go. Something was

154

being done. But Linda's eyes had filled with uncontrollable tears at his jovial remarks. Of everyone there, she knew that Andy was far from having stage fright. Last Sunday, when they had wandered on the long grass slopes on the outskirts of the town he had been difficult to manage. He had wanted her to lie down in the grass and let him make love to her there and then, as if they were already married. She had refused indignantly—that sort of thing just wasn't done before marriage, it was wicked, or so her mother had always told her. But her own body had gone soft and limp, and if only he had pulled her into his arms . . .

But that was for tonight, decently, in a bed, she told herself, blinking away her tears.

Mrs. Buchanan said briskly, "There'll be a time for a cup of tea, now that boy's so late. Come and help me, Miss Rose. I've been saving a bit of Earl Grey."

Alice, at the window, exclaimed, "Here's Amy Brown. Church must be over!"

That meant that by now the Reverend Weekes would be waiting, too.

Amy came in saying she had hurried over from chapel to see if there was anything she could do. They were singing the last hymn. She had slipped out.

"We have no bridegroom, as yet," Mrs. Buchanan said in her dry voice. And suddenly Linda bent her head, whispering, "He's dead. I know."

Everyone twittered about her, denying such a tragic fancy, except Mrs. Buchanan, who was standing still, her face stone. As if she, too, could not pretend any more.

Lizzie made a decision.

"I'm going to the hospital. I'll see if anyone has been brought in."

Alice tugged at her skirt.

"No, wait till Bertie gets back. He'll find out. He'll see Colonel Baden-Powell, if necessary."

"But Andy's only late," Amy murmured in distress.

"He's dead," said Linda, in that same flat voice. "I know."

She pulled off the coronet of yellowing orange blossom, disturbing Miss Rose's careful arrangement of her hair.

"I must take off this silly dress."

155

Daisy began to cry, lifting her arms silently to Lizzie. "That cry-baby," her mother said.

Linda was standing in her petticoat when the young officer, looking harassed and nervous, came up the road and turned in at the gate of Mrs. Buchanan's house.

He stood at the door, refusing to come in. He wasn't used to assignments like this one. It was bad enough breaking bad news by letter, but to have to tell it to a man's bride! He would rather have faced Paul Kruger's army single-handed.

Andy had been found only an hour ago. A sniper's bullet had gone cleanly through his forehead. Tit for tat, in a way. He had been a clever marksman himself. The body had been brought in and would be buried that evening, at the usual time.

So the flowers, thought Lizzie, would do for the funeral.

XIV

With the new year, the shelling grew more prolonged. The hospital was hit again, and an improvised one was made in a ruined convent, a gaunt red structure near the railway station. It had gaping holes in the walls and broken windows. What had once been a garden was a jungle of weeds and thorns. But there were several rooms on the ground floor which were undamaged. These, with the assistance of Mr. Weil, who sent crockery, kitchen utensils and food, were made ready for eighteen patients.

Lizzie was one of the volunteer nurses who was moved to this rather desolate structure. Within minutes of the patients' being installed, a shell burst near, showering them with the inevitable dust. As a consequence, an upstairs room was used as a lookout, with a soldier always on duty. He would clatter down the stairs shouting, "Gun pointed at convent!" at regular intervals. But Creaky's shooting had remained inaccurate. Usually the shell burst in a cloud of dust half a mile away.

The weather was hard to bear, blinding heat dispersed by heavy thunderstorms, then the heat again and a plague of insects, the horrible flies and mosquitoes being joined by locusts and other species of winged beetles. A tarantula crawled up the wall of the ward, and Lizzie had to scream for the help of one of the more mobile patients. She shuddered for minutes after it had been dispatched.

But the frequent rain showers had made the grass on the veld green and lush, and in the early morning, after the long hours of keeping watch in the ward, listening to the snores and groans, the tramp of the guards on the stairs, the whistle of the wind and the faint sputter now and then of the paraffin lamps, it was wonderful to go

157

outdoors and breathe the clean air blowing straight from the Kalahari desert.

That was, if there was not a fusillade of shots from the Boer lines, the bullets ringing on the tin roofs of houses, or the early morning roar of Creaky, hoping to catch the sentries walking single file in the long grass as they came off duty.

The Boers had thought of a new form of torture for the weary prisoners in the town. Creaky was moved to another position, but instead of firing immediately after its muzzle was raised, it remained in that position for minute after minute until a whole hour after the alarm "Gun in position!" had elapsed. Then, at last, came the roar of the shell, and people were able to lift their heads and emerge into the daylight once more.

The waiting stretched people's nerves intolerably. But much much worse was to come. On the third of January a day-long bombardment took place.

Alice thought it was the most terrifying day she had ever spent in her life. Her ears ached with the noise, her eyes smarted with dust, and she was exhausted from trying to keep the children calm. She thought it would be a miracle if she emerged from this with Bertie's son still secure in her womb. Early in the day news had come that Mrs. Ryan had been hurried to hospital for the birth of her baby.

Billy had inevitably joined the Partridge children, and for once Alice didn't fuss about his grubby hands on Daisy's frock or the possible presence of livestock in his long-unwashed hair or the germs he might carry. He was a little boy as frightened as all of them, although he pretended otherwise, whistling through his teeth in imitation of Colonel Baden-Powell, and going through his usual repertoire of tricks to make Daisy laugh.

But even he tired as the day wore on and the unremitting crash of shells continued. The shelter was foul with the warm air, the forever seeping dust and the sweat of nervous people. There had never been so many shells in the women's laager. It was being remarked that the Dutch women seldom seemed to have to fly for cover —they had usually taken it before the alarm was given. Had they secret information about the time the gun would be fired?

158

Suspicion didn't make the situation easier to bear. Miss Rose, her flat figure sagging a little, although it could never be said to droop, made valiant efforts to keep the imprisoned children occupied. By midafternoon even she had had to give up and sit in the torpor which had overcome them all. Daisy was as white as her muslin dress. She had whimpered for a while, then sat curled on her mother's lap, silent. She felt hot, Alice thought. Or was that imagination? They were all as hot and uncomfortable as it was possible to be.

It seemed as if not six hours but a whole week had gone by when at last it was safe to come up into the blazing afternoon sun and assess the damage.

A little boy was seriously hurt; a woman had had a shell splinter through her heart, dying instantly; her sister had had an arm shockingly mutilated.

That seemed to be the extent of the injuries suffered in the women's laager, but no one knew what had happened in the town. It wasn't until Lizzie came out that evening, anxious for the welfare of Alice and the girls, that the damage was told.

Dixon's Hotel had been hit again and there had been no less than thirty-four shells in the vicinity of the auxiliary hospital. One had fallen through the roof of the Convent, and for a little while, in the choking cloud of dust and falling bricks, it had been impossible to know how many had been hurt.

Lady Sarah Wilson and her husband, both recuperating from a sharp attack of fever, had nearly lost their lives. They had emerged like dusty ghosts from the rubble.

Alice wept silently as she listened.

"Will we ever get out of this dreadful place? Supposing we're still living like this when my baby is born. He'll never live."

"You were crazy to start having a baby at a time like this." The long, tortured day had left Lizzie, too, with finely stretched nerves. Alice's tears irritated her unbearably.

"What would you have done?" Alice wept. "Would it be better to be like poor Linda Hill?"

"Don't be silly. There's no comparison. You have a husband and three children. You could have waited."

"I didn't know things were to be like this. And neither did you. If you had a husband, I'm sure you'd have behaved in exactly the same way. That is if you loved him and wanted to be a good wife."

Lizzie said nothing. She had done neither of those things for Humphrey. How could she have? The marriage had been a disaster from start to finish. "Supposing you were married to that Tom Wheeler you're always thinking about, although I think he drinks too much, and Bertie says he's the kind of man who's had a past—"

"You aren't anything without a past," Lizzie said. "You're a nothing."

Alice's tears dried in her surprised eyes.

"You say that as if you're speaking about yourself."

"I suppose I am, in a way. You don't know me very well, Alice." Lizzie stretched wearily. She was tired to the bone and knew she would never sleep.

"But I wouldn't have let myself get pregnant, in your situation," she said stubbornly. "You're a fool, Alice. Let's hope the siege is over before your baby is born. And get some rest now. I'll listen for the children."

"My head's still ringing with all that noise. How many graves are there in the cemetery now, Lizzie?"

"I don't know. I don't keep count."

"Is it awful watching someone die?"

"Of course it's awful! What do you think?"

"Lizzie, I'm sorry. You must have had a terrible week with all those wounded. And here I am sitting complaining. I'm ashamed of myself. Scold me, if you like."

"I don't want to scold you. I'm not very good-tempered myself. I worry all the time about Tom. That's the truth, and I'm not ashamed of it. He nearly died the last time he went out. He came back a skeleton. You should have seen him."

Alice came to put a hand on her shoulder.

"Poor Lizzie. I know you love him, and I wish you wouldn't, because that sort of thing has no future. But is there any future for any of us? Look at that moon. It's quite perfect. It makes you feel that everything's peaceful. But I suppose you must want the seige not to end, because when it does you'll have to say goodbye to Tom."

"Yes," Lizzie whispered.

"What a terrible thing."

"I don't even know if he loves me. But I think he does."

In the night Daisy woke and said her head ached. Lizzie felt it and found it alarmingly hot. She didn't want to disturb Alice, who was sleeping at last. But she was filled with dread. Daisy was sickening for something. Fevers were no light matter here. They usually turned into typhoid or enteric. Not one of those horrible diseases for gentle shy Daisy!

The probability was all too likely. The surprising thing was that the Partridge children had so far escaped an illness. It must have been only their mother's attention to hygiene that had saved them.

By morning Daisy was turning her face away from food and saying she was so thirsty. She didn't want to get up, either. Her legs ached.

Alice's face, pale with her own morning nausea, was full of fear.

"Lizzie, it isn't typhoid?"

"I don't know. Keep Henrietta and Fanny away from her. I'm going to ask Doctor Macpherson to come."

"Won't he be too busy at the hospital?"

"He'll come if I ask him."

At another time Alice would have shown intense interest in this revealing statement. Was Doctor Macpherson an admirer of Lizzie's?

But now she couldn't take her eyes off Daisy with her alarmingly flushed face.

"How long will he be?"

"I don't know. We'll try to borrow a horse and cart. If there's an alarm, wrap her up warmly before you take her into the shelter. I'm going to ask Miss Rose to come over and stay with you."

Alice's lip quivered. "See if you can find out where Bertie is. Tell him we need him."

Lizzie kissed her swiftly.

"I'll try."

It wasn't always possible to find a husband occupied in defense duties to go to the aid of his family in trouble. Yesterday Mrs. Ryan had given birth to a puny baby who had only lived two hours. She herself, on hearing the new little girl had so quickly followed her sister Annie, had turned her face to the wall and looked as if she, too, might quietly decide to die. Her husband was still missing and must now be presumed dead.

It was a fair morning with a cool breeze that would soon enough turn into burning tongues of air. Yesterday the temperature had reached over a hundred degrees. It was not likely to be less today.

Lizzie, in her anxiety for Daisy, refused to follow nursing etiquette. She searched the hospital for Doctor Macpherson, and at last finding him holding a consultation with Doctor Hayes at the bedside of a trooper whose thigh wound was giving off the deadly sweet smell of gangrene, broke unceremoniously into their discussion.

"Doctor Macpherson, may I speak to you."

In his disciplined way he finished what he had been saying to Doctor Hayes.

"I agree that we'll have to amputate. The patient understands that there's no alternative. I'm sorry, my boy. Yes, Miss Willoughby? Is this an emergency?"

"Please, doctor!" Lizzie drew him away from the bed. "I'm so afraid little Daisy Partridge has typhoid."

"Then tell her mother to bring her in."

"But it's Daisy! She's special. We all adore her. And supposing Henrietta and Fanny were to catch the disease, too." Lizzie grasped his sleeve, thinking he had never been so much the doctor, so deliberately removed from the untidiness of human emotions.

"Oh, those little girls. Yes, they're very charming. But not hardened to an African summer. I should think this was inevitable."

"Don't be so *callous* about it!" Lizzie was in tears. "I'm asking you to come and see her."

Now he did show surprise.

"All the way to the women's laager. But I'm operating in an hour." He lowered his voice. "That man will die before tomorrow if we don't do something quickly. Don't you care about him?"

"Of course I do, but not enough to waste time standing here talking. I've a mule cart outside. Do hurry."

Doctor Macpherson spoke with sudden briskness.

"Wait for me outside. I'll be with you in five minutes."

What he arranged about the wounded trooper, Lizzie didn't know, nor, at this time, did she care. She had thought she had disciplined herself not to panic, but the thought of Daisy's flowerlike face red and ugly with fever was too much to bear. Typhoid! How many survived?

Doctor Macpherson had discarded his white hospital coat and appeared in shirtsleeves. He got in the cart beside Lizzie, took the reins from her and whipped up the reluctant mule. Startled, it tore away in a shower of flying dust and gravel.

"Where did you find this grand outfit?"

"Lady Sarah helped me. It's the one she drove back to town. The poor beast's half dead from starvation, I'm afraid."

"We all are—or will be. You know that, don't you?"

"Never mind about us." Lizzie clung to the seat, her bones rattling. "I'm thinking of the children."

"And perhaps I am too. Perhaps I'm not as callous as you think," he said quietly.

Nor was he. For he sat up all that night with the sick child, sharing the vigil with Lizzie and with Bertie Partridge, who kept appearing at Daisy's bedside, then tiptoeing heavily away again, his limp worse than it had ever been. Alice had been persuaded to stay with the two other little girls and Miss Rose. She mustn't risk infection either for them or for herself and the new life she carried. She must trust Daisy to the skill of Doctor Macpherson and Lizzie's loving nursing.

Some of the women in the laager grumbled that their children had been gravely ill and had not got this special care.

But in spite of it Daisy could not be saved. At midday the next day her little body shuddered with a long convulsion, then was still.

It had been a particularly virulent case, Doctor Macpherson said. The child should never have been subjected to all the rigors of a siege and its attendant evils of malnutrition and disease without having developed some sort of immunity.

That day in Capetown when Alice had so optimistically set out on her reckless journey seemed a very long time ago.

The journey had this little withered flower at its end. Daisy's blue eyes, welling with their constant silent tender tears, were closed, and she was going into the arid red dust to keep Annie Ryan and the scrap of a newborn baby company.

It was unbelievable and true.

Mrs. Ryan died that day, too. Creaky had begun the mid-afternoon shelling, and during one particularly loud crash Mrs. Ryan just rolled up her eyes and died, as if she were too frightened to go on living.

So Billy was virtually an orphan. He celebrated this fact by disappearing for two whole days.

No one knew whether it was his mother or Daisy he was grieving for, though it was more likely Daisy. He reappeared at last, looking as wild and bony as a starved mongrel. Miss Rose fed him a bowl of the new porridge they were making, a tasteless concoction made from the husks of oats.

Food was really beginning to get scarce. The seven thousand natives in the kraal were almost starving, and soup kitchens had been started for them. They had resorted to killing and eating dogs. Although not reduced to that desperate measure, the two thousand people in the town found their daily ration of oatmeal biscuit, horse sausages and brawn almost too distasteful to eat. For those who had money, a few luxuries could still be purchased. Flour was fifty shillings a bag and potatoes forty shillings a hundredweight. An egg, a great prize, cost a shilling, and there was a little blackmarket liquor to be had if anyone had a purse deep enough to pay for it.

The children were pale and pinched and fretful; the adults, even the young healthy soldiers in the trenches, were getting weak. All horses killed by enemy action were handed over to the food commissariat to be used for rations. But the horses were badly fed, too, and their flesh disgustingly tough. Occasionally the Barolongs went hunting and came back with cattle cleverly stolen from the Boers. The order was given that they could keep one in ten of such animals driven across the veld into their stad.

Billy Ryan had an agony that was even worse than the agony of losing his playmate Daisy. Star was starving.

Alice had insisted on moving out of the women's laager back to her house. Nothing her husband could say would prevent her. She hated the laager as another species of hell, and if she had to stay there she would either die or go mad.

She preferred to expose Henrietta's and Fanny's lives to shellfire rather than to that filthy disease that had taken her beloved Daisy.

They were going home to live decently with a roof over their heads and clean sheets on the beds. She intended to start giving them regular lessons—reading, spelling and arithmetic in the mornings and piano lessons in the afternoons.

They were not to become little savages.

She was as thin as a rail above the now-visible swelling of her stomach. Her eyes were enormous and filled with a frenetic light. She never let Henrietta and Fanny out of her sight, teaching them, or hustling them into the nearest shelter when the alarm bells sounded, or taking them on the long walk to the cemetery every Sunday to see the dry little mound that was Daisy's grave. When they were in bed at night she sat up sewing and washing and ironing, as if immaculate frills and starched lace could banish the dirt and germs and horror from her mind.

Bertie was afraid she really would go out of her mind.

But the siege couldn't last forever, although Colonel Baden-Powell had given orders that supplies must be stretched as far as possible. It was only the beginning of February and he expected to have to hold out until May at the earliest.

The day he made that announcement, Lizzie knew he must have new information about the whereabouts of Colonel Plumer and the relief force. Her heart beat wildly with excitement. She was almost certain what had happened. Tom was back.

XV

She had no pride about seeking him out. She intended to go to his house immediately when she came off duty that afternoon. If he were not there, Joey would know where he was.

But the house was deserted. The back had been struck by a shell. The kitchen was a heap of rubble and dust mixed with pots and pans. In the bedroom the double bed, left by the previous owners, ludicrously stood on its end, its brass knobs glinting in the sunlight.

The living room had escaped any damage except a liberal shower of dust. The table, littered as usual with Tom's papers, had a frosting of grit. Lizzie's feet made prints in the thick dust on the wooden floor. There were other prints there, she saw with relief. Someone had recently walked across the room and looked into the destroyed kitchen just as she had. Tom?

Uncertain whether to wait here for him to come back or to go and search for him, Lizzie's mind was made up for her in the most definite way. The alarm sounded. Creaky was about to fire. Minutes later there came the roar of an approaching shell and an explosion so close that another shower of dust clouded the air and made her sneeze and choke.

In the quiet before the next shell she fled out of the house and ran for the nearest shelter. It was a shallow trench dug at the end of the street, and in it already, crouching out of the direct rays of the blazing sun, were a handful of people, including Tom Wheeler.

He literally caught Lizzie in his arms as she tumbled in just before the next crashing roar of an approaching shell.

"So Miss Lizzie turns up again."

166

"Turns up is right," she said, smoothing down her skirts.

The dust settled and she was able to look at him. His hair had gone gray, she noticed with shock, then realized that it was only filmed with dust. Her own probably was, too. They must look like a pair of gray ghosts, with thin faces and overlarge eyes.

"You got back safely, thank goodness."

"Do you, Lizzie?"

"Do I what?"

"Thank goodness?"

"Oh, yes. And God, too. I've just seen that your house has been hit. I didn't know."

"And Joey has gone."

"Gone? Where?"

The muted thunder, increasing to its climactic explosion, sounded again. Lizzie pressed her hands to her ears and waited for the silence.

"Back to his tribe?" she asked.

"No, the Boers got him. Caught him trying to drive off cattle. Shot him there and then. And set fire to huts in the stad as a reprisal. At least that's what his wife told me when I went to look for him." Once more a shell was approaching, and Tom's flat voice was drowned. "When I got back and found the house had been hit I thought that might have been the way he died. But it wasn't. It was by a bullet. A Mauser bullet in his spine."

"Daisy Partridge is dead, too," Lizzie said.

"Daisy? The smallest one?"

"Yes."

"This damnable war!"

Lizzie put her hand in his. His palm was gritty with dust. She felt the particles drive into her flesh as the pressure began. It was his wounded hand, and she was conscious, among other confused emotions, of relief that it had so much strength. Doctor Macpherson's fears about atrophying muscles were not so far realized.

"Let's get out of this hole in the ground."

"Where to?"

"Somewhere where we won't die by suffocation." He was already halfway up the steps leading into the bright afternoon light. He put down a hand to assist her. "Are you prepared to run the gauntlet?"

"Anywhere."

"Good. Let's get out of town."

Their wild run down the main street, across Market Square and the recreation ground toward the grassy slopes far outside the town but still within the defended perimeter was such an escape from tension that they both became hilarious. Hysteria, Lizzie thought, with one small sober part of her mind. This transition from sorrow to a high ebullience of spirits was not sane behavior.

Who wanted to be sane?

Once they had to fling themselves flat as earth and stones showered over them. Once Tom dragged her into a ditch, and they heard fragments of shell striking with sharp pings on nearby roofs. At least their escape was unobserved, for everyone was underground.

Did it matter who saw them?

At last Lizzie flung herself down in the long coarse grass, gasping that she couldn't run another step. And at the same time the shelling stopped. Tom watched the big gun's muzzle being lowered before he slid down beside Lizzie and took her into his arms.

The sober part of her mind had vanished with the breath from her lungs. Now she was completely, gloriously mad.

She helped his fumbling fingers with the buttons of her blouse, the laces of her stays. The grass made a striped shadow over them. It was still blazingly hot, and her body was on fire. His was thin, thin. She could feel his ribs, the delicate structure of bones over his pounding heart. His cheekbones were like knuckles, his eyes sunken but burning with such brilliant intensity that there was no doubting the violence of life within him. His lips tasted of dust, mingling with the dust on her own. His seeking fingers found her breast. It seemed to start beneath his hand. Faces passed through her mind, Linda Hill with her look of quenched youth and remorse, silly romantic Alice welcoming her pregnancy, Katie Roos turning traitor for her young Dutch husband, the dying soldier crying for his black-haired Molly.

Then all the faces faded and there was only Tom's above her, the dusty hair, the sharply boned cheeks, the violent eyes. Protecting her from the glare of the sun although it blazed through her, burning her up, stabbing her with acute pain that turned into a long intolerable ecstasy.

The violence slowly died from Tom's eyes. They became tender, concerned, loving.

She wanted this moment of peace prolonged forever.

But he moved away. "Lizzie! You never told me."

"Told you what?"

"That this was the first time. I thought you were married."

"Married?" She was so indolent, so peaceful, it seemed a pity to talk. "That's just a word."

"A word that usually means something."

She felt her lips curving in a slow smile.

She looked into his eyes.

"Would you have loved me if you had known it was the first time?"

"I don't think anything on earth would have stopped me. Is that what you want to hear?"

"Oh, yes, Tom, yes."

"Then?"

"My husband—Humphrey—had had a war wound. Apparently his doctors had told him the result, but he refused to believe them. He thought a young wife—" She hadn't quite got over the long unhappiness of it all, she discovered. She could still shiver a little, in spite of the burning heat. "It was no use, so he began to hate me as if I were to blame. He both loved and hated me, poor man. But perhaps he loved me most and that's why he finally sent me away. I believe I see it now."

"He didn't love you enough to give you a divorce," Tom said violently.

"He couldn't. The humiliation would have killed him."

"Damn the humiliation! What about yours?"

"Tom, it's over now."

"It's not. You're still married to him."

"And you to Milly."

"Don't bring Milly here, too."

Lizzie sat up, feeling the sun on her bared throat and breast.

"It's a funny place for anyone to be. Primitive. Wonderful."

"Wonderful," he echoed. "Take down your hair."

"Now? I'll never get it up again."

"It doesn't matter. You can say a passing shell blew it down. I once helped you do up your hair, remember?"

"After that night I fell asleep in your house? I don't think I expected you to remember."

"Why not?"

"You must have known I've always been in love with you. But I wasn't at all sure about you."

"Then you weren't very observant."

"You were often pretty offhand."

"I didn't want to complicate things any more for you. Or for me, for that matter."

Lizzie took his hand, turning it over, examining the long, ugly scar.

"How dirty we are. Filthy."

"You look like a chimney sweep. A rather beautiful one, however."

"Tom!"

"Yes, little sweep."

"I could give you a son."

He leaned forward to kiss the tip of her nose.

"But I have one," he said.

His voice was no less gentle than it had been. Yet the withdrawal in it was unmistakable.

"You wouldn't want mine?" An ache was growing around her heart.

He turned away from her.

"Don't be a little fool."

"Perhaps I have it in me already," she said stubbornly. Even Alice had not been so reckless as this.

"Lizzie—if you have—oh, God!"

"We could stay in South Africa after the war. No one would need to know who we were. It's a big country. We could get lost in Bulawayo or Natal."

"I have a boy in England. I don't think I could be a deserting father. Do you understand that?"

She leaned over him, drawing his tense face into her hands.

"I suppose I must." She knew he loved her, at least. The torment in his eyes showed that. "We have the war," she added.

He began to smile, but with a cynicism she didn't like to see.

"Yes, we have the war, and we live on food not fit for

170

animals, and innocent people get killed by shellfire, and babies like Daisy Partridge die." He waved his hand in a wide circle. "This perimeter of Baden-Powell's is our monstrous wedding ring, and Creaky's shells bestow a blessing on us."

She pulled him to her. "At any place in the world I had met you and in any circumstances, I would have done this."

"Would you, Lizzie? I'm not sure. I'm not sure that I would have."

"It's living. It's being alive."

"That's the point. We have a too constant awareness of death."

"Tom, Tom, Tom, let's be happy about it."

He pulled the pins out of her hair, burying his face in it as it fell down.

"Let me have this cloud of sweet darkness," he murmured.

She turned into his arms, fitting herself against his hard body, crying out as he gripped her. The darkness was painful as well as sweet. But irresistible.

Was what had happened written all over her face? Two hours late at the hospital—Sister Casey had been tart and impatient with her.

"I know that you're not trained as a nurse, Miss Willoughby, but so long as you agree to do this job, you'll make an effort to do it properly."

Doctor Macpherson, coming from the operating theater, his face drawn with fatigue, said, "You look as if you've caught the sun, nurse. Better put some oil on that burn. By the way, what's the latest news from England?"

"I haven't heard any, doctor."

"I thought you might have. I heard English papers had arrived. Two months old, I believe, but it might be pleasant to read about December fogs."

She hadn't thought to ask Tom any news at all, not even the whereabouts of the relief force. But it couldn't be very near since Colonel Baden-Powell had warned people that there might be another three months of hardship ahead.

It turned out that Tom had brought some newspapers in, also some precious letters. There was another one for Alice from her parents. It made her cry because it made

171

loving inquiries for Henrietta and Fanny and, "darling Daisy, is she still so tender-hearted?"

"You'll have another baby to tell them about before long," Lizzie comforted her.

"Lizzie, that's the first time you've spoken sympathetically about the new baby. What's made you change your mind about it?"

"I never meant to be unkind," Lizzie said slowly. "I was just tired and bad-tempered. Perhaps it's nice that you're having it."

Alice's eyes, still drowned in tears, but far from being blind, looked at Lizzie curiously.

"I believe it's that tragedy about Andy Buchanan and that poor child bride that you have on your mind. You've got a far-off look. Or is it that your precious Tom is back safely?"

"Perhaps. I believe he'll take a limited number of letters when he goes out again. So you ought to take the opportunity to write home."

"But what shall I say?" Alice asked, her tears flowing again. "That horse sausages are a delicacy? That we might be reduced to fried locusts? Oh, what a *horrible* place this is."

It was true that the horses were being weeded out for human consumption. Beginning with the oldest and weakest, they were being slaughtered and cut into steaks, and their bones boiled for soup to save the Barolongs from complete starvation. This, however, did not make the horse compound safe from an occasional raid by hungry natives. Trooper Hardy's big gray gelding, the pride of his heart, went missing, and then the shaggy, aged, half-starved pony Star, belonging to Billy Ryan.

At first Billy thought Star must simply have wandered farther afield in search of grazing. The summer heat had dried up the grass, and what was left provided poor picking.

Billy haunted the compound all one day, a ragged, large-eyed, unwashed little boy with fear in his eyes. Trooper Burch had to drive him away at night.

"Get off home, lad. You can't sleep here. Where's your mother?"

"Dead," said Billy.

"I'm sorry to hear that. But there must be someone looking after you."

Whoever it was, thought Trooper Burch, didn't have much respect for the properties of soap and water. Probably there wasn't much soap to be had, but there was water drawn up from the emergency wells and carried by buckets to the various houses and tents. Young Billy didn't need to be quite such a filthy scarecrow.

"I look after myself," he said.

"Then where's your Dad?"

"He went missing before Christmas, and my sister died. I'm an orphan."

"But you must have friends."

Daisy had been his friend. Daisy and Star.

Billy dug his bare toe into the hard earth.

"Have you seen my pony?"

"No, lad, I haven't. Not for the last day or so."

"She can't be far. She doesn't go far. She comes when I whistle."

"Then she'll turn up. If I remember right she's a bit too skinny to interest—" Trooper Burch stopped, and bit his tongue as he saw the naked fear in the boy's face. "Have you had your dinner today?"

"I had some porridge this morning," Billy said uninterestedly.

"And nothing since? You're suffering from a hollow belly, son. Come along to the cookhouse. We might scratch up a bit of stew for you. And then be off with you. Your pony will turn up in her own good time."

She did. At least, a portion of her did. A Barolong boy, a long skinny youngster with his ribs showing like wickerwork beneath his shiny black skin, was arrested and charged with horse stealing. He had removed most evidence, but not quite all, of his theft. A hoof lay between him and his captors. A little hoof scarred with age but still dainty and petite. In youth its owner must have pranced very prettily on it. By its size it had belonged to a pony, and there had been only one pony in the horse area at Mafeking.

The ragged scarecrow haunting the camp had to be brought to look at it. Only this evidence would persuade him to give up his useless vigil and go home.

They all expected the kid, who couldn't have been

173

more than seven or eight, to burst into tears. But instead the dirty freckled face turned to stone. Without a single word Billy turned and walked away, a curious slow stiff walk, like an old man's.

Two days later he was brought into the hospital. He had been found hiding in the back of a half-destroyed house. The woman living next door saw a movement and thought it was a jackal. But it had been Billy, driven from his retreat in search of food. Of which evidently he had found little for he was nothing but bones held together by parchment-colored skin. Although he was conscious, he seemed to have lost the use of his tongue. Or perhaps it was his hearing that did not function, for he ignored everything said to him. Washed at last, and now unnaturally clean, he lay in bed and stared at the ceiling.

At first he had had to be fed slowly with milk diluted with water; then he had progressed to gruel, which everyone hoped he wouldn't recognize. It had been made from boiled-down horse bones. After that his healthy boy's appetite returned and several of the nurses sacrificed part of their rations to give him adequate meals. With the nourishing food the physical damage would be repaired. The damage to his mind was another thing.

A week went by, and still he could not or would not speak. The face on the pillow, with the staring freckles and the too tidily brushed hair, was a gargoyle's.

Alice was persuaded to bring Henrietta and Fanny to lure him out of his silence. But that was a mistake. They were frightened by his appearance. Henrietta exclaimed, "He looks so funny, Mamma. I don't like him." And Fanny burst into tears.

A fleeting expression that might have been scorn passed over Billy's face. Then he turned his head to the wall.

"It was wrong, it only reminded him of Daisy," Alice said in distress.

"That wouldn't have mattered if it had shocked him into speaking," Doctor Macpherson said. "Our problem is that he's well physically and we can't keep him here. We haven't room. Who will volunteer to take care of him?"

Miss Rose. Lizzie didn't know whether her idea was an inspiration or a blunder.

Miss Rose was sent for and the position explained to

her. She listened, her sharp eyes glinting. Always thin, she was now painfully so, her shoulder blades holding her cotton blouse like a coat hanger, the belt nipped around her narrow waist. It was to be accurately guessed that she had not been availing herself of her full rations. She had never stopped teaching such children as could be persuaded to learn through the terror and confusion of alarms and shelling. Some of these children were becoming almost as emaciated as Billy Ryan. Some of them had recovered from fevers. Some had died. But all who struggled with the lessons she gave were hungry. She obviously did what she could about that.

And now there was Billy, who had forgotten how to talk.

Miss Rose stood looking down at him in bed. She must have looked as tall and straight as a flag pole above him.

"Get up, Billy Ryan," she said in her hectoring voice. "You're not sick any longer. There are other children who need your bed. Aren't you ashamed of yourself, a great boy of eight lying there like a baby. Get up at once and get dressed."

It seemed that they had all been wrong. They had treated the boy with too much tenderness. It was only the voice of authority that would penetrate his numbed brain.

For he did get up and put on the decent clean cotton shirt and pants that had been found for him. Then he followed Miss Rose out of the ward, walking a few paces behind her on his stick legs.

"I am alone in the world, too," she was saying in her dry, emotionless voice. "But I don't lie in bed worrying about it. I go on living. So will you, Billy Ryan. I've been needing a useful boy to put up some shelves for me. Can you use a hammer and nails?"

"Yes."

"Yes, Miss Rose. Address me properly, if you please."

"Yes, Miss Rose. I can hammer straight."

"Good. Then let's be on our way."

Lizzie had once seen a baby hare, rescued from a trap, mothered by a stable cat, emaciated and thin-coated from too many litters of kittens. She had little milk to give her nursling, but a great deal of love tempered with instruction.

175

The tall plain woman striding out of the hospital grounds, turning occasionally to see if her protégé followed, reminded her exactly of the cat seeking to bestow its mother love on any creature, even the most unlikely.

"It's the first time he's spoken since he was brought in," she said in amazement.

Sister Casey sniffed. She had to give credit where credit was due, but she would rather it had been Doctor Macpherson than Miss Willoughby who had had the improbable idea of bringing the schoolteacher here.

"If you'd worked in hospitals as long as I have, Miss Willoughby, nothing in human nature would surprise you. Make up the bed. There'll be a new admission soon enough if General Snyman has his way. And don't get maudlin," she added sharply, "about a crafty little boy who's been fooling us all for a week."

XVI

The Sunday truce continued. It was reported that General Snyman had had urgent messages from Pretoria to hurry up and capture Mafeking. But he replied that he would be a fool to ask his men to walk over dynamite mines. It was much better to continue in his policy of starving the English out and subduing them by the constant nerve-wracking shelling.

Since the women's laager had been shelled so frequently, Colonel Baden-Powell sent a message to the Boer headquarters that if this continued he would move the suspected spies, already jailed, to a new jail set up within the women's laager. Then, any shelling would endanger friends as well as enemies.

For ten days after that no shells fell in the laager. Instead, fire was concentrated in the vicinity of the hospital, and eventually a shell went through one of the wards, involving the moving of patients to the already overcrowded other wards.

Spasmodic gunfire went on for most of the daylight hours, but by evening there was usually a period of peace. Counting on this, the officers decided to give a ball on the thirteenth of February.

Preparations for such an excitement revived the flagging spirits of the women. It could scarcely be a fashionable affair, although the officers in uniform would add dash. The women who had ball gowns got them out and aired and ironed them. Others hastily bought up the remaining materials in the draper's shop. These were not very elegant, but a borrowed sash or a treasured piece of lace could do wonders to a length of gingham.

Mrs. Buchanan, trying to persuade Linda to go, offered the girl her garnets, a heavy necklace and earrings, which would add dignity to a simple muslin dress.

Linda was too young to indulge in long-drawn-out grief. It was true that Andy had been dead only six weeks. But this was wartime. If everyone kept up the convention of mourning, the women would all look like crows, and there would be no black material left in town.

Linda was seventeen and must get back her gaiety. Let her go to the ball and find that there were still a great many good-looking young men above ground.

But the girl could not be persuaded. Since Andy's death she had left home (where there were six brothers and sisters to fill the house) and had come to live with Mrs. Buchanan. The old lady didn't intend to allow this arrangement to go on forever. It was unnatural and bad for a young girl. But in the meantime the surroundings of Andy's home seemed to comfort her. She had begun to help at the hospital, where she had quickly discovered that she was not the only one bereaved. A premature maturity had come to her young face. Mrs. Buchanan recognized that she would have been a splendid wife for Andy. This knowledge made the bitterness of his death more intense. But she hid her grief beneath her usual tart emotionless exterior and tried not to allow herself to become too dependent on the girl for company and affection. It was very hard to grow old alone. She must resist the temptation to make Andy's death an excuse to keep Linda prisoner.

"No, Granny, I couldn't go to a dance," Linda said. "The music would only make me cry. But I'll offer to do night duty at the hospital so Lizzie or one of the other nurses can get away."

"You'll cry there too," the old lady accused.

"Not if I'm working. I see people there worse than me."

"Well—you're a good girl. Don't be too good. You won't get much fun that way. But I suppose you've got time."

Time. The one thing too many hadn't got.

Alice hadn't wanted to go to the ball, either. Bertie talked her out of that morbid nonsense. He had been grieved enough at Daisy's death. She had been a pretty creature, although to his mind a bit of a cry-baby. But life went on, and there was the other child coming, who with luck might be a boy. And he couldn't bear a woman moping about and spoiling her looks. Decking herself out with a bit of finery and showing off at the ball would do Alice all the good in the world.

Lizzie was going, of course. She was the least reluctant of them all. She knew that Tom would be there and wanted to show him how she could look at her best. He had scarcely seen her other than travel-stained, exhausted and downright dirty. They had made love with dust smudged all over their faces.

She intended, too, to have a real ball gown. She ruthlessly cut the sleeves out of the blue silk dress she had worn to the Christmas dinner and made the neck low so that her shoulders would be exposed. Alice, who was always generous, unpicked the lace from one of her own gowns and lent it to Lizzie to ruck around the neck. Lizzie had her own long evening gloves, a feathered fan and the aquamarine pendant her mother had given her for her coming-out. Miss Rose would do hers and Alice's hair. Miss Rose, apart from going to the ball herself, which would have been a very unlikely event, got quite carried away with the preparations.

She had arranged to sleep the night at the Partridges'. She had brought Billy with her, not because he wanted to come—the sight of the little girls sent him back into his painful silence—but because he refused to stay alone in Miss Rose's austere tent in the women's laager. He had got into a state of terror at the thought. So she had to bring him along that evening after the day's shelling had ceased.

She apologized for his presence, saying in her tart voice that she was ashamed of him, a big boy like that afraid to let her out of his sight. But there was a lurking and unfamiliar softness in her eyes.

"At least I see that he's clean," she said. "And he's coming on with his reading. We might find that he's educable yet."

Billy poked out his tongue at her behind her back to make Henrietta and Fanny laugh. But he was still only a shadow of the tough outlaw, and halfway through the game Henrietta had organized, he ran away and hid. He refused to appear even to see Alice and Lizzie and Bertie Partridge in all their finery depart.

The ball was something of a travesty, although the

179

music was spirited and the officers did their best. Colonel Baden-Powell and Lady Sarah Wilson led the dancing. All the town's more eminent citizens were there. There was plenty of wine to drink and even food of a kind. The hall had been decorated with such greenery as could be gathered. The floor had been assiduously polished.

But it was scarcely the Duchess of Richmond's before Waterloo, Tom said to Lizzie. It was a stifling room in a raw little frontier town, and everyone was too badly fed and tired to put much spirit into the evening.

Tom was in a queer touchy mood. Lizzie's elaborate toilette seemed to make him angry rather than admiring.

"I liked you better with dirt on your face and your hair falling down," he said bluntly.

"Oh, Tom. And I took all this trouble for you."

"What are we doing prancing here like lunatics when we should be winning this bloody war?"

"Why did you come if you feel like that?"

"News. I'm a reporter. They'll love this in London. 'Undefeated citizens of Mafeking turn out in their finery. Show defiance to the enemy.' "

Lizzie disliked sewing and had spent a long time at the tiresome occupation in order to look charming tonight. She hadn't seen Tom since the afternoon in the long grass outside the town. She had been uneasily afraid that he had been avoiding her. She was almost sure that he regretted what had happened. She was quite sure that he would never have touched her had he known she was still a virgin. It made what should have been a light, forgettable affair too complicated. Now he had her on his conscience and was probably hating her. She had feared this for several days. It was the only way to explain his avoidance of her. Her early happiness had dissolved away like a rainbow in too harsh a light.

"You're a coward," she said.

He grimaced. "I hoped it didn't show."

"Not physically. Morally. You're running away from your wife, and now you're running away from me, too."

His fingers dug into the small of her back.

"Not because I want to. Only because it's expedient."

"Expedient?"

"Don't raise your brows in that polite social way!"

She answered containedly, "Alice is watching. And

180

other people. If you tell me you hate me, I'll still nod and smile."

"I believe you'd even be capable of it," he said with admiration.

"I've learned how to wear a public face."

"You well-bred Englishwomen. Do you never make a scene?"

"Oh, yes. I can promise you that if you go on running away from me."

His eyes went dark. "I told you it's only because I can't involve you in something temporary. The war will end and so will our affair. I was wrong to begin it. It was a weak moment."

His brutality did make her composure crack.

"Did I have nothing to do with beginning it?"

"Then we were both wrong. Lizzie, look at you! Beautiful. Well-bred. With more than your fair share of trouble already. I can't add to it."

"Isn't it a little late—Certainly, Colonel. With pleasure."

Smiling with her aching composure, Lizzie left Tom and glided away in Colonel Hore's arms. She loved dancing. It was almost possible to let her pain float away in the rhythm of the waltz. Colonel Hore danced well. Much better than Tom did. And he didn't talk beyond the required small nothings. She supposed he had better manners than Tom. But over his shoulder her eyes were following Tom. She saw him make his way across the room and go outside.

She was almost certain he wouldn't be back. She didn't know how to stop herself following him. She stayed only because at that moment Colonel Baden-Powell smiled at her, and she remembered that she had a duty toward making the evening a success. Everyone, she supposed, was playing a part, but most of them were concealing only their fear of physical things—starvation, disease, being mutilated by a shell. Not agony of mind, as she was.

The orchestra was playing the rollicking song "Goodbye, Dolly, I must leave you, though it breaks my heart to go . . ."

Tom, if he were listening, would be substituting the name Lizzie for Dolly. It fitted very well.

Bertie Partridge, coming to partner her in spite of his

bad leg, was an accomplished performer. He made the usual polite compliments. "By George, Lizzie, you're looking well. You almost outshine my wife, and I never thought anyone could do that."

Then Doctor Macpherson, whom she had left at the hospital, unexpectedly turned up and claimed a waltz. He, too, danced well. And he didn't attempt to talk. She was grateful and thought that perhaps she had misjudged him. He had more sensitivity than she had realized.

When the music stopped he lingered beside her.

"Can I get you a drink? Whatever liquid is available."

"Thank you, Alex."

"You're looking very well tonight."

"I tried to. I thought it one's duty." She thought his eyes too observant and added, "To the colonel and the regiment. They're making a very good show."

Abruptly he said, "You're doing well, but not well enough. Have you quarreled?"

"Quarreled?"

"I saw Tom Wheeler leaving as I came."

"Did you? I don't think he cares for functions like this. He came so that he could report it to his newspapers."

"Good. I'm glad to see the back of him," said Doctor Macpherson briskly. "Now, my dear. I suspect that innocuous mixture is a form of Mafeking lemonade. I think we both prefer a glass of wine."

It was about midnight when a tremendous volley of riflefire stopped the dancers in midstep and made the orchestra cease on a medley of discordant notes.

Colonel Baden-Powell hurriedly left the hall, followed by all his officers, after hasty apologies to their partners. In the much depleted gathering there was little panic. There had been too many alarms in the past weeks for one more to have much effect.

But Bertie Partridge, taking charge, ordered all the lights to be put out, and it was eerie sitting in the dark, with only a little moonlight coming through the windows, listening to the distant cracking of rifles. Amy Brown huddled against Lizzie. Lizzie could feel the tremors going over her body, although she didn't make a sound. Alice had wanted to rush home to the children, but her husband refused to allow her to go. Henrietta and Fanny would be as safe with Miss Rose as they could be with anyone.

He wasn't, of course, keeping people prisoner here, he said in his jovial voice. Anyone who wanted to make for a shelter could do so. But personally he thought this bit of a flare-up was simply the unsporting Boers' way of spoiling their evening.

He had scarcely finished speaking before there was another fusillade, then isolated shots came at intervals, as if from nervous fingers on triggers. Doctor Macpherson had groped his way to Lizzie and bent over her.

"I'm going back to the hospital. I may be needed. Will you risk the walk with me, or do you prefer to stay here?"

Lizzie felt Amy Brown's fingers clutching her. She kept wondering where Tom was.

"I'll stay here."

Doctor Macpherson, after the briefest pause, picked his way out of the dark room. Alice, huddled in her chair and wishing Bertie would sit beside her, thought that that quiet, rather dull man had more than a professional interest in Lizzie. He certainly was dull but he seemed respectable and reliable. Lizzie might do worse. It was time she settled down. And it would be nice for the ladies to prepare for another wedding that wouldn't end in the tragedy of poor Linda's. It would give them all something pleasant to think of. Sickness and death were becoming too much their daily fare.

She must speak to Lizzie, she thought, wincing as another shot rang out. She would play matchmaker, she decided, twisting her fingers together until they hurt. If only all this fear and tension and grief didn't hurt her baby. He felt lively enough, and her stomach was swelling as if he were going to be quite big, in spite of the dreadful diet. If only his little fair head against her breast would eventually make her forget Daisy whom she had killed by bringing her to this awful place. And would make Bertie give her his eternal grateful love . . .

Gradually the night became quiet. It seemed as if the last shot had been fired. Bertie was just deciding, in his ponderous way, that people might safely make their way to their homes, risking no bigger dangers than tripping over unseen obstacles in the dark, when a messenger arrived from the Colonel's headquarters.

It had all been a false alarm. The Boers had been taken in by a ruse. Inspector Marsh of the Police Force had shouted through a megaphone that echoed around the perimeter, "Men in first trench fix bayonets!" Expecting an attack, the Boers, crouching at their loopholes, had loosed off a sharp volley to deter the attackers.

But no one had come. With stretched nerves, the Boers had fired again at intervals, until gradually they became aware of the fact that they had been hoaxed.

The town would suffer tomorrow, the women said wryly, as they gathered their shawls and wraps and prepared to go home from their spoiled evening. There would surely be increased shelling. The trouble was, the Boers had no sense of humor.

Lizzie told Alice that she was going to sleep at the hospital to save the journey back in the morning. It was only midnight, but she was tired. She would be perfectly all right walking there alone. She was used to finding her way about in the dark.

To prove her intention she set off, walking rapidly across the recreation grounds. But the moment the little knots of people around the hall had dispersed, she turned, taking another direction, a solitary woman hurrying along with purpose. This was the long way around, but it would take her past Tom's house. She had heard that he was living there again in spite of the damage the house had suffered. He had made the front room habitable and had his meals, such as they were, at Dixon's Hotel.

Expedient, he had said, in their brief conversation. What a word. And she had promised him a scene. Now, if he were in his poor shattered home, he was to get it, and probably the rest of the roof would fall in and crush them both.

She was walking so fast, intent on her thoughts, that she didn't hear the footsteps behind her. When she did, her pursuer was almost on her, and she cried out as her arm was grasped.

"It's only me. Not General Snyman or one of his henchmen," said Tom. "Why are you in such a hurry?"

"I was going to the hospital."

"Wrong way."

"Making a detour past your house," she admitted.

"There's no one home."

"Tom, I won't spend the rest of my life pursuing you."

"A pity," he said.

They stood facing each other, although it was too dark to read expressions. Lizzie knew only that the bitterness had gone out of Tom's voice. He had got over his difficult mood.

"Well, what's amusing you?" she asked tartly.

"Nothing. I'm not amused. This isn't a joke, it's too cruel. It surely shouldn't need the armies of Queen Victoria and Oom Paul Kruger to bring Lizzie Willoughby and Tom Wheeler together. I thought there was going to be an attack just now. I thought I or you might die in the middle of a quarrel."

"It wasn't a quarrel."

"It was nothing else. You held your head so high, I wanted to hit you. Don't do that grand lady stuff with me."

"If you use words like 'expedient,' I'll retaliate in whatever way I please."

" 'Expedient' was right."

"It isn't any longer. You've just said so. You or I might die, having wasted the time Queen Victoria and Oom Paul Kruger have given us."

"You're too clever, Lizzie."

"So are you, Tom. And you don't trust me. As if I would keep you away from your little boy. That's the real trouble, isn't it?"

"It's something that can't be solved," he said quietly.

"My trouble is worse because it makes me a monster. You know what it is." She pulled him to her, pressing her face against his shoulder. "Oh, dear God, I don't want the war to end."

"If that's a crime, we're both guilty."

"You, too?"

"I love you. I told you."

"Tell me again. I can't hear it often enough. We have so little time. Let's go to your house."

"It's full of dust. The ceiling might fall."

"I don't care."

"Nor do I. Then let's hurry. The sun will be up before we know it."

" 'It was the lark, the herald of the morn,' " she said dreamily.

"It will be a shower of hot lead, more likely."

Much later he said regretfully, "Your grand dress . . ."

"You said you liked me better dirty." She sneezed and laughed and said with happy tenderness, "Don't move. It only stirs up the dust."

XVII

At last the tonic the town needed had come. Kimberley had been relieved on February 15 and Ladysmith not quite two weeks later. A native runner had brought in the news, along with a bundle of ancient newspapers, and the additional news, of special interest to Mafeking, that at a great battle at Paardeberg, their old antagonist, General Cronje had surrendered.

There was wild jubilation, although not too much energy was expended in shouting and throwing up hats. The people were too weak and tired. Their own turn to be relieved must come. But would it come in time? The miserable rations kept them alive, but increased their vulnerability to disease to a frightening extent.

More disturbing, it was not only food of which the little garrison was getting short. Ammunition was also running out. And Colonel Baden-Powell had optimistically informed the new Commander-in-Chief, Lord Roberts, by runner, that he could hold out until the end of May. Nearly three more months.

It was all very well getting messages of congratulations from Lord Roberts, and from Queen Victoria herself, on their courageous stand. How many of them would be lying horizontally by the end of May?

At least there had been a temporary lull in the shelling. Creaky had been moved again but remained singularly inactive. There were rumors that Snyman was in Pretoria. During his absence the Boers seemed content to sit and observe Mafeking from behind their pipe smoke. But on his return a week later the bombardment began with renewed force. In addition, the weary residents experienced another trial, which was not a complete disaster.

During all of February and March there had been

thunderstorms mixed with the almost intolerable heat. There had been flies and mosquitoes and winged beetles and scorpions. But toward the end of March a small mysterious cloud appeared low in the blazing sky. It grew rapidly nearer and larger and resolved itself into a million locusts that descended on the town, making the women scream in hysterical horror. They were everywhere, darkening hastily shut windows, blundering inside the flaps of tents, falling down chimneys, crackling underfoot.

But the Barolongs fell on them with cries of joy. Food! The starving blacks, subsisting almost entirely on the daily brew of horse soup, found this plague a gift from heaven.

Following their example, some of the women queasily experimented with frying the loathsome insects and found that they tasted surprisingly good—as an alternative to the obnoxious porridge of oat husks, at least.

Alice would have starved rather than eaten them, but, steeling herself, she prepared a meal of curried locusts for her family. Bertie pronounced them quite a delicacy.

But Alice thought that the crackling of their brown bodies underfoot would provide her with a recurring nightmare for the rest of her life.

Captain Girdwood, the amiable officer who had been so efficient and tactful in administering food rationing, was dead, hit by shell splinters in Market Square. Trooper Elkington, with the reputation for being the best-looking man in the garrison, was tragically blinded by another chance shot. The death roll mounted in ones and twos. A few people even died of old age, though this cause of death was the exception rather than the rule.

It was a miracle that Colonel Baden-Powell himself escaped harm. No one dared think what would happen if he failed to come back from his nightly inspection of the forward trenches and forts, or from one of his lonely forays onto the veld, literally to the doorstep of the Boer encampments. Or if, when he climbed up to his lookout post a dozen times a day in spite of constant shelling, he were hit.

None of these disasters happened. His cheerful whistle was constantly heard. He seemed never to sleep. Nor did he show exhaustion or anxiety. He was truly "the wolf that never sleeps."

And the siege was nearly six months old.

Then a spasm of hope flared. On the last day of March there was the sound of distant firing. It didn't come from the Boer defenses but from farther away.

It was Colonel Plumer and the relief force!

Everyone who had an accessible rooftop was on it. Eyes strained into the distance. The afternoon sunlight bathed a seemingly peaceful veld. On the horizon tiny puffs of smoke rose and dissolved. There was no mistake about what was happening. The relief force *was* on its way. And Colonel Baden-Powell had said they must wait until the end of May. For the first time he was wrong. Here was Colonel Plumer and the armies of Her Majesty the Queen a good two months early.

All troops were at the alert. The armored train was steaming and waiting the order to set out. Horsemen scouted warily.

But between Colonel Plumer was Snyman's mounted force, outnumbering the British forces by thousands. This was the way the Boers liked to fight, on horseback, moving speedily, firing with deadly accuracy. This was not the groping in the dark, and the detested bayonet.

They must have welcomed the unexpected action, especially when they discovered that Plumer had only three hundred and fifty men and two small guns. The gallant little action was soon over. Plumer fell back on Ramathlabama, leaving forty-nine casualties behind him, and a great many sinking hearts in Mafeking. The dashing of suddenly raised hopes was too cruel.

It was not much use for Colonel Baden-Powell to repeat his famous injunction to sit tight and shoot straight. Nor to make a suggestion, carried out by his efficient staff, that a concert be organized for that evening. People responded because they must. The Colonel, they said, could do everything but command them to be cheerful. That was not possible on this night of dashed hopes.

The next day the ambulances, bumping slowly over the veld, brought back Plumer's wounded and dead. The hospital and the Convent of the Sisters of Mercy were now so crowded that beds had to be made on the floor. Medical supplies were short, but shorter still was nourish-

189

ing food for men badly weakened by exhaustion and blood loss. Too many died from wounds that should not have been fatal.

Lizzie was furiously glad to be working so hard that she had no time to think. She and Tom had been given a reprieve. That was the thought she tried to evade. They could not have happiness at the expense of so many. It was not their fault that Colonel Plumer had failed, that the siege went on, yet she felt guiltily that it was. She had dared to think selfishly of her own happiness.

Yet it wasn't really happiness. The times she and Tom were together were brief and frenzied. They were both too tired, and too undernourished, to be tranquil or content.

The day after Plumer's failure Tom had arranged a small dinner for two in the dusty living room of his ruined house.

He had a bottle of white wine, which he had tried to cool by standing it in a bucket of freshly drawn well water. He had also managed to obtain two eggs and a small piece of meat (horse, almost certainly), which he had stewed with fresh vegetables. The biggest prize was an ounce of real coffee.

There were even candles in silver candlesticks on the table. Tom said he had borrowed them from the mayor's wife.

"But what did you say you wanted them for?" Lizzie asked.

"Never you mind. Do you usually ask a host where he has acquired his silverware?"

Lizzie laughed, loving his lighthearted mood. It might be an act, but it was done for her benefit. She was very happy about that. For a little while she was able to respond to it. She drank enough of the wine, lukewarm in spite of Tom's efforts, to make her remember less vividly the hideous wounds she had helped to dress that day. This snatched hour of happiness was not going to hasten anybody's death or increase anybody's already unbearable pain. The candlelight fluttered and across it she saw Tom's tender eyes. What a beautiful face he had, she thought, with its high bony brow and jutting chin. Its thinness gave it a sculptured look.

"You're beautiful, Tom."

"You're drunk, Lizzie."

"It's your lean, bony look. You might be a statue by Michelangelo. If your eyes were closed."

He closed them obligingly, and she cried, "No, no! Open them." In the shadowy light he had looked dead.

"Then pay me cooking compliments instead. We might never have a meal like this again."

"But we will. When the war's over. Where shall we go for our first meal? The Ritz, Paris?"

"The Ritz, London, would do very well. Or the Savoy, or we could have a good English steak and kidney pie at the Cheshire Cheese in Fleet Street. Or a baron of beef —isn't that a marvelous description—a baron, not a plain knight or an esquire. Very rich and juicy."

"Followed by fruit," said Lizzie. "Pineapples and oranges and grapes and figs and strawberries."

"And then a piece of Stilton or Camembert."

"And very hot black coffee."

"And an 1863 brandy."

"That was the year I was born."

"A vintage year." Tom raised his glass. "To you."

"To us," Lizzie amended.

"Not to me. I'm only a worthless newspaper reporter, who excels at only one thing. Making women unhappy."

"Then are we never to have that meal at the Ritz or the Savoy, or anywhere?" Lizzie said. "I'd be content with the humblest place."

"You know I'd take you to Buckingham Palace if I could."

"With Her Majesty looking at us with that cold eye of hers!" Lizzie quickly sought the fantasy mood again. She hadn't liked the angry resentment in Tom's voice. "I only met her once and I'm sure she didn't approve of me even then. She thought I had a frivolous look."

"She guessed correctly. It was extremely frivolous of you to fall in love with such an unsuitable person as me. Lizzie, can you stay all night?"

"I'm supposed to be back at the hospital."

"Tell them Alice was ill. Tell them anything." His voice had urgency. "Lizzie, it may be the last time, who knows?"

"Are you going out again?"

"Soon."

"Oh, Tom."

"Take that worried look off your face. I'll be back with the relief force."

"They say that won't be for two months."

"I'll hurry them up."

"Oh, Tom," she said again.

He came around the table to bend over her, putting his lips on the back of her neck. His hand lay over her breast. She flung around on him.

"Never let's talk of endings!"

"No, Lizzie."

"Let's talk of beginnings. God can't be so unkind."

"I don't think God is on our side any more than He's on the Boers'. He's keeping a nice balance between."

"God is supposed to be love," Lizzie said with trembling lips.

"That's it." Tom's fingers were busy with the buttons of her blouse.

"And if He gives us a child I'll thank him forever."

"If *I* give you a child," said Tom. Then he snatched her violently to him. "I just want you. You!" He kissed her hard between words. "You. You."

When she awoke hours later, although it was still dark, he was gone.

She began to cry, thrusting her knuckles into her eyes like a child.

"Oh, no, Tom. Not yet."

But it was true. When her shaking fingers had found matches to light the lamp, she saw the note propped against the empty wine bottle on the table.

Be a good girl and return the candlesticks to Mrs. Whiteley. Keep your chin up and your eyes dry, and when I come back perhaps we'll talk of beginnings after all.

He had written that only to give her courage, she thought. But perhaps not. Perhaps he meant it. And it did give her courage, for she was able to stop crying, and dress herself, and blow out the lamp, and step out of the darkened house into the street. The moon was setting over the sleeping town. Presently the first gunfire of the morning would begin. Before that happened she could reach Alice's house and slip in quietly. The same cool dawn wind that blew in her face would also be blowing in Tom's. That thought was comforting. She wondered if this time she might have his child in her womb.

She was glad she hadn't had to watch him go.

The Queen had sent another message to Colonel Baden-Powell.

> I continue watching with confidence and admiration the patient and resolute defense which is so gallantly maintained under your ever resourceful command.

"Does she think we can live on glory?" Alice wanted to know.

Alice was six months' pregnant now, and the difficulty was to persuade her to eat more than her share of the family's rations. Bertie was doing his best. It seemed that he had a gift for foraging and finding small delicacies that one would not have thought still existed. Once he came home with a tin of caviar.

"Imagine!" Alice said weakly to Lizzie. "Bertie never was honest, you know. I don't mean he's dishonest, he just has that knack of knowing how far outside the law he can go. Papa always said he would either make a fortune or have a succession of bankruptcies. Perhaps a succession of fortunes, too. I suppose it's because I've never quite known where I am with him that I go on loving him. An enigma is always so much more fascinating."

One would scarcely have called Bertie Partridge, with his predictable conversation, his exaggerated moustache, his mannerisms and his slightly less than frank gaze, an enigma. Lizzie thought that he was just the very ordinary brand of deceiver. Alice, a cut above him socially and a beauty into the bargain, was his shop window.

But even Lizzie had to admit that he had shown devotion and kindness to Alice during the last trying weeks. And he did have a genuine longing for the son they both hoped Alice was carrying.

The question of whether or not she could deliver it safely under these trying conditions was another matter.

Henrietta and Fanny didn't know anything about the little brother who might soon arrive. They only knew that Mamma was always tired and lay on the couch a great deal. She supervised their piano lessons from there, and always swooped them up in a great hurry when the alarm bells sounded. For their part, they welcomed the signal that Creaky was going into action. The shelter was preferable to those tiresome scales. They almost thought that Daisy was the luckiest. She was safely in heaven, where she wasn't tired or hungry or thirsty or hot or frightened or anything. Or so Mamma said.

Then there came the day when the guns never stopped firing. Three hundred and fifty shells were fired, a great many falling in the women's laager.

But, although nobody realized it during the long numbing day, this was Creaky's last display. The very last shell of all, ironically, hit the Dutch church. And in the morning Creaky had disappeared. Everyone anticipated that the big gun was merely being moved to a new position. This was not so. As far as Mafeking was concerned, the long barrel being slowly and menacingly raised ready to spout flame was a sight belonging to the past. Days later, news came that Creaky had been moved to Pretoria.

This was not entirely an occasion for rejoicing, for the lesser guns, the Maxims and the Krupps, still poured fire into the town. They had yet to be routed and sent to follow Creaky's retreat.

The runner who had brought the news of Creaky's whereabouts brought also a message from Lord Roberts. The relief column, he stated bluntly, would be unlikely to reach the town until the middle of June. Another interminable seven or eight weeks.

Immediately, Major Goold-Adams, Major Godley, Major Lord Edward Cecil and Captain Ryan formed a board to examine rationing. Food supplies were precariously low. There was almost no sugar, salt or coffee. Tea was finished. Milk was so scarce that it was reserved for the children. There would be enough horse meat for about half a pound a day for each person. A kind of oatmeal biscuit, made from forage oats, had to take the place of bread. And there was always the unappetizing "sowens" porridge, which disagreed badly with a lot of people.

Not only the women and children were getting weak.

194

The troops in the line, subsisting on a diet that would scarcely have satisfied a cat, were becoming dangerously weak if they were to withstand an attack.

And an attack was all too likely, for it had just come to the garrison's knowledge that Sarel Eloff, a grandson of President Kruger, had come from Pretoria with French and German reinforcements. He was reputed to be young, brave and impatient. He was not likely to sit contentedly with General Snyman, waiting for the population of Mafeking to starve to death.

But at least the terrible heat no longer plagued people. There had been a series of rainstorms and after they were over the hot season was over, too. Another runner got through the Boer lines with letters and newspapers from England. The papers were full of admiration for Mafeking's stand. The world waited breathlessly, they stated, for its relief. Colonel Baden-Powell was a hero of the highest order. So were the gallant residents who were fighting and suffering and standing firm with him. They could not all be decorated for gallantry, but they had everyone's prayers.

There had been a letter for Lizzie, the first she had had since her arrival in Mafeking. She looked at it in surprise, her numbed brain not at first recognizing that the handwriting was her brother Evelyn's.

Thank God he was alive. She tore open the envelope, and eagerly read the letter.

Humphrey, her husband, was dead, she read.

Since no one had known Lady Elizabeth's whereabouts, the information had been sent to her brother.

Sir Humphrey had suffered another apoplectic stroke soon after her departure from England. He had lived, completely unconscious, for three months. Then he had died.

She was a widow. She was free.

She had been free at the time she had first made love with Tom. She had not been committing adultery after all.

Her hand was trembling as she folded the letter. How would this news affect Tom? He was not similarly free. Milly was still his wife. There was still the little boy waiting for his father to come home.

But even while thinking her as securely married as himself he had talked of discussing beginnings.

She told herself that she must not dare to hope. Yet she was hoping all the time.

Hurry and come back, Tom. There's at least one person we can no longer hurt. So surely . . . surely . . .

One weapon did not exist for her. She was not yet going to have Tom's child. How could she have expected, in this state of semistarvation, to conceive? Yet she was intensely disappointed that she had not. She would have been as recklessly delighted as Alice had been with her ill-advised conception. Especially when Tom came back to be told.

He was overdue. He had never stayed away as long as this. Perhaps he really intended to come in with the relief force.

"I hope your letter had pleasant news," Doctor Macpherson was saying. He had been present when one of the Boys' Brigade had come to the hospital with the letter.

"Oh—yes, it has. My brother says he's well and has escaped injury except for a nick in an ear lobe. Isn't that a mercy!"

"It certainly is. What about your family in England?"

"I have no family in England."

"You told me your parents were dead. You must have other relatives."

Lizzie folded the letter and tucked it deep in her pocket.

"None," she said calmly.

"Well, then, it's doubly important that your brother continues to keep out of the way of gunfire," Doctor Macpherson said briskly. "Unless, of course, you form another attachment."

"Of course," said Lizzie vaguely.

Doctor Macpherson snapped his fingers suddenly. He stood there looking at her, frowning slightly, and snapping his fingers with that air of suppressed tension. It was the first time she had seen him lose his calm. Although one could hardly call this a loss of control, for he made no further comment. But when he walked away his shoulders seemed too straight, his back too stiff, and Lizzie had a sudden feeling of compassion. The man was vulnerable, after all. And he had too much delicacy. He would not intrude, much as he must have longed to. She respected him for that. Tom would not have had that delicacy. Inquisitively, he would have demanded to know what was in Evelyn's letter.

She wondered idly if his face would have showed the relief and joy that she was almost certain Alex Macpherson's would have, had she told him her news.

XVIII

Casualties kept on nibbling away at the forces. Another man died of gangrene after a leg amputation. Some natives were killed by stray shots. The first week of May went by, and Colonel Baden-Powell received an impudent letter from Field Cornet Sarel Eloff saying that he had heard about the cricket matches played in Mafeking, and thought he would bring his own team.

Instead of keeping that unlikely promise, he broke the Sunday truce and ordered the Boers to open fire on the town in order to distract attention from a small party who were rounding up horses grazing in the valley near Cannon Kopje. In the ensuing fracas another man was killed and another grave had to be dug in the ever-widening cemetery that night.

People wondered uneasily what next the reckless Eloff might do. They had not long to wait.

Before dawn on the twelfth of May all but the heaviest sleepers were awakened by a rattle of musketry. They started up resentfully. This was too much. At least General Snyman had had the courtesy to wait until dawn before beginning his day's intermittent bombardment.

The moon was just sinking. It was dark enough for the flash of gunfire to show up startlingly. Everything indicated that a Boer attack on a large scale was about to begin.

The alarm bells rang with a great clangor. Bugles sounded, calling troops to their posts. The Town Guard was summoned in full force. It was a sharply cold morning. Alice called to Bertie to put on his greatcoat. She wanted to make him a cup of the precious coffee she had been hoarding but he wouldn't wait.

"Must go, old girl." He kissed her, then Henrietta and

Fanny, who were standing in their nightgowns, shivering. "Get the children dressed and into the nearest shelter."

Fanny began to sob. Henrietta demanded in her high voice, "Are the Boers coming, Papa? Are they going to shoot us?"

"Nothing of the sort, my dear. Do what your mother tells you."

Then he was gone, and Alice held her hands against her stomach, feeling the baby move. It felt as agitated as she was. Supposing it decided to come today, in a sordid bomb shelter.

"Do as Papa said. Get dressed," she said sharply to the trembling children.

The clangor of bells, overlaying the far-off rattle of guns, was making her head confused. She scarcely knew how to dress herself. She must put on warm clothes for it was very chilly. Her merino dress and a woolly shawl.

"Mamma, Fanny's putting on her *yesterday's* camisole!" Henrietta was exclaiming in horror.

"Never mind. You do the same."

"But it hasn't been washed!" Henrietta's voice was full of distaste.

"You're a very pampered little girl. No other children in this town have clean underclothes every day. It's only because of my slaving for you."

Two horrified pairs of blue eyes gazed at her.

"But, Mamma—you've always said we had to be clean. You always said we must never get like Billy Ryan—"

With a supreme effort Alice made her face grow calm.

"Yes, darlings, you're perfectly right. But today there's no time. Now hurry."

They obeyed, but with sidelong glances at their mother. She had never before spoken to them like that. It was because Daisy was dead, Henrietta decided. Mamma had loved Daisy best.

By the time they tumbled into the shelter, the alarm seemed to be over. It was growing light, and now there was only an occasional shot in the far distance. Had all this been for nothing? Alice didn't think she could bear it any longer. She felt ill. Her back was aching quite badly.

The alarm was far from being over, although the citizens of Mafeking didn't know this immediately. The first shots had been a ruse, the real attack was taking place out of hearing beyond the native kraal on the way to the Police Fort. The Police Fort was the objective.

The previous day Sarel Eloff had hung up a notice in the laager at Jackal Tree: "We leave for Mafeking tonight. We shall breakfast tomorrow at Dixon's Hotel." He had also, with superb insolence, sent a message to Reuter's correspondent, telling him to telegraph the fall of Mafeking to London.

It was not yet breakfast time, but the thatched huts in the Barolong village were on fire, and the attackers were well on their way to the Police Fort, a stone house made into a defense post, standing midway between the native village and the town.

If it fell, there was nothing to prevent the Boers breaking triumphantly into Mafeking.

Colonel Hore was in command at the Police Fort. He had a force of three officers and thirteen men. Major Godley's small force had already fallen back from the outposts. There was little sixteen men could do against the advance of at least one hundred and fifty.

Urgent telephone messages were received by Colonel Baden-Powell at his headquarters, and within minutes he had his defense plan put into action. The Town Guard, the Bechuanaland Rifles, and the Railway Division were dispatched to their particular posts. In addition, the jail was opened, and all prisoners who were not Boer sympathizers were armed and sent to the rifle pits to fight for their Queen.

By this time the glare of the burning village was clearly visible, and people had realized what was happening. The long-dreaded day had arrived. The Boers were really coming this time. But they had held out too long to be defeated now. Not only prisoners from the jail were being armed. Every man, no matter how old or infirm, wanted a gun. So did the youngsters who previously had been only messenger carriers. The Boys' Brigade was ready for its baptism of fire.

Intense excitement was one way of overcoming fear. It was left for the women, crouching in shelters, trying to protect their children, to tremble with apprehension and inevitable boredom as the hours went by.

Within half an hour of the beginning of the attack,

200

while the fires burning the huts in the kraal were at their brightest, the telephone rang again at headquarters.

A strange, insolent voice spoke to Colonel Baden-Powell.

"You can't touch us. We hold Colonel Hore a prisoner."

The Boers had succeeded in entering the fort!

This presented Colonel Baden-Powell with an agonizing dilemma. So swiftly and completely had his defense plan been put into action that by this time the Police Fort was surrounded by his own men, and consequently not only Colonel Hore and his men, but a large number of the attacking force were already trapped within.

If the fort were fired on, he would, in all probability, be murdering his own men.

But Mafeking must not be allowed to fall. There was no alternative. Dispassionately, Colonel Baden-Powell gave the order. The fort was to be attacked ceaselessly until it fell. And that must happen before General Snyman made up his reluctant mind to come to the aid of the President's grandson.

The sun rose high in the sky, and no move came from the distant laagers. The little stone-walled fort was under constant fire. Eloff and his companions now knew what it was to be besieged. They had caught themselves in their own trap.

At midmorning Major Panzera went toward the fort, waving a white handkerchief. He carried a message begging Eloff to surrender without further bloodshed. The fort was surrounded with a ring of rifles. It was obvious his countrymen were not coming to his rescue.

To this, Eloff sent an arrogant reply. He saw no reason for surrender. Shortly, not only the Police Fort but the whole town would be in his hands.

Fire opened again. But the resistance had become a species of tragi-farce. Inside the fort, among the polyglot attacking force were Frenchmen, Germans and Portuguese. As the day wore on and the heat grew, the men became thirsty. There was no water. The water tanks had been hit by riflefire and emptied hours ago. However, an enterprising French nobleman, the Comte de Fremont, found a case of Burgundy and immediately broached it. The same man, who obviously did not take war seriously despite the dead and wounded about him, then opened the mess piano and began playing delicate little sonatas, as if he were in a Parisian salon.

What the dedicated Eloff thought of this, or of Snyman's failure to support him, was not known. But as the day went by it must have been clear to him that his brave and reckless plan had failed as completely as had the plan of an equally reckless man, Doctor Jameson, some years earlier.

Spasmodic firing continued until six o'clock. Then Eloff, deserted by half his men who had mutinied and escaped, had no alternative but to surrender to Colonel Hore, his prisoner.

Handing him his rifle, he said wearily, "If you go out and stop the firing I will give in. I have been deserted by Snyman and half my men have run away."

So the dejected band marched into town, seventy-three men, some of them stumbling from genuine weariness, some from the consumption of too much red wine. They were a curious company. When Colonel Baden-Powell courteously invited Eloff and his officers to dine with him, he found he was entertaining a French baron and a German count. The two noblemen's pleasure in the deplorable food served could not have been great, but they may have appreciated the cultivated conversation after the rough and ready existence among the earnest, pious Boers.

Eloff, disappointed, disillusioned, brave, but remarkably brash, said flatly, "You must be taken, Colonel."

"I daresay you think so," Colonel Baden-Powell replied politely. "But I rather imagine Lord Roberts or the British Government will one day hear that I'm besieged and send a force to relieve me."

Eloff laughed loudly. "I've heard all about the relief force. It set out from Kimberley a few days ago. We're planning to smash it at Koodoos Rand."

The Comte de Fremont had had enough of the lowering look of his young commander. Too much fighting was excessively boring.

"Then come, *mon ami,* let us drink to it. This is very excellent wine for a thirsty man, if not exactly—forgive me, *mon Colonel*—for a connoisseur."

It was pure comedy the next morning when Lady Sarah Wilson was invited to join the distinguished captives for

202

breakfast. She thought Eloff an unprepossessing fellow with unkempt hair and sandy whiskers. He was also overcome with dejection, and angry with General Snyman. The fool had merely scratched his head and said, *"Morro is nocher dag"* when begged for reinforcements. Tomorrow was certainly another day, Eloff said gloomily.

But the Comte de Fremont was a gay and sparkling companion. He bemoaned the terrible African climate and said that he could not get back to his beloved *la belle France* quickly enough. Perhaps Lady Sarah had been to the Paris Exhibition? Perhaps she had recently dined at Maxim's?

He was a most unlikely person to shut up in the primitive jail. But there he had to go, along with Eloff and his countrymen. The jail was full to bursting point now, because the prisoners who had fought so gallantly the previous day had also had to be returned to their cells to complete their sentences.

One of them, however, had snatched an extra half hour before meekly submitting to being disarmed and locked up. This was Henry Carter. He had escaped from his guard to call on Amy Brown.

Amy was in a terrible fluster.

"Mr. Carter!"

"I wanted you to see me with my head held up."

His head might have been held up, but it was filthy, sweat and dust making runnels down his face, a half-shaved beard blackening his chin, his clothing ragged and sweat-stained.

With his glittering black eyes and his smile of triumph, he looked alarming, a villain of the deepest dye. Amy shrank back, longing to run inside and close the door in his face.

But something kept her. Not politeness. A sort of fascination that she couldn't begin to understand. A weakness in her knees. A feeling that his black eyes were hypnotizing her.

"Miss Amy, you've been an angel of mercy. You haven't known whether I was guilty or innocent but you've treated me with kindness. Today every time I fired my rifle I thought it was you I was protecting. One more shot for Miss Amy I'd say to myself, and loose off."

"Which one are you?" Amy stammered.

"Which what, ma'am?"

"Innocent or guilty?"

"Well, I took the diamonds. I admit that. It was a temptation I wasn't able to resist. But I swear I never did that man any harm. What hurt he had was an accident."

"You—k-killed today."

"Of course. That's war. That's a different matter altogether. You must know that, innocent as you are. But war changes you. It makes you want to lead a good life. I promise to do that if you'll marry me, Amy Brown."

"Mr. Carter, I *couldn't!* How dare you ask me!"

Amy's horrified refusal was out before she could prevent it. It was shock that made her so regardless of his feelings. And he had feelings, rough and criminal as he was, for at her answer all the reckless light went out of his eyes. He was suddenly as he had been in jail, surly and contemptuous.

He stepped back, saying, "I see the fright in your face. Don't be scared. I won't touch you. I never forced myself on a lady that didn't want me." He held his ridiculous half-shaved chin in the air and said with dignity, "I thought I was making myself a hero for you today, but I see I wasted my time. Good day to you."

"Mr. Carter—"

"Don't waste words," came his contemptuous answer. "You with your sympathy and your religion. All that God is love business, and not despising a criminal. I thought you might be real. But you're not. You're only a paper lady. Be careful or you might blow away."

Amy did find strength, at last, to slam the door. Then she began to cry. She heard her mother calling, "Who was that, dear?" and couldn't answer.

He was a vile horrible man. How could she ever have put on her best bonnet for him? Or allowed that shameful sweetness to steal over her? To think he would have had the impertinence—oh, it didn't bear thinking of. Some women did crazy things in wartime, like Lizzie Willoughby quite blatantly having an affair with Tom Wheeler. Everyone knew about that.

But she, Amy, was too timid to snatch at life, even if she were to die tomorrow. She had denied it just now. That made her virtually dead already.

All the long day the wounded had had to be cared for.

There was no watching the battle from a rooftop for Lizzie this time. By evening she was numb with exhaustion. She did not, as did two other indefatigable women, go out on to the battlefield to try to save lives, nor did she have the grim task of the trained nurses at emergency operations. She kept away flies, and held hands, and wiped away the sweat of agony. She worked in a dream, seeing Tom's features in every new casualty brought in. At first, when he had gone, she had counted the days one by one, estimating the approximate date of his return. Lately she had been afraid to continue. The number was growing too high. Much too high for his safety.

Rumors were that the relief force was not far away. She was pinning her hopes to that, longing, after all, for the siege to end. For Tom's long absence could only be explained by the probability that he really did mean to enter the town with the relief force.

The day did come to an end at last, and the count of dead and wounded among the British forces was mercifully low. Four dead and ten wounded. But the Boers had suffered heavy losses, in wounded and killed and in those taken prisoner. The more lightly wounded had been helped away by comrades. The graver cases could not be left to die while the slow Boer ambulances lumbered over the veld. They were brought into the overcrowded hospitals and some of their lives were saved.

"There's a young fellow here asking for his wife," Doctor Macpherson said to Lizzie. "No one seems to know her. He calls her Katya."

"But of course. She's in jail for being a Boer sympathizer."

"Then I'd better send a message for her to be fetched. He isn't going to live."

Poor Katie Roos. Now what would she do? Go on reviling the British or turn back to them as her own people?

Katie, Linda, Amy, Alice, herself. All scarred by a war in which they had wanted no part. Poor us, thought Lizzie, picking up a pail of stained dressings, trudging wearily down the corridor. But tonight she would sleep from sheer exhaustion. That was one blessing. Her nights lately had been too wakeful. And when she had at last slept she had dreamed too much, one dream in particular, of those

205

horrible vultures, with folded wings, standing before a corpse.

"Nurse!" called Sister Casey urgently. "Nurse Willoughby! Go and find Doctor Macpherson."

"I don't know where he is, Sister. It's an hour since I saw him."

"Then look, girl, look. Tell him one of his operation cases is hemorrhaging."

It was odd for Doctor Macpherson not to be on duty. Lizzie looked in all the wards, then in the small office next to Doctor Hill's. That was where she found him, fallen asleep over his desk. His sandy head lay in the crook of his arm. His pen had rolled away out of his loosened fingers.

She was loath to wake him. She had an unexpected feeling of tenderness. Once more he was showing that he, too, could be vulnerable.

"Doctor Macpherson!" She had to shake his shoulder. "Alex!"

"M-mm? What is it?"

His speech was thickened with sleep, but long discipline brought his head up, almost with alertness. She was shocked at his look of exhaustion.

"Alex, are you ill?"

"No, only tired. Was up all last night. Operating all day. Didn't mean to do this, though." He shook his head, trying to disperse the heavy drowsiness. "What is it?"

"Sister Casey wants you in ward one. She says a patient is hemorrhaging."

Instantly he was on his feet.

"Corporal Smith? I'll be right there."

"Doctor!"

Again discipline automatically made him pause.

"I'll try to find some coffee if you come back here."

"Good girl. That would be wonderful."

It was nearly an hour before he came back. Lizzie had heated the deplorable coffee and let it grow cold again. But he came at last, looking almost fresh, as if that short doze with his head on the hard desk had been all he needed.

"Is that the coffee you promised me?"

"It's got cold."

"It's liquid. It will keep me awake. That's the main thing." He looked at her through his light-colored lashes.

"Sorry you found me like that."

"I suppose you're human like the rest of us."

"Oh, yes, I'm human. You look done in yourself."

"Are things under control now?"

"More or less. If no more cases come in. I've stopped Corporal Smith's bleeding. With luck he'll live."

"They shoot each other and we patch them up. It's crazy."

"Yes. Makes you want to go and live on an island. After this is over I believe I might do that."

"How nice."

He looked at her again, his tired eyes faintly derisive.

"Do you mean that, Lizzie?"

"I suppose so. I've never lived on an island. But you've got nothing to run away from."

"Have you?"

Her eyes stung with sudden tears. Why hadn't Tom thought of taking her to live on an island? It was such a wonderful solution. She must suggest it to him.

"Have I something to run away from? Yes, I had, but not any longer."

He didn't ask questions. He merely said, "Well, time takes care of everything," and leaned forward and startled her by kissing her forehead. "Now back to work. Thanks for the coffee. You would be surprised how it has rejuvenated me."

Everyone was tired that night, but Alice was quite sure no one could be so achingly prostrated as she was. Twice that afternoon she had been sure her baby was going to make a premature arrival. When they had heard at last that the Boers had surrendered and had been taken prisoner, such a pain shot through her that it was as if she had been hit by riflefire herself. She sat quite still, praying that the birth was not beginning, because if it were, the baby would be much too small and weak to live.

Gradually she recovered and was able to get the children to bed. Poor little things, they had had a miserable supper of cold horse sausage and half a mug each of precious milk. When the war was over, she promised them, they could have all their favorite things to eat every day.

"For the rest of our lives?" Henrietta wanted to know.

"I shall have a chocolate mousse for breakfast every morning," Fanny said sleepily.

"That was Daisy's favorite thing, not yours."

"Mamma said I could."

"When will the war be over, Mamma?"

"You must ask Papa. Perhaps tomorrow. Who knows?"

Bertie came in just after they had fallen asleep. He was full of the story of the Boers' capitulation.

"That fellow Eloff looked as if he would have liked to have shot the lot of them. Snyman first. It's lucky for our skins Snyman let him down. I must say Eloff doesn't cut much of a dash as a grandson of Kruger. But Kruger's no oil painting himself. A crass sort of fellow. Well, I don't envy B. P. his dinner guests."

"I've told the children the siege might be over tomorrow," Alice said, speaking out of her daze of weariness.

"You're a bit optimistic, old girl. I hardly think the relief force is that close. But better to hope than to cry. How was the day?"

"Very long."

"I suppose it was. Hadn't you better get to bed?"

"When you do. I thought once today that the baby was going to come."

Bertie shot her an alarmed look.

"Thank God it didn't."

"I willed it not to. I sat very quietly."

"Good girl. Do you know, Alice, you've changed."

"I expect so. I'm much larger than when I arrived here."

Bertie gave his low haw haw. "You're certainly that. But then you were a willful child. Yes, that's what you were. A beautiful willful child. I adored you. I was always proud of you with your looks and your way of dressing. Now you're different."

"How?" said Alice uncertainly.

"Well, just think of the Alice you were then, sitting in a trench all day and not having hysterics."

"I'm shabby now. And plain."

"Shabby, yes. But not plain. I believe you're better-looking this way. You've a look of—well, I don't know. I never was a clever chap at words. But I'm deuced proud of you."

208

Alice's lips were quivering uncontrollably.

"For what? Having your son?"

"I don't care whether the little blighter's a boy or a girl, actually. I wouldn't mind another Daisy, to tell the truth. Oh, look here, Alice, let's come to bed. I'll just hold you, shall I? I feel like holding you."

And who could have guessed, Alice thought drowsily, that the nightmare day could end like this, in complete bliss.

XIX

The next day, Sunday, the dead from the battle were buried, and there was a thanksgiving service for those who remained alive. But no sports were held. Everyone was too tired after the exertions of the previous day and the lack of adequate food. If the relief force were to appear, Bertie Partridge said, they would scarcely be able to raise a cheer.

But there was no sign of the force, no messages came in, and the prospect of a slow death by starvation became too possible to ignore.

Mrs. Murphy sacrificed the last of her treasured hens, though it was almost too skinny to eat. But it made some good broth for invalids. Miss Rose said she couldn't eat because of a gastric upset and gave Billy Ryan all of her day's ration. When, however, he seemed to be more distressed by her illness than by hunger, she had to admit that she was perfectly well.

"Good gracious, what's a small stomach upset?"

"I don't like people being sick," Billy said stolidly. "My mother died and my sister."

"I'm far from dying, I assure you." Behind her spectacles Miss Rose's sharp eyes blinked rapidly. It would be funny if she got too fond of this irritating child. Funnier still if he got too fond of her. At present he was being too dependent on her, too agitated if she were out of his sight for long. She would have to drive him out. Somehow he must be given back the wild independence that had so alarmed his mother. Not that Miss Rose hadn't secret longings to keep him by her. She was thinking that when the siege was over she would get another room built on to the schoolhouse. A boy needed his own room. And a sharp little boy like Billy needed a good education. She was already planning a syllabus.

But that didn't mean that the boy would be molly-coddled. She intended speaking to Major Cecil the moment she could catch him in an idle moment. Billy was a good deal younger than the average age of the boys in the Boys' Brigade. But a tough youngster like him could be put to some use.

The result of this was that Billy was allowed to sit on a rooftop and watch for clouds of dust in the distance. There was great rivalry as to who would be the first to spot the relief force approaching.

The Boer guns, since the failure of Eloff's attack, had been almost silent. Sunday passed without incident, also Monday.

On Tuesday the monotony vanished. A runner came in with news that a relief column under Colonel Mahon was already past Vryburg. A little later a carrier pigeon brought the additional news that Colonel Plumer at Sefetili was planning to rendezvous with Colonel Mahon at Massibi.

The news spread through the town in a flash. When it reached the hospital Lizzie was feeding a patient from an invalid cup. He began to choke and when he recovered his breath, said tolerantly, "You nearly poured the whole cupful down my throat. But I'll forgive you, nurse, under the circumstances."

Lizzie said she was sorry but she was so excited about the news. She hurried out of the ward, intent on finding out only one thing—not the whereabouts of the relief force, but whether the runner who had come in was Tom.

Without asking for leave, she threw off her uniform, straightened her hair and set off for the town. Dixon's bar, Tom's house, Market Square, where excited knots of people were gathered—in any of these places she might find him.

"Lizzie!" called Amy Brown. "Have you heard the news?"

"Yes, I have. Where—I mean, who brought it?"

"A runner from Colonel Mahon's company. An Australian, I believe. They say both Australians and New Zealanders are among the forces arriving. Papa says it's wonderful how the Empire is so united. Lizzie, what's the matter? Aren't you pleased?"

211

She had better go back to the hospital, Lizzie was thinking dully. Finish feeding the poor sergeant who had had both hands badly burned when trying to put out the fire in the kraal last Saturday.

"Oh, I guess I know," Amy exclaimed. "You hoped the runner might be Tom Wheeler."

"Yes, I did."

"He has been away an awfully long time, hasn't he? Perhaps," Amy said brightly, "he's gone to Capetown."

"Running away?" Lizzie's voice was harsh. "Don't be ridiculous."

"I only thought—I was only trying to make a helpful suggestion."

"Well, it wasn't a very sensible one. You'd better go and make helpful suggestions to the Boer prisoners in jail. They'll be the ones needing sympathy."

Lizzie's hard tone had brought the quick tears to Amy's eyes. She hung her head, thinking what a failure she was at everything. Even when she was being tolerant about Miss Willoughby's quite shameless love affair she didn't seem to do it properly or acceptably. The horrible war had done this to her, she thought painfully. If it hadn't happened, she would never have had these impossible emotional situations forced on her. She would have lived a quiet neutral life unaware of her terrible limitations.

Even now she wanted to turn away and not face the desolation in Lizzie's eyes.

"I expect he'll come back safely," she murmured, but Lizzie hadn't stayed to listen. She was walking back toward the hospital, her step slow and listless.

The sun was high in the sky, and in the blue brilliance, as always, the tiny black specks of the scavenging aasvogels were circling.

Her heart ached with physical pain.

For the rest of that day people watched from rooftops, exclaiming excitedly at every cloud of dust on the horizon, whether it was made by a party of Snyman's horsemen taking up defense positions or by Boer reinforcements from General de la Rey's contingent.

They were certainly not yet caused by the relief force, for by the next morning people were still waiting. By afternoon, however, distant gunfire was heard. All of the town's forces were on the alert; waiting silently with loaded guns. Then, at sundown, a message came. The heliograph might have been a heavenly star winking, so heartened were the watchers.

From Colonel Mahon's Force—How are you getting on?

The exciting news of this message had scarcely had time to spread through the town before a small troop of men in khaki mounted on tired horses trotted up the main street, coming from the direction of the western defenses.

This was a familiar sight in Mafeking. It was a little while before the observant Billy Ryan screamed that these troopers were strangers. They were burned almost black with the sun and marked with exhaustion, but they hadn't the look of starvation common to all in this town. They must be the first arrivals of the relief force.

Before the little band could reach its destination, Colonel Baden-Powell's headquarters, the cheering began, and became wilder and wilder, its sound carrying to the distant hospital and Convent; and even as far as the women's laager.

Bertie Partridge was inspired to begin singing "Rule Britannia" and in a moment everyone had joined in.

Weakened by exhaustion, sickness, the atrocious food and deferred hope, there was still a remarkable volume of sound left in people's throats. If the triumphant song could have echoed as far as the distant Boer laagers, it must have struck bitter irony into the hearts of the remaining aggressors.

If they had time to listen. For it was safe to assume that if they were not massing to support de la Rey's force, they were in hasty retreat.

They had sat in that monotonous spot for long enough.

The little troop was led by Major Karri Davies of the Imperial Light Horse. After a conference with Colonel Baden-Powell he immediately sent two troopers back to report to Colonel Mahon and Colonel Plumer. His message said that the way in through the western defenses was clear . . .

But people had better go home to bed. The march in

213

would not take place until after breakfast the next morning.

"Why don't you get some sleep?" Doctor Macpherson asked Lizzie at midnight.

Lizzie, who had been walking up and down outside the hospital in bright moonlight, turned on him with the exacerbation of stretched nerves.

"I believe you deliberately follow me about! I wish you would stop it."

"I care about you too much to do that," Doctor Macpherson replied gently.

Lizzie rudely pressed her hands to her ears.

"Not now! Please!"

"You're torturing yourself about Tom Wheeler, aren't you?"

"Haven't I every reason? He's been gone"—her voice dropped desolately—"so long."

"He'll probably make a dramatic arrival tomorrow, sharing the honors with Colonel Mahon."

Lizzie didn't miss the sarcasm in Doctor Macpherson's voice.

"You don't like him, do you," she accused angrily. "You think he's foolhardy and an exhibitionist and drinks too much. You'd like him never to come back, wouldn't you?"

"You're quite wrong, Lizzie. I have no feelings for him at all except that he's a rival. But a not-too-formidable one, since he can never marry you. I," he added with quiet deliberation, "can do that."

Lizzie stared at him in disbelief.

"You can say that to me—*now!*"

"Now is the time. It will help you through tomorrow—if Wheeler doesn't come back."

"How *can* you talk like that?" she whispered, and began to sob with such intensity that she could not shake off the arm laid across her shoulders.

"Lizzie, are you pregnant? I'll marry you at once if you are."

His calm voice had the shock of cold water thrown in her face. She became quiet at once, although she couldn't speak. She merely shook her head, and he said briskly, "Come, my dear. I'm going to prescribe for you. A half

214

glass of emergency brandy. Then you must rest. The sun will be up soon."

It was the lark, the herald of the morn . . . The words were like a whispering ghost in her head, from a time that was infinite years ago.

XX

But there was not to be much sleep for anybody that night. The whole town was aroused when the moon was still high and shining brilliantly by the sound of many horses' hooves and marching feet.

What seemed to the bewildered townspeople, rubbing sleep out of their eyes, an enormous number of horses and men and guns had assembled on the recreation grounds. Under cover of darkness the relief force had marched in, through the way that lay open past Israel's Farm, where Colonel Plumer had fought and won the day yesterday.

Tired men were already lying down to rest before the final battle in the morning when, it was hoped, General Snyman and all his burghers would be sent flying for their lives.

It was too soon to indulge in wild greetings and celebrations. The two hundred and seventeenth day of the siege was dawning, and it would be the last. But the final action had still to take place.

The unwholesome sowens porridge was eaten without complaint that morning, and no one noticed whether his precious remaining ounces of sugar had been mixed with Kalahari sand by a crafty shopkeeper, or not. Hungry as everyone was, it was a condition one had learned to live with, and it could well be forgotten this morning. There wasn't really time to eat. One had to be out on a rooftop watching the enthralling sight of real batteries of twelve-pounders trotting briskly out onto the veld and going into action.

Indeed, anyone who had lingered over breakfast would have missed the battle altogether, for it lasted only half an hour.

Then a great cloud of dust that wasn't due entirely to exploding shells appeared around the Boer headquarters.

People stared incredulously, scarcely able to believe what it meant. General Snyman was trekking! One by one, the wagons, with bullocks and mules being whipped up to greater speed, were moving off in the direction of the Transvaal border.

They vanished so quickly that by the time the dust had cleared the veld was empty. The laager which had been there for so long that it had seemed a permanent feature of the landscape had simply vanished. Wagons, men, horses and cattle had gone. Mounted troops, exploring the debris left, found nothing but filth and litter, a few chickens and a few abandoned cattle. It seemed incredible that such a short time ago ten thousand men had gathered there.

Some of them remained, of course. There were a number of graves, some of them mass ones. Not many were marked. Soon, with wind and weather, they would be lost sight of altogether. The forts that had bristled with guns and the scrubby trees that had concealed many an expert sniper were empty, too. The veld was suddenly dreamlike in its emptiness and loneliness.

It was a relief to turn from it and see the flags flying triumphantly in the town.

There was to be a welcome for the relieving force and a parade, something for the starved, exhausted people to feast their eyes on.

It was not, however, an entirely happy day. The dead and wounded from Colonel Plumer's action at Israel's Farm were still being brought in, the wagons avoiding the center of the town so as not to dampen the celebrations.

Thirty had died in the battle. As always, joy was mixed with tragedy.

Lizzie, after a brief rest at Doctor Macpherson's insistence in the night, had worked without ceasing.

At first, when she had heard that the entire relief force had arrived, she had wanted to rush out and search their numbers for Tom. Then she had found herself unable to. She knew that if he had come back he would look for her at once. So she must wait. She must learn self-discipline by attending to the needs of the gravely wounded and dying. Her brief rebellion in the night was over. Her face had a new austerity. She couldn't smile false reassurance at the badly mutilated. But she could give them quiet and completely dedicated companionship in their agony. She had accepted at last that her suffering was no greater than anyone else's.

She had learned that lesson just in time. For by daylight she knew that Tom was not coming back.

It was, inevitably, Doctor Macpherson who had to confirm her intuition. Perhaps he had asked to be the one to do so.

Sister Casey called her from the bedside of a boy with half his face shot away.

"Doctor wants to speak to you, nurse."

Lizzie straightened her aching back.

"Very well, Sister," she said quietly.

"Lizzie." Doctor Macpherson had drawn her a little way down the corridor. He took a letter from his pocket and held it out to her. She read the address written in a precise feminine hand. "Mr. Thomas Wheeler, Mafeking, South Africa."

"It's from his wife. He hadn't opened it."

Lizzie heard herself saying quite containedly, "Where was he found?"

"About halfway to Vryburg. On the veld. He had been shot."

"The—the vultures—" Lizzie's lips were suddenly too stiff to frame words. She had always known that nightmare would come true.

"He would have died instantaneously."

"How can you *know?*"

"Lizzie, my dear." Doctor Macpherson's voice had a tenderness she had never before heard. "There's no use torturing yourself thinking anything else."

"No, you're quite right. You're always right."

She pushed back her hair from her damp forehead and held out her hand for the letter.

"Will you let me answer this, Alex? It's the least I can do for that poor woman in England."

He hesitated. She said, "Don't look at me like that. I won't behave badly again. Tom used to taunt me with being a lady—so now I'll try—to prove it."

"Lizzie, Lizzie, cry!"

She shook her head. "Later. There's time later."

He looked at her anxiously, helplessly, then silently handed her the letter with the English postmark.

Although, in the end, the Boers had shown no fight, the townspeople were not to be denied their spectacle.

During the morning the relief force made an official march to Market Square. Headed by the three Colonels, Baden-Powell, Plumer and Mahon, and followed by many distinguished officers such as Prince Alexander of Teck, Sir John Willoughby, Colonel Frank Rhodes, a brother of Cecil Rhodes, the former Prime Minister of the Cape Colony, and also Colonel Baden-Powell's own brother, who had been one of the first of the relief column to arrive in Mafeking, they moved down the dusty road into the town center.

Behind them rode the Royal Horse Artillery, the Canadian Artillery, the Imperial Light Horse and the Diamond Fields Horse. A little dust stirred by the horses' hooves settled lightly on the men on foot, volunteers from across the world—Canadians, Scots, New Zealanders, Australians, Irish, South Africans and Britain's own Royal Fusiliers. Fit lean brown men, walking with the long easy stride of many marches.

Behind them again—they should have led the procession, some people said—came the garrison troops, ragged, thin as skeletons, heads held high. The Protectorate Regiment, the Bechuanaland Rifles, the Cape Police, the Cape boys.

The Union Jack flew from every flag pole. The band played. The mayor was dressed in his formal clothes, waiting to make a speech, waiting to say that he ventured to think there would be a great deal of excitement and jubilation in England this day. He wanted to thank Colonel Baden-Powell for his unexampled leadership, and Colonel Mahon and Colonel Plumer of the relief force for their successful operation. And the town's citizens, without whose patience and courage Mafeking would never have stayed firm. And the dead. Those who had fallen in battle and those, the very old and the very young, who had been victims of the diseases attendant on war and privation. Three hundred and twenty-six fighting men had died, and one hundred and eighty-two civilians.

Who would have thought there would have been five hundred graves dug in the cemetery that had been scarcely begun seven months ago.

After the mayor had spoken, Colonel Baden-Powell

stood up tó say his last words to the people he had lived with and endeavored so hard to protect for seven long months.

He stood on the platform, a slight, sunburned figure, trim and soldierly, silhouetted against the brown empty veld that he had examined so often through field glasses that he must have known every hump and rock and hollow.

"We have been a happy family. The time has come for breaking up. When we were first invested I said to you, 'Sit tight and shoot straight.' The garrison has sat tight and shot straight with the present glorious result. Many nice things have been said about me, but it is an easy thing to be the figurehead of a ship. The garrison has been the riggings and the sails of the good ship Mafeking and has brought her safely through her stormy cruise."

Later in the day, a service was held in the cemetery, the wind billowing gently in Father Ogles's surplice. Once more the melancholy notes of the "Last Post" floated over the town and the veld. There were no Boers in the vicinity to hear the volley that rang out over the graves. There would be no more furtive interments by lanternlight.

People could walk about freely in the daylight. They could scarcely believe it and still kept their ears sharpened for alarm bells. The women could move back to their houses, counting the damage of fallen chimneys, broken windows, scattered plaster. They could even begin to remake their gardens.

It was all over. The war had flowed past them. But no one was unscarred.

Of the women who had made uneasy acquaintance in the train that had failed to reach safety on the first day of the siege, only one was dead. Mrs. Ryan, with her tediously whining child Annie. But old Mrs. Buchanan had turned from a vigorous, aggressive old woman to a feeble, silent one, waiting only to rejoin her husband, her son and her grandson. Linda was slowly recovering from her grief. She was too young for it to mark her permanently.

Katie Roos, whose husband Piet had been brought in to die in the hospital and to be buried in this cemetery, was stony-eyed and hostile. She was never going to forgive her countrymen for what they had done. She would outspan to her husband's family on their farm near Vryburg, if

220

they were still there. She declared violently that she would never be British again.

It seemed that Amy Brown might have escaped unscathed. No one knew of any emotional crisis which she might have suffered. But she was oddly quiet. She walked about with her eyes down, as if she had a great sorrow. She looked odd, to say the least. Too much religion, the women said. And she was a poor, impressionable creature, anyway. You could picture her sitting, pedaling away at that organ in the Brown parlor until she was a thin old woman.

Miss Rose, on the other hand, had had a new lease of life. She had decided to adopt Billy Ryan, since the boy seemed to have no objection. She had discovered that he had no real intellectual ability, but he had a great talent for carpentry. Give him wood, a hammer and nails, and he would build not only another room on to Miss Rose's house, but later, in this growing town, houses themselves. When he was old enough she would apprentice him to a builder. In the meantime he must learn his three r's, and good manners, and a fear of God.

Lastly, there were the two outsiders, who were not outsiders any longer. They belonged to the town now, since they had helped to shape its history.

Alice had somehow contrived to go through the whole siege in a pregnant condition and not lose her baby. But she had a small, much-too-new white cross in the cemetery to visit.

After the ceremony was over she lingered to put some yellow poppies, all the flowers she could find, on the small grave.

Lizzie thought how forlorn she looked standing there in her muslin dress and her floppy sun hat.

"Poppies," Lizzie said. "They'll make Daisy sleep well. Where are Henrietta and Fanny?"

"With Miss Rose and Billy. I wouldn't let them come. It's too sad for them. I've told them about the new baby. They think it's going to arrive on the doorstep. They run every morning to look. Lizzie!" Alice's strained blue eyes looked up. "I can never leave here now, do you realize that?"

"You mean you have to stay with Daisy?"

"Yes. Partly. And partly because Bertie wants to stay.

221

He has his business here. He says it will boom after the war. I don't mind, because it's where we've found each other, in a way. In spite of everything being so terrible. What about you, Lizzie?"

"Me?"

"Darling, we know about Tom. We're terribly sorry. Did you love him very much?"

"Yes."

"It's awful." Alice was feeling for words, saying earnestly, "But you would have had to say goodbye sometime soon. If you can take any comfort out of that."

"I don't know. I don't know anything. It shouldn't have needed Tom to be dead."

"No. Nor Daisy." Alice began to shiver. "Come away from here. Bertie says I mustn't be morbid. Let's go home. The hospital can do without you tonight. You look so tired."

Lizzie looked out across the brown flatness of the veld, at the outcrops of rock catching the last sunlight.

No need to worry about Tom shivering out there tonight . . .

She put out her hand to take Alice's.

"It's so long since we came here together."

"We were so innocent," Alice said.

"I was never innocent."

"Oh, you pretended to be worldly. I never believed it. I suppose we both are now, if going through so much makes one worldly. What will you do, Lizzie? Marry Alex Macpherson?"

After a long time Lizzie said, "I expect so. Sometime."

"He's a decent man," Alice said warmly. "I believe he'll make you happy. Much more than Tom would have done. Yes, I will say it whether you like it or not. Tom Wheeler would never have made you happy."

"I know." Lizzie wrapped her arms around herself, shivering in the cool wind. "For one thing, there would always have been his son. Even if I'd managed to give him one."

"Sons mean a lot to a man," Alice said with sure knowledge.

Before Lizzie could go home with Alice there was one last painful thing to be done.

The door of Tom's house stuck a little. When she had

succeeded in pushing it open the dust shivered down and settled. She stood in the gloom, in the familiar place.

Tom's books and papers were still here, covered with dust. There was the sketch of the three little Partridge girls and the terrible one of the aasvogels preparing to tear at the corpse. When Father Ogle had spoken in the cemetery, saying of the siege, "Some have broken, some have grown strong. Let us not talk about the enemy, but what has happened to ourselves . . ." she had been in her nightmare again, seeing the aasvogels standing piously over Tom and hearing his ironic voice—"Grace before meat."

She picked up his pen and shook the ink bottle to see if the ink had not all dried up. There was a tiny trickle in the bottom with which she was able to write:

MY DEAR MRS. WHEELER,
 You will by this time have had the tragic news of your husband's death. I knew him, and I now write to tell you how much and with what affection he spoke of you and his son. . . .

The evening was very quiet. Almost no sounds came from the street or the Market Square. After the long day of celebrations and emotional turmoil, people were tired. They were too undernourished to be able to stand long activity. But thinly from across the street Lizzie could hear the sound of an organ. Amy Brown was playing in the Brown parlor.

> *Shall we gather at the river,*
> *Where bright angels' feet have trod . . .*

The sentimental tune would remind Lizzie forever of Mafeking, the Place of Stones, and the deadly river that had flowed over it, certainly not one marked with angels' footprints.

Daisy, Annie Ryan, Peter Moody, Andy Buchanan, Tom Wheeler . . .

Lizzie bent resolutely to her task. She must get the letter finished because she couldn't stand this dusty room. Tom was in every corner.

She must hurry back to the hospital, where there was still plenty to do. Alex would be looking for her. She realized that she was glad, for the first time, that she was not pregnant with Tom's baby. It would be better with Alex if she did not have to be grateful to him. She might even find that she could make him happy.

It was almost dark when she had finished. She sealed the envelope and straightened her tired back.

"Goodnight, Tom," she said very quietly, and went.